SIDE HUSTLE TANGO

BOOK 2 OF THE GRAND HUMAN EMPIRE

JOHN WILKER

EDITED BY
CHRISTINA SHORT

Rogue Publishing

Copyright © 2021 by Rogue Publishing, LTD
All rights reserved.

No part of this book may be reproduced in any form or by any electronic or mechanical means, including information storage and retrieval systems, without written permission from the author, except for the use of brief quotations in a book review.

For permissions contact:
rights@johnwilker.com

Cover art by: Vivid Covers

V 1.1

ISBN: 978-1-951964-11-5

CONTENTS

Introduction ix

ONE

CHAPTER ONE

Flair 5
Pleasantries and Threats 9
This is Not a Drill 12
Sideways 17

CHAPTER TWO

This Planet Sucked Anyway 23
Home Sweet Space Station 28
Grocery Shopping 32
Detours 35

CHAPTER THREE

Mornings After 41
Now Departing 44
Lunch 48
Are You kidding me 51

CHAPTER FOUR

Space Walk 55
Back on Track 59
Now Arriving 62
You Could at Least By me a Drink 65
Interesting Tastes 69

CHAPTER FIVE

Planet Fall	75
This is fancy	80
Walk about	83
Nightlife	88

CHAPTER SIX

Changes in Direction	95
Wrong Door	99
This is unexpected	101
Manhunt	104

CHAPTER SEVEN

Strangers	111
Meet New People	114
Bustin' Out	118
Makin' Plans	121
Breakfast of Champions	125

CHAPTER EIGHT

And We're walking...	131
Robbing	135
Memories	139
Wrinkles	144

TWO

CHAPTER NINE

No Rest	153
Party Time	157
This Part Took a Turn...	162
Awkward Cab Rides	167
Time to Go	169

DEDICATION

*To my fans.
Thank you!*

CHAPTER TEN

We've been robbed	175
Transit	179
Reviewing The Tapes	182

CHAPTER ELEVEN

Red Turtle Shell Power	187
Welcome To Columbiana	191
Shopping	197

CHAPTER TWELVE

Data Transfer	203
Side Quests	208
Small Packages	212
Won't be here long	216

CHAPTER THIRTEEN

Tea	223
Questions and Answers	225
Welp	229
Now What?	233
This is bad	237

THREE

CHAPTER FOURTEEN

I have an Idea	245
You're Invited	250
Lots To Do	254
Reunions	257

CHAPTER FIFTEEN

Jitters	263
Distractions	267
The Frame up	271
Slipping Away	274

CHAPTER SIXTEEN

Dress the Part	281
Show Time	285
Sales Hustle	289

CHAPTER SEVENTEEN

Mugging	295
It's Complicated	299
Bear Poking Never Goes Well	303

CHAPTER EIGHTEEN

Springing The Trap	309
Bad News	312
Hack the Hacker	314
Proper Paperwork	317

CHAPTER NINETEEN

Closing the Trap	323
Turning of Screws	327
Fake News	331

CHAPTER TWENTY

TTFN	337
They Never Learn	340
Welcome Home	344

Continue the Adventure	349
Stay Connected	351
Offer	353
Other Books by John Wilker	355

You're about to embark on a fun adventure!

When you're done reading, I hope you'll take a minute to leave a review!

If you liked the story and want more, joining my newsletter is a great way to get free samples, and exclusive short stories.

If you like supporting things you love by sporting merch or buying direct, well you're in luck! I've launched a shop, take a look. **Use, discount code "Osprey" and you'll save %15!**

ONE

CHAPTER ONE

FLAIR

"Of all the things to make it this far from Earth, TGI Fridays isn't one I'd have bet on," Jax said as their client approached. The well-dressed woman was threading her way between screaming children and flair-adorned servers. He watched as she side-stepped a toddler with ranch-covered hands.

Naomi nodded. "First time here." Her often unwilling business partner looked at her, his mouth hanging open. She shrugged. "What? I didn't really have a normal childhood, remember?" She held up her hands. Blue lines that traced her arms, neck, and face glowed. The bio-circuit tattoos faded as she looked around. "I kinda like it." She watched a server zip past, balancing a tray of drinks in her hand, buttons and other trinkets jangling as she moved. "It's fun."

Jax raised a hand, patting the air. "Okay, okay, calm down. Maybe if you're good, we can come back another time. I think there's one of these at the Jericho station." Their client had almost reached them, dodging a distracted father with an infant cradled in one arm and another child tethered by a leash that was straining. Jax reached into his jacket and retrieved a portable data storage device, placing it on the table.

"Mr. Caruso, Ms. Himura," the well-dressed woman said, dropping into the open chair across the table from them, exhaling. "Welcome to Nuevo Santiago," she said, likely with less enthusiasm than when she had entered the building.

"Lovely colony you have, Madame Governor," Naomi replied.

Nuevo Santiago was one of the older pre-Empire colonies. Colonists from Chile and Argentina originally settled it during the early exodus from Earth. The government's open immigration policy caused the population to boom quickly with people from all over Earth looking for a fresh start. The original settlers made sure new arrivals felt welcome and that they knew that the cultural center of the planet was South America.

If Jax remembered correctly, during the war, Nuevo Santiago had remained neutral. At least, as neutral as possible. Being a bit out of the way helped.

He smiled his best fake smile. "It is, great place." He raised an eyebrow. "You have our payment?"

The governor, very much descended from the fairer-skinned settlers of the colony, nodded as she slid a hand into her purse. As she removed an anonymous credit stick from it, she looked at the data store sitting on the table. "That's everything?"

She slid the credit stick across the table just as a server came over. "What can I get you folks?" The twenty-year-old's smile looked like it was painted it on his face at the beginning of each shift. "Mozzarella sticks are half off for another hour," he offered.

ONE

Jax looked up. "Two..." He tapped his chin. "Sagerstown Ambers." He looked at the governor, eyebrow raised.

"Nothing for me," she said, doing her best to avoid eye contact with the server, likely hoping he didn't recognize her.

The server nodded and headed off, stopping when Naomi shouted, "You know what, throw in some mozzarella sticks." The young man turned, his smile still in place, and inclined his head before continuing away from them.

Jax reached for the credit stick as Naomi slid the data storage device toward the governor. The small device could hold terabytes of data on specially designed crystalline nano-wafers. Status lights on the leading edge of the rectangular device blinked to show device health.

Unbeknownst to the three of them, as they were trading goods for payment, three well-dressed men and a woman walked in, taking seats in the bar. They were way too well dressed to be Friday's patrons. The bar was between the main dining area and the door, and was full of football fans in varying degrees of fan regalia. When the bartender walked over, one of the men waved him away, scowling.

Jax held the onetime use credit stick up to his gPhone. The two devices detected each other via lower power local networking. After handshaking, the two devices linked, and his banking app showed the amount of money contained on the onetime stick. A blinking button let Jax know he could transfer the funds to his primary account. He tapped the button, then dropped the now empty credit stick in his half empty glass of water. The governor and Naomi watched the entire process quietly.

Jax smiled. "Payment received."

The governor was doing something similar at her end of the table, accessing the data storage unit from her own gPhone. The status lights on the unit blinked as the governor verified the data.

"Here you go." The server was back, a tray balanced in one hand. He deposited a frosted mug in front of first Naomi, then Jax, placing a basket of steaming breaded cheese in the center of the table. "Careful, those are hot," he said as he placed three plates and napkins on the table.

When the server moved on, the governor exhaled. "This place is exhausting." She gestured to the storage device. "This is incredible. With this, we'll be able to put Jellico away for a long time." She nodded to each of them. "Thank you."

Jax sipped his beer, then said, "That's outstanding. Glad we could help."

Naomi smiled. "From what you told, that's good news."

The governor nodded, and after looking around, said, "Okay, then we're done here." She stood up, smoothed her blazer, and plucked a mozzarella stick from the basket. "Safe travels." She turned and almost collided with a woman chasing a shouting child. She shook her head and walked away.

Jax looked at Naomi, holding his mug up. When she clinked hers against his, he said, "To getting paid."

As Naomi popped a mozzarella stick in her mouth, someone behind them said, "Hello, Mr. Caruso."

PLEASANTRIES AND THREATS

"Mr. Ichiko says hello," a muscular man said from behind Jax. He nodded to Jax and Naomi's table as three other well-dressed syndicate enforcers moved to surround the table. The server approached and turned around when one of the men gave him a look. A heavyset woman leaned down and plucked a mozzarella stick from the basket between two tattooed fingers. "Good call. These are amazing." She bit into the steaming morsel.

The leader nodded to the woman and a younger man. "Go get the car."

The woman nodded, grabbing one more mozzarella stick as she headed for the door, her younger colleague falling in behind her.

The taller man, obviously the leader of this team, reached for a mozzarella stick but stopped when Jax said, "You gonna pay the bill? You're eating my appetizer."

The man smiled and grabbed Jax's beer, taking a long drink.

Jax winked. "I tend to backwash." The gangster put the glass down, frowning. Jax shrugged, batting his eyes. He looked around, then said, "I have to pee. Thinking I should do that before we leave?"

The taller man looked around until he spotted the restrooms, near the back of the dining room. He pointed to the men's room and nodded to his colleague. "Make sure he washes his hands."

The other man, shorter than the leader, chuckled. "Sure thing." He hitched a thumb toward the restrooms. "Let's go." Jax stood, and both men headed to the restroom.

As Jax and his captor walked away, Naomi looked up at the man who was the head goon of the team. "So, what's the deal?"

The man's smirk made Naomi's skin crawl. "We take you to Mr. Ichiko, collect our bonuses. You two, well, I'm guessing you'll die." He moved to intercept the server. "We're done. Check, please." The server nodded. The goon turned to Naomi. "It'll probably be painful. He has a nasty streak, and you two really pissed him off. We had to abandon our Themura operation."

"Sorry to hear that," Naomi deadpanned.

Outside the restroom, the Crimson Orchid operative said, "Don't do anything stupid, okay?" He pushed the door open and looked inside. Empty.

Jax smiled. "Who, me?" He pushed past the man, looking inside. "You gonna come help?" He winked.

The man shoved Jax, following him inside. "Hurry up."

Jax moved to the urinal. "Oh, dammit!" he hissed.

"You piss yourself?"

Jax turned. "Someone took a dump in the urinal." He motioned the other man over. "Who does that? So fucking gross!"

Curious, the Crimson Orchid operative came up next to Jax. The moment he leaned past Jax to look, the much smaller Jax grabbed the man's necktie, pulling his head down as hard and fast as he could, slamming it into the top of the urinal.

Jax drove a fist into the man's midsection before pulling him again, face first, into the top of the urinal. The man fell to the ground, unconscious and bloody. The urinal sported a few new cracks.

"Idiot," Jax mumbled, stepping around the prone form. After washing his hands, he opened the door and slipped out. Moving quickly back toward the table with Naomi and the other Crimson Orchid goon, he spotted the perfect distraction.

He reached up and pulled the fire alarm.

THIS IS NOT A DRILL

The fire alarm rang out, followed by the automated voice. "May I have your attention, please?" The alarm blared, then, "This is an emergency. Please walk quickly and safely to the nearest exit." The alarm rang out again, then repeated the message.

Naomi's goon looked around frantically, which was all the opening she needed. She grabbed his belt in one hand while her nearest foot lashed out, knocking his feet out from under him. As he fell, she used his belt to guide his upper body to collide with the table. Mugs of beer and mozzarella sticks bounced up into the air. Her captor momentarily stunned, she stood, grabbing his hair and slamming his head into the table twice, then once more for good measure. She let go of his belt, allowing him to fall to the ground, limbs like wet noodles. Leaning over, she slapped his cheek. No reaction.

Naomi looked at the panicked restaurant goers rushing to the exit, food and drinks all over the floor. "Okay, this place is less fun," she said to herself.

ONE

Jax walked up. "Guess you didn't need me."

Naomi turned, grinning, "Never do." When she saw his face fall, she added, "If it helps your fragile male ego, I needed the distraction. So, thanks." In the background, the alarm was still droning, the automated message repeating. The restaurant was almost empty now. She looked around. "Back door." Jax nodded and followed her.

The back of the restaurant was not an alley, but another street. "This place is an entire block?" Jax looked around at the back of the TGI Fridays. "Jeesh." He looked up and down the street to get his bearings. "Spaceport is this way." He headed off up the street.

As they crossed the street, a matte black luxury sedan came around the corner. An older model, no hover engine. It rolled on smart material tires similar to Rudy's rollerball. "Uh oh," Naomi said, pointing. The sound of approaching sirens drowned out the whine of the sedan's motor increasing power as it bore down on them. Naomi grabbed Jax's elbow, guiding him the opposite direction, down a small alley between two boutiques offering the latest in Nuevo Santiago summer fashions.

Jax tapped his earpiece. "Baxter, we've got ourselves a situation here."

"You need me to save you," the droid replied from aboard the *Osprey*.

"We wouldn't object," Naomi offered after tapping her own earpiece to join the conversation.

Rudy cut in, "I'll guide you." There was a pause, then, "Turn right when you exit the street and cross the street. There's an alley."

As they entered the alley that Rudy told them about, a blaster bolt struck the building to their left, raining chips of concrete down on them. Naomi and Jax moved from a jog to a sprint as the black sedan roared past the mouth of the alley. One of the goons from before leaned out the passenger side window to fire on them.

As Naomi and Jax ran through alleys ducking occasional blaster fire, Baxter was leaping from building to building, already halfway between the spaceport and Jax's location. *Almost there*, he beamed to Rudy.

"You're gonna have to move quick for this next block," Rudy said. "There's an open-air market between you and Baxter. Try to blend in and make it to the other side."

Naomi and Jax exited their alley, coming to a stop. Hundreds of shoppers were milling about across the street from them. They walked as quickly as they could across the street just as the black sedan slid into view. With no regard for traffic laws, the car came to a stop, and both Crimson Orchid operatives exited the vehicle.

"Excuse me, coming through," Naomi repeated over and over, trying to move through the midday shoppers. She glanced over her shoulder when they hit the halfway point through the shopping area. "Crap, they're almost on us!" she hissed as she not-politely shoved a suited man aside. "Sorry, nice suit," she said over her shoulder. The man made a rude gesture.

Jax looked around. "Rudy?"

"Keep going. When you get to the street, cross and go left."

"The spaceport is to the right," Jax protested.

"And Baxter is to the left," the navigation droid retorted.

"There!" Naomi pointed across the street to a large electronics store and the alley next to it. As they left the crowded shopping area, they turned their fast walk back into a sprint. "At least they're not shooting the place up," Naomi said as they crossed the street.

As they reached the alley, a hover car honked as both Crimson Orchid operatives crossed the street. The woman from the restaurant slammed a hand down on the hood and cursed the driver.

"Uh, Rudy, this alley is a dead end," Jax said as he and Naomi got halfway down the length of the narrow space. Several doors lined the sides of the cramped space. Rudy didn't answer. Jax tried a door handle. Locked. Naomi tried a handle on the opposite side, also locked.

At the open end of the alley, two suited thugs stopped. "Well, this was easier than I expected," one said loud enough for Jax and Naomi to hear. Both operatives pulled pistols from under their suit jackets.

Jax and Naomi backed all the way to the brick wall at the end of the alley. With their backs to the wall, Jax said, "Look, guys, I'm sure we can come to some sort of arrangement. We just got paid for a job. I can transfer the credits to you."

As the two organized crime goons came closer, a matte black shadow dropped from above, landing with a metallic thud. Both stopped, turning to look behind them as Baxter stood up from his landing. With a metal-on-metal *snikt* sound, blades deployed from both forearms. "Oh, shit," one said as he raised his pistol. The woman said nothing, raising her pistol and opening fire.

Knowing better, Jax closed his eyes as Baxter bolted toward the two criminals, their blaster bolts doing little to slow the combat droid down. He raised a hand to Naomi's face to shield her eyes. She swatted his hand away, then tightly closed her eyes. The screams truncated into low gurgles, then fell silent.

Naomi opened her eyes. "Ew," Naomi moaned, turning to look at Jax, his eyes still closed.

Baxter's blades made the same noise retracting as they did deploying. "Two fewer problems of the Crimson Orchid variety," he said nonchalantly.

SIDEWAYS

Exiting the alley as Baxter scaled the wall to return to the *Osprey* the same way he'd come, Naomi scolded, "I told you we needed to be more careful, that the moment we leave Kelso, they're on us." She hitched her thumb over her shoulder to the two bodies.

Jax waved her concern away. "They didn't show up last week on Sandusky."

"That's because no one likes Sandusky," Naomi retorted, turning toward the spaceport. "I'm just saying, unless we deal with this, they're gonna keep showing up."

"You make it sound like it's an overdue library book," Jax replied, flagging down an auto-cab. The door slid open, and he extended a hand for Naomi to get in first. "It's the freaking mafia. You know, the mafia that tried to frame and kill us on Jebidiah. The mafia that we outsmarted, sorta. The mafia that still wants us dead."

Naomi slid into the cab, making room for Jax. "Fair, but we gotta do something." She wrinkled her nose and lifted a foot off of something squishy.

"Destination?" the Rudimentary Intelligence, or RI, in

control of the vehicle asked. The dash had a pixelated face on it.

"Castellón Spaceport," Jax grunted, getting settled.

"Acknowledged," the vehicle replied as it pulled away from the sidewalk. The face turned into an 8-bit display of their progress toward the spaceport.

Jax looked at his business partner. "I'm open to ideas."

"I hate to interrupt," Skip, the *Osprey's* Sentient Intelligence, or SI, interrupted. "But in the last two hours, three different pairs of well-dressed men and women have walked by our landing pad. I believe our fake ident was not as airtight as we thought."

"Crimson Orchid?" Naomi asked.

"One would assume, unless an impromptu fashion show is taking place nearby," the ship's SI quipped.

"Gah," Jax groaned. He turned to watch the city pass by. He sighed, "Okay, keep us posted and see if you can't tell where they're hanging out. Bax, you may need to intercede, clearing us a path. We're about fifteen minutes from the port."

"Copy that," the deep baritone of the combat droid replied.

"Next time we're here, let's stay in the Old Town district," Naomi said.

Jax was silent a heartbeat, then turned. "What?"

"Old Town. Let's stay there next time," she repeated.

"Next time...we're here? Nuevo Santiago?" He rubbed his face.

Naomi stared at him. "Never mind, we're here." She tilted her head to the window. The cab had passed into the secure perimeter area of the spaceport, the road narrowing to one lane each way. Castellón Spaceport was the first spaceport of the colony. The first colonists made the ring

ONE

wall of rough-hewn brown brick, carving openings for businesses and administrative offices.

The Old Town district was on one side, much closer to the spaceport. As the colony grew, a new town that blossomed into the capital city was built a few kilometers from the port.

A few minutes later, the cab came to a stop at the pedestrian entrance to the spaceport. The pixelated face was back on the dash, grinning. "We have arrived. Thank you for riding with CabCo." The side door of the cab slid open.

Jax put his hand to his ear. "Bax, we're here."

"You're clear," the droid replied.

Inside the spaceport, Baxter, perched on top of a fifty-year-old bulk freighter, was watching four Crimson Orchid operatives confer. He had followed one pair after they had passed by the *Osprey* earlier. *Targets acquired*, he beamed back to the ship.

What do you want from me? Do what you do, Rudy sent back.

Don't track blood around the hold if you can avoid it, Skip added.

Baxter stepped off of the top of the freighter, dropping to the duracrete landing pad with a thud. As he stood, he said, "Hello, my name is Baxter. Prepare to die."

"Huh?" one of the goons said, turning to the others, who shrugged.

"You need to watch more old movies," the droid replied as his matching combat blades slid out of his forearms. The segments of the blade deployed, and for a split second, hung limp until the internal chain pulled the segments together into one solid blade. Both blades were honed to a point the human eye cannot see, able to cut through most metals and definitely skin and bone.

The moment the blades clicked into place, he lunged forward, skewering the two nearest men. The man and the woman behind them pulled their pistols and opened fire, striking their dead friends as often as Baxter.

One of his powerful railguns rose and swiveled into position over his shoulder. At full power, the slug would pass through the humans in front of him, vaporizing them, and plow through the ship a hundred meters beyond, a personal yacht of some kind. At thirty percent power, the slug flew through the nearest attacker and fell to the ground a dozen meters beyond. Before the third operative hit the ground, the railgun pivoted, taking aim on the fourth and final operative.

"Woah, wait," she said, raising both hands above her head.

Baxter cocked his head, then turned and walked away. The operative let out a loud sigh of relief as Baxter's railgun spun one hundred and eighty degrees and fired. With a wet splat, the fourth Crimson Orchid operative fell to the duracrete. *All clear*, he sent wirelessly.

CHAPTER TWO

THIS PLANET SUCKED ANYWAY

As Jax and Naomi reached the *Osprey*'s boarding ramp, Baxter appeared. "Four fewer Crimson Orchid goons to worry about on our next job."

Jax grunted, raising his hand so Naomi could go up the ramp. "If only I thought there was a chance of them running out of goons anytime soon."

"Truth," Naomi said, entering the small boarding room at the lowest section of the Valerian Coop Interceptor.

From the speaker in the ceiling, Skip scolded, "Wipe your feet, Baxter."

Jax shook his head as he entered the small space, pushing past Baxter to slap the control to raise the boarding ramp. "Let's just get off this planet, please." He followed Naomi up the spiral staircase to the cargo and engineering deck. Behind him, he heard Baxter's heavy footfalls on the staircase.

"Skip, get the preflight started, and let traffic control know we're leaving."

"The magic word?" the ship's SI replied.

Jax wiped his face, groaning. "Please." He turned to

Naomi when he heard her chuckle. He raised a finger. "Don't." He headed up to the common deck one level up. "This is your fault."

The preflight checks and departure clearance took less than five minutes to complete. "We're good to go, boss," Skip said as Jax flopped into the pilot's chair in the small flight deck of the *Osprey*.

Jax prepped his station, letting the flight controls slide into place. "Then let's get the hell out of here."

The repulsor lifts built into the *Osprey*'s wing roots powered up. The whine rose in pitch until the nimble ship rose from the landing pad. As it did, the two powerful landing gears retracted. Heavy hull plating slid into place to cover them.

Naomi came up the spiral staircase into the narrow flight deck. "Rudy, were you in my quarters?"

The navigation droid's squat cylindrical head spun 180 degrees to look at her. "Why would I be in your room?" He was secured into the custom designed frame built into the navigation console. "Like I'm some kind of human pervert or something."

Jax coughed. "Uh, here we go." He pushed the throttle control for the main engines, giving them power. The *Osprey* leapt forward, roaring over the top of the spaceport as she gained altitude, her atmospheric engines leaving thick streams of exhaust in their wake.

"I don't know why you'd be in there, but Baxter was with us, and, well, Skip is Skip," Naomi retorted. She leveled a finger at the meter-high nav droid. "Just admit it."

Two metallic clicks came from the navigation console, releasing Rudy. His body spun to line back up with what passed for his face. "Fine! I was organizing your closet!"

"You were what?" Naomi growled.

ONE

Jax pursed his lips, focusing on piloting the *Osprey* up and out of the atmosphere.

"The other day, we were talking, and I saw your closet. It was disturbing. Since you and Jax were busy, I thought I'd lend a hand." He spread his arms, palms up.

"I don't need…I have a system…"

Rudy's arms fell to his side. "Is the system, make piles not organized by color or size or style, then shove them into one enormous pile?"

Naomi threw her hands up. "Gah!" She stormed down the staircase, her footfalls ringing back up to the flight deck. From the deck below, she shouted, "Go in there again and I'll reprogram you!"

The moment Jax was reasonably sure Naomi was somewhere on the common deck, he exploded with laughter. He looked over his shoulder. "Dude."

Rudy spun to face him. "What?" He rolled back to his station, locking into place. "It was distressing."

Jax shook his head, turning back to his console. "We good for wormhole transition?" Behind him, he could hear Rudy mumbling. One of the small displays set in his flight console updated with a flight path, taking them past the orbit of Nuevo Santiago's two moons. After laying in the course, he pressed the ship wide intercom. "We're thirty minutes from wormhole."

Opening a wormhole near planets and moons, while doable, was not advised. The interplay of gravity and rent space-time tended to have unpredictable effects. The Empire did its best to enforce no-wormhole zones in most systems.

The time until wormhole passed without incident. The Crimson Orchid apparently didn't have a ship in orbit to intercept them, and the Imperial frigate that was in the system didn't even acknowledge them as they broke orbit.

Jax was about to engage the wormhole drive when Skip said, "Incoming comms."

Naomi came up the stairs. "Aren't we supposed to be in wormhole?" Jax looked at her, and she said, "I like the light show."

Before Jax could say anything, Skip said, "Governor Singh is calling."

Jax reached for the communications controls, opening the channel. "Hi, Auntie."

"Hello, Jackson. Where are you?" Her voice came through the overhead speakers.

"We're just leaving Nuevo Santiago. Heading home." Jax looked over his shoulder as Naomi dropped into the third, usually empty, duty station on the bridge. Over the past few months, she had been making it her own, which mostly included stickers on the side of the console and a fake plant epoxied to the top.

"Oh, good. I need a lift. You and your cute girlfriend can take me to the Governors' Summit."

"Auntie, you're on speaker. Also, what summit?" Jax blushed, not turning to look at Naomi. He could sense her ear-to-ear grin.

"It's time for the emperor's independent colony Governors' Summit," the aged Indian woman said.

Jax rubbed his face. "Oh, right, Unification Day. Can't you hire a shuttle?" He knew immediately that that was the wrong thing to say.

Governor Singh's voice was deeper, sterner. "Of course I can hire a shuttle. But I'm not, so I'll see you when you arrive. Jeffry and I will be ready. You can come for dinner."

ONE

The console beeped twice, letting him know the channel was closed.

"What's this summit?" Naomi asked, adding, "Why is it on Uni Day?"

Jax reached for the wormhole generator controls, opening the rift in space-time that the *Osprey* leapt into. Looked over his shoulder, he said, "It's the emperor's way of reminding the few remaining Indie stations and colonies of the armistice and who *won* the war." He used air quotes for *won*. He sighed. "Free trip to New Terra."

She thought for a moment. "Cool."

HOME SWEET SPACE STATION

Two days later, a bored sounding voice said, "*Osprey*, you're cleared for approach," from the overhead speakers of the flight deck. Ahead of the small ship, the rolling pin in a donut of Kelso station was growing.

"Copy that, Kelso control." Jax closed the channel. He pressed a control on his console and watched as the massive doors of the Caruso family mechanical bay slid apart. Orange lights in the ceiling and floor of the space swirled, warning anyone who might be in the bay that the static atmosphere barrier was active.

The *Osprey* slid into the massive bay, passing through the barrier that kept a breathable atmosphere inside the bay when the enormous doors were open. Once inside the bay, she turned slowly so she was facing out before settling on her outstretched landing gear.

Jax pressed the control that told the enormous doors to close, then put the entire console into standby. He turned. "Home sweet space station." Naomi smiled as she placed her own station into standby and moved to the spiral staircase.

ONE

As the pair moved from the bridge to the common deck, then to the cargo hold, Jax said, "Rudy can oversee getting things re-supplied here. You mind going grocery shopping?"

Naomi stepped out of the staircase in the cramped boarding room, pressing the control that lowered the boarding ramp. "Sure, no problem. I need to pick up some padlocks to keep our freaky little organizer out of my stuff."

"I heard that!" Rudy's voice came from the overhead speaker.

Naomi looked up at the ceiling. "Good. Stay out of my stuff, you mechanical freak!" She descended the ramp, muttering about droids and privacy.

Jax shook his head and looked up. "Rudy, Skip, get everything squared away. I suspect we're leaving tomorrow."

"Copy that, boss," the droid and the SI replied in unison.

From just above them in the cargo hold, Baxter said, "I'll go with Naomi." He stomped down the stairwell, pushing past Jax.

As Naomi crossed the bay toward the hatch that led out into the station, Jax shouted, "Shop for four!"

She turned as the hatch slid aside, revealing the corridor beyond. "Four?" Baxter caught up and moved into the corridor.

"Auntie doesn't go anywhere without Jeffry," Jax said.

Naomi smiled. "Of course." She turned and left, the hatch sliding closed behind her until a hand slid in, blocking it. Jax looked over, sighing, as the hatch retracted, revealing a Kelso station customs agent.

The heavyset woman walked in. "Mr. Caruso," she greeted.

"Oh, hi, Shirley. Where's Lewis?" He met her closer to the hatch than the *Osprey*.

The customs agent consulted her tablet, then looked up at Jax. "He's off today. I think he has his kids this week." She cleared her throat. "So, Nuevo Santiago? Anywhere else?"

Jax shrugged. "Nope, there and back again."

"Anything to declare?" She looked past Jax to the *Osprey*.

"Nope. Didn't even get any souvenirs."

She offered her tablet to Jax, the screen showing her completed report and a rectangle waiting for his thumbprint. "Okay, welcome back." After he placed his thumb on the screen, she nodded as she slid her tablet into a pouch on her pant leg.

As Shirley reached the hatch, Jax's gPhone buzzed. He removed it from his pocket, looking at the screen. He pressed a button and said, "I'm on my way, Auntie." As he lowered the phone, before tapping the screen to end the call, he heard her say, "Hurry up."

As the hatch closed behind Jax, Rudy rolled down the boarding ramp. Wirelessly, he told Skip, *I scheduled a sonic cleaning. They'll be here in an hour.*

You're my favorite, the SI that managed the *Osprey's* systems replied.

Rudy rolled underneath the ship to the wall of the bay. A panel slid open at his approach, revealing several tubes. He dragged a waste removal umbilical back to the underside of the *Osprey*. Rudy was far too short to reach the bottom of the ship from the ground, but having gotten used to Jax leaving these types of tasks to him, he had made improvements to the mechanical bay. A wide ramp with wheels on it came racing over, parking in perfect position to

ONE

allow the small navigation droid to reach the *Osprey*'s underside.

As Rudy attached the umbilical, Skip asked, *You know what the worst part of being installed in a starship is?*

Rudy reached up and pressed a button that activated the bilge pump system that would flush the ship's waste tanks into the space station's main waste system. *Humans pooping inside you?*

There was a pause, long enough to be noticeable to beings who process things in milliseconds. *Okay, the second worst thing?*

Rudy rolled down the ramp, sending it a signal to line up under the main data and power trunk connection. *What?* He rolled to the wall, fetching the thick trunk cable.

You all get to go off and do things, and I just sit here.

Rudy's head spun a full circle. *I am connecting umbilicals to you to suck human poop out and recharge your reactor. It's not as glamorous as you think.*

GROCERY SHOPPING

"Is the governor vegetarian?" Naomi asked as she and Baxter meandered through the first row of stalls in the market sector in the lower spoke of the station.

"Not that I know of, but I have not eaten with the governor," the matte black droid deadpanned. He pointed to his head. "No mouth."

Naomi looked up at the swishing red optical sensor and made a face. She turned to a stall up ahead. "There." She reached over toward Baxter, offering the shopping bag for him to hold. An older, dark-skinned man that Naomi thought might have come from India on Earth ran the stall. "Hello," she said as he looked up at her.

"Hello, young lady. What are you looking for today?"

"I'm going to be traveling with Governor Singh and don't know what she likes."

The man flashed a toothy grin. "And I would know because I'm Indian?" When he saw the look on Naomi's face, he pressed on, "Would it surprise you to learn that I grew up in Cleveland?"

"Oh, my God!" Naomi said, a flush rising up her neck

and cheeks. "I'm so sorry, I didn't mean to..." She turned away, about to bolt from the stall.

A weathered brown hand landed on her shoulder. "You young people, such easy marks." The man chuckled. "My dear, I came to Kelso from Pune when I was three. I don't know the governor personally, but she has visited my shop in the past." He turned and picked up a few things: spices, a bag of snacks, a bottle of something Naomi didn't recognize, and a few other things. He looked past Naomi to Baxter. "Mr. Robot, come, come." Baxter stepped closer, offering the shopping bag.

After the shopkeeper deposited the goods into Baxter's shopping bag, he reached for a tablet. As he entered the order, he said, "The governor should like those things."

As Naomi and Baxter left the Indian man's stall, she looked at her mechanical companion. "What about Jeffry?"

Without looking down at Naomi, Baxter replied, "He looks bland. We can grab a few things at Spacer Wares. Jax shops there a lot." She nodded.

The primary market of Kelso station was below the space dock facilities, a deck above what the residents often called The Below. Eighty percent of Kelso station's population were middle class by most standards. The market spanned the entire deck it occupied and comprised hundreds of stalls, selling anything from replacement parts for reactors to the foodstuffs of every nation on Earth. The bulk of Kelso's population originally emigrated from India and surrounding countries, so the smells of Indian food permeated the market space.

Spacer Wares, however, was above the space dock facilities in the more formal commercial district. Where the market was a swap meet, the commercial district was a shopping mall. Spacer Wares anchored one end of the spacious tree-lined walkways of the shopping area.

"I hate this place," Naomi complained as they entered the massive space. She was surveying the various signs indicating which aisles contained what. Baxter tapped her shoulder and pointed off to the left. She nodded. "It's just so impersonal and corporate." Baxter said nothing.

They walked until Baxter said, "This is the area Jax frequents."

Naomi looked around. Junk food, beer, and other high calorie snacks surrounded them. She sighed, "Yeah, no." She looked around, then pointed. "There. Come on."

DETOURS

"You took your time."

Jax leaned down to hug the short Indian woman standing in the doorway. "It's good to see you, Auntie." He straightened as she stepped back to smooth her pink and yellow sari.

She gestured to the table. "Come." She turned and walked into the room. Her living quarters were on the same level as her office.

A hatch in the living room connected the two spaces. It opened, and Jeffry walked in. "Hello, Jackson."

"Hey, Jeffry," Jax greeted as he took a seat at the dining table.

"Your job on Nuevo Santiago went well?" the young man, Governor Singh's administrative assistant, asked.

Jax smiled. "Oh yeah, and we got to stop at TGI Fridays."

"Lucky you," the other man replied, straight faced.

Governor Singh placed a plate in front of Jax, then motioned to an empty spot at the table. "Jeffry, sit down." She placed a plate where her assistant sat and one at her place opposite Jax. She turned to her adopted nephew. "Fridays?"

Jax shrugged. "Mozzarella sticks were half off." He looked down at his plate. "This looks great." He held up his fork, a kofta held on the end.

Governor Singh smiled. "I thought a home cooked meal before our trip was in order."

Jax nodded, chewing. Between bites, he asked, "So, I admit, I'd forgotten about these summits. When was the last one? He hasn't been doing them annually, right?"

Governor Singh thought as she chewed. "They were more frequent back in the day, when you were little. The emperor tired of our complaining." She frowned. "This is the first in..." She tapped her fork on her plate as she thought. She looked at Jeffry, who shrugged. "I guess five years? They petered out when his grip on the galaxy solidified." She was uncertain.

The three of them ate dinner, chatting about station hubbub and Empire gossip. Jax filled them in on their job playing private investigators on Nuevo Santiago. After dinner, he cleared the table and said, "Okay, you two get packed, and we'll meet up tomorrow. Sound good?"

Jeffry nodded. "I'll make sure we're there."

Jax left the executive levels of the station and headed down to the grittier levels below the space dock.

"Jackson Caruso!" Lucas the bartender of the Angry Spacer shouted, waving to Jax with his mechanical arm.

Jax smiled and took a seat at the bar. "Hey, Lucas."

The bartender grabbed a frosted mug and filled it. He slid it over. "Haven't seen you in a bit."

Jax took a sip. "Naomi and I had a gig."

"That working out, then?" the man on the other side of the bar asked.

ONE

Jax nodded and tilted his head. "I haven't killed her yet, so..."

"That's a good thing, I guess," Lucas chuckled.

"Jax! Hey, loser!" someone shouted from deeper inside the bar. Jax groaned. Lucas walked away, shaking his head.

Jax turned. "Hey, Marshmallow." He spotted Steve and a guy he assumed was Steve's boyfriend, not that he had been stalking Steve's SpaceBook page. "Hey, Stevie."

The younger Delphino waved. "Hey, Jax."

Jax smiled, looking at the man next to Steve. "Hi. I'm Jackson."

The other man, older than Jax by five years, at least, and sporting a rugged jawline with sandy blond hair, smiled. "Hi." He offered his hand. "Walter Benton."

Jax raised an eyebrow and looked at Steve, then back to Walter. "Of the founding Bentons?"

The older man smiled. "Indeed."

Marshall laughed, slapping Jax on the shoulder. "Stevie traded up."

"Hey, my family is a founding family, too, Marshmallow." The large Delphino scowled at the repeated use of a nickname he hated.

Walter looked at Jax, then Steve, then back again. "Oh, I see." He smiled. "Awkward."

Steve's cheeks burned bright red.

Jax smiled. "Not at all. Steve and I...uh..."

"Dated," Steve offered. "Sorta, well..."

"They hooked up," Marshall offered. "A couple months back."

Before anyone could say anything else, a familiar voice said, "Well, this is a sausage party."

Jax turned. "Hey, partner." He raised his beer glass. "Shopping done?" He mouthed the words *thank you*.

She nodded to Lucas as he offered her a beer. "Baxter took everything back to the ship."

"Cool." Jax finished his beer and nodded to Lucas. He turned to the surrounding group. "Walter, nice to meet you. You and Stevie look good together." Jax made a face as he accepted a mug from Lucas. "Marshmallow, you still suck." Jax turned to Steve. "Good to see you, man." Standing up, he said, "I've got a bunch more beer to drink, then a bed that isn't mine to find my way into." He raised his glass. "Goodbye." Naomi rolled her eyes as Jax made his way towards a group that looked like might be spending their first time in the Spacer.

CHAPTER THREE

MORNINGS AFTER

Something buzzed. Jax opened his eyes, then clamped them closed as the dim light felt like ice picks being jabbed into his brain. More slowly the second time, he opened them to see an unfamiliar bedroom. Trying to not jostle the bed too much, he looked around, trying to put the pieces of the previous night together. He had been successful in his mission to get drunk and make a new friend.

From the size of the room, he was in The Below, which wasn't surprising. Anyone he met at the Angry Spacer was likely a local, and not from the upper levels. He finally got to the other side of the bed, blond close-cropped hair facing away from him. Strong, mahogany shoulders.

The thing that buzzed, buzzed again. "I think that's your phone," his host said, rolling over. He smiled. "Good morning."

Jax's ears flushed bright red. "Sorry." He slowly slid out from under the thin sheets, looking around the floor for his clothes. "And, yeah, good morning." He smiled.

His host slid out of bed and padded to the small kitchenette in the corner. "Coffee?" he asked over his shoulder.

Jax watched him for a few heartbeats until his phone, wherever it was, buzzed again.

He finally found his pants, half under the bed. He pulled his gPhone out of a pocket and looked at the screen. *You're late. Make it a run of shame. – Love, Naomi.*

"Damnit," he hissed, then shot a glance over to the kitchen. "Sorry, gonna have to rain check on the coffee..." He drew out the last breath, drawing a blank on his host's name.

"Tony," the other man smiled.

"Sorry, I suck with names," Jax apologized, slipping his T-shirt on.

"I don't know that we exchanged them last night," Tony admitted, taking a sip of his coffee. He held up a disposable cup. "For the road?" His brown eyes twinkled at his guest's obvious discomfort.

Jax got his shoes on and walked over. Taking the cup, he nodded. "Thanks. I gotta run, but let's catch up when I get back?"

Tony grinned. "I'd like that. A proper date maybe?" He walked Jax to the door. As the hatch slid open, he held out his own gPhone, swiping on the screen. Jax's beeped, notifying him of an incoming data stream. "Don't be a stranger."

As the hatch to Tony's quarters closed, Jax looked at the phone filing the other man's contact details for later. Another message appeared. *Where are you?*

He tapped the message, then put the phone to his ear. "I'll be right there." He took a sip of the coffee Tony had given him. Pretty good stuff for someone living down Below.

"You need to set an alarm before you go out sleeping around," Naomi scolded.

"Okay, Mom. Relax. I'm only a few levels away. I'll be

there in a minute." He closed the channel, putting the phone in his back pocket.

The door to the Caruso family mechanical bay slid out of the way, allowing Jax into the bay. The *Osprey* was sitting in her normal place, facing out toward the large outer doors. Rudy and Naomi were waiting near the cobbled together living room space next to the small office in the corner.

He grinned as he set his coffee cup down on an end table. "She's already here, huh?"

Rudy made his nodding gesture, a small metal hand in a fist, bobbing up and down.

Naomi looked at the cup. "Your hookup runs a coffee shop?"

Jax tutted, "My *hookup* runs a none-of-your-business." He took another sip. "Though that would make sense. This is a damn good cup of coffee." He headed for the *Osprey*'s boarding ramp. As he reached the embarkation space, he had to stop to climb over a mountain of suitcases. He looked down. Naomi and Rudy had followed him. "What the hell? It's just her and Jeffry, right? She didn't bring the rest of her staff?"

Naomi stared at him. "Just her and Jeffry."

Jax looked up toward the opening in the deck where the spiral staircase passed through. "Hey, Baxter! Can you help with this?" He rubbed his face as the mild hangover he woke up with reasserted itself.

From the cargo deck above, "Kill people and haul luggage. I have the best existence."

Jax rubbed his face, then climbed over the luggage to take the stairs up to the common deck.

NOW DEPARTING

"Jackson, you're late," Governor Singh said from the sofa in the common area. She and Jeffry were sitting together, an assortment of tablets laid out in front of them. When she saw him, she grinned. "Busy night last night?"

"Morning, Auntie, Jeffry," Jax said as he passed the seating area, heading for the only restroom on the ship, in the forward most section of the common deck. "Just need to splash some water on my face, and we'll get going."

As the door to the ship's head closed, he heard his adopted aunt say, "I hope you used protection!" He was glad she couldn't see his face.

When Jax emerged from the head, Baxter was coming up the stairs with more suitcases than Jax could ever hope to carry, balanced and clutched. The bot turned to Jax. "Where are these going?"

Jax opened his mouth, but Governor Singh beat him to the punch. "My bags go in Jackson's room. Jeffry's can go in one of the other rooms."

"Uh, what now?" Jax asked. He looked at Naomi, who

was trying to hide her grin. She turned around before he could address her. "My room is, well, my room."

"Not anymore." The ancient Indian woman grinned. "I'm old. I can't sleep on one of those narrow uncomfortable cots in your guest rooms."

"They're called berths," Jax corrected, not knowing what else to say.

"I don't care." She turned to Baxter. "You heard me, big bot." Baxter turned his swishing red optical sensor to Jax, then turned and went down the corridor to the aft of the ship where the living quarters were.

Jax looked at the ceiling, taking a deep breath. "Okay, I guess—"

"Don't forget, my quarters are mine now," Naomi interrupted. She pointed to Jeffry. "You two can share the other guest berth."

Jax looked at the younger man, who just shrugged and said, "Fair warning: I snore."

Jax groaned and followed Baxter. "I'll get my things!" Then, he added, "Rudy, get us ready to go!"

The navigation droid, who had kept to the corner of the room out of sight, bounced on his roller ball, then headed for the open center of the spiral stairwell connecting the decks of the ship. He shot up to the bridge without a sound.

Baxter needed two trips to haul all the luggage from the small embarkation room at the bottom of the *Osprey* and get it sorted into the various berths. Jax had moved some clothes and personal items into the only remaining guest berth, now that Naomi had laid claim to one of them and replaced the double bunk bed setup with a more comfortable, larger bed.

As Jax dropped into the pilot's seat, he consulted his console. "We good?" He turned his head slightly to look at Rudy, secured to his navigation console.

"Yup, space control cleared us for immediate departure," the droid replied.

Jax tapped the intercom. "We're cleared for departure. Make sure you're seated."

Down in the common area, Governor Singh and Jeffry were back in the lounge area going over tablets spread over the coffee table and between them on the sofa. Naomi was sitting in the large chair, watching them. She asked, "So, what's all this?" She pointed to the tablets. "Stuff for your meeting or whatever?"

The governor looked up. "Oh no. This is just station work we're trying to get ahead of." She smiled. "No matter what, we always have a backlog." She waved to the assorted devices. "Work never stops."

Naomi's eyes bulged. "Running for governor is off my list now. That's a lot of paperwork. You're only going to be gone a week."

The rumble of the reactor powering up reverberated through the common deck.

Jeffry clucked, "You've no idea. This is just the stuff I didn't trust the rest of the staff to manage on their own in our absence."

The ship lurched as it lifted off the deck. The sound of the landing gear retracting echoed. Jeffry looked around. "Is that normal? Should the ship make those kinds of noises?"

From the overhead speaker, Skip replied, "Don't worry, that's just the landing gear retracting. You're perfectly safe inside me."

Naomi pursed her lips, eyebrows arched. She looked up at the ceiling. "That's probably not the way you should say that."

"Oh, sorry," the ship's SI replied but offered nothing further.

ONE

Governor Singh rested a hand on Jeffry's knee. "Jeffry doesn't leave the station."

Naomi nodded. "Don't like space travel?"

"It's not my favorite thing, no," the young man admitted. As the ship shifted again, something downstairs in the cargo deck groaned. Jeffry's face paled.

LUNCH

The door to the ship's head opened. Jeffry stumbled out. From the small dining table, Jax said, "I hope you didn't miss." When Jeffry made a face, Jax continued, "Lunch is ready."

Naomi helped Governor Singh up from the couch and walked her over to the table. The older woman took a seat as Jax placed a specially designed magnet bowl on the table. She inhaled. "Chili?"

Jax shrugged as Jeffry and Naomi sat down. "We've got a few days for you to curry up the kitchen. I figured I'd treat." He took his own bowl and stood leaning against the countertop. He nodded to his adopted aunt. "What can you tell us about the summit?"

The governor finished chewing, then said, "The emperor likes to give lip service to the regional governors by occasionally hosting these summits." She took another bite of her lunch, then continued, "They're really just an opportunity for the emperor to show off how big his dick is." Jeffry coughed, setting his spoon down. The governor continued, "He started holding them after he assumed

ONE

power. They were his way to show the galaxy that his rule was benevolent. That he cared what the colony and station governors thought. Crap like that." She grunted. "Then, once he solidified his hold, he was free to drop the pretense."

"Sounds shitty," Naomi offered.

Governor Singh nodded. "It is." She shrugged. "Such is life. If nothing else, it's a chance to visit New Terra, all expenses paid." She took a bite. "I am curious why, after all this time, he's decided to hold a summit."

Jax perked up. "So, I can submit an invoice for this trip?" The look the elderly Indian woman gave him was enough to make him look at the deck and take a bite of his chili. He added, "Yeah, it is a bit troubling, him holding a summit all of a sudden." He took a drink, then asked, "Think he's up to something hinky?"

"He's always thinking of something hinky," Governor Singh replied.

Naomi rubbed her chin. "Like you said, free trip to New Terra."

Jax looked at her. "I kind of assumed you wouldn't be that keen to go to New Terra."

Naomi tilted her head. "I probably wouldn't go there on my own." She looked at Jax. "But I have some business I can do while we're there."

Jax raised an eyebrow but let the topic drop at a look from his new business partner. "Anyone need seconds?"

Jeffry raised a hand, then puffed his cheeks out and lowered it, waving Jax off.

Naomi asked, "So he expects the independent station governors to attend but have no voice or role in the thing?" She thought for a moment. "For that matter, why are there independent stations?"

Jax groaned, "You had to ask." He opened the refrigerator and grabbed a beer.

The governor clucked, "Never mind him." She took a bite of chili, then continued, "After the war, the remnants of the Indies wrung a few concessions from soon-to-be Emperor Stenson. One was the independent stations and colonies." She looked up at the ceiling, then said, "As a show of good faith, those not in favor of unification could have a place. We still, for the most part, are subject to the laws of the Empire, but are more," she tapped one manicured fingernail on the table, "protectorates, I suppose."

Naomi opened her mouth but was interrupted by the ship lurching to the right and something somewhere making a sound like metal tearing. The lights flickered, then went out a split second before the artificial gravity died.

"Skip!" Jax shouted as he grabbed the edge of the cupboard he was standing next to. The ceiling speaker crackled.

"Jackson?" the governor asked, clutching the table, her legs moving up over her head.

"I'm gonna hurl," Jeffry warned.

Naomi pushed off away from him. "Keep it together, Jeffry." The emergency lighting turned on, bathing everyone and everything in diffuse red light. "Captain?"

Jax kicked off toward the staircase. "Skip, what's going on?"

The speaker in the ceiling crackled again, then Skip answered, "I'm trying to run a diagnostic. It is not going well. What I can tell you is that something went wrong with the wormhole generator."

"Oh, God!" Jeffry moaned.

ARE YOU KIDDING ME

Jax pulled himself into his seat at the flight console. It was entirely dark. "Skip, you said the issue was the wormhole generator. What's up with main power?"

"I don't know. Baxter is down there looking," the ship's SI replied.

"But I am not an engineering droid," Baxter added over the channel.

Rudy, still secured in his console, said, "I've been able to get a fix on our position."

"We weren't in wormhole long enough to be anywhere close to New Terra," the nav droid said. "We're in deep space. The nearest star looks like it's at least fifteen light years away. According to the star charts, the system is uninhabited."

Naomi drifted up to the bridge. "I got your aunt and Jeffry situated." She looked around. "What's up?"

"We're in deep space. The nearest system we can't reach is uninhabited," Jax offered, then turned. "Hey, maybe your blue juju can help figure this out. Skip is running a diagnostic and Baxter is in engineering…" He trailed off and shrugged. "And until we get main power back online, and ideally figure out what the hell is wrong, we're dead in space."

Naomi nodded. "I'll go down to engineering, see if the reactor control system has anything to say." She turned and pushed off back down the spiral staircase.

Moments later, "Jax! Jax! Come down here!" Naomi shouted from the base of the staircase on the cargo and engineering deck.

"Be right there," Jax replied.

As he passed through the common deck, his aunt asked, "Jackson, what's going on?" She and Jeffry were seated on the sofa, strapped in with safety belts that were normally tucked under the cushions out of sight.

He paused long enough to say, "We're working on it." He pulled himself down to the next level, where Naomi was waiting.

"Do you know what an alluvial damper is?" she asked as he followed her through the cargo hold, past the small med bay into the engineering compartment.

Baxter was standing near the reactor control panel, his feet magnetized. He moved to the side when Jax and Naomi entered. "Oh, good. Unless you need me to break this, I don't really know what else I can do here."

Jax looked around the engineering space. He pointed to something. "That it?"

Naomi followed his finger, shaking her head. "It wasn't a pop quiz, and no, that's not it."

Baxter, now standing near the hatch, said, "I didn't do it."

CHAPTER FOUR

SPACE WALK

Jax looked at his mechanical friend and smiled. He looked around again, bracing himself as he floated. "This isn't my forte, either." He turned to the ceiling. "Skip? What's an..." He looked at Naomi.

"Alluvial damper," she said.

"Alluv—"

"I heard her," Skip interrupted. "The alluvial damper manages power flow between the reactor and the wormhole generator." There was a pause. "I'm a little embarrassed that Naomi could identify the issue faster than I could. My thanks."

"You're very welcome, Skip," Naomi replied sweetly. "I'm sure your diagnostic would have gotten to it. Directly interfacing with the reactor at the firmware level let me take a shortcut that isn't available to you."

"When this meeting of the mutual admiration society concludes, let me know," Jax groused. From the hatch, Baxter barked a metallic sounding laugh.

"Be nice," Naomi hissed.

Skip continued, "Anyway. The alluvial damper failed,

rather spectacularly, I might add." A monitor came to life showing a camera view of the topside of the *Osprey*. Normally, the view would show the sleek curves of the ship's hull. Right then, it showed a jagged tear in the hull, something inside sending sparks into space. Skip continued, "It caused a cascade failure along the main power trunk, which is why most of the power is out, and the reactor automatically scrammed."

"That's not supposed to happen, right?" Jax asked.

"Yes and no." The *Osprey*'s SI paused. "The reactor scramming is exactly what was supposed to happen. Likewise, the main fuses tripping. Had those things not happened, the cascade would have destroyed the entire main bus and possibly put the reactor into overload." The ship's SI paused to let that sink in, then added, "The alluvial damper failing is definitely not something that should happen. That is likely a result of the secondary fuse assembly failing. Something, I might add, I warned you could happen if the primary fuse tripped."

Jax made a face. "I thought we fixed it?" He pushed himself off of the display he was using to get closer to the main reactor panel.

Skip made a noise. "We did not." From the speaker came Jax's voice: *We'll fix it later, I'm sure it'll be fine for a while. Those are expensive.*

Naomi looked at Jax, her mouth pressed into a fine line. She was hovering motionless in the middle of the space.

Jax rubbed his face. "Okay, no more recording our conversations."

"That's your takeaway?" Naomi put both hands on her hips, which caused her to rotate in place until she grabbed something on the ceiling.

Jax waved her off. "No. Skip, what are our options? And

I'm sorry I didn't take your warning seriously before."

"Thank you. Luckily, we are not completely screwed. I believe we can fashion a temporary fix. We'll need to effect actual repairs on New Terra, but getting there should be possible."

Skip explained what needed to happen and how to make the repairs. Once they knew what the problem was, getting the reactor and gravity back online took little time. After that, the industrial fabricator in the corner of the engineering space came to life.

In the common area, Jeffry was hyperventilating after being told he'd have to space walk with Jax to fix the broken alluvial damper and fuse assembly. The younger man moaned, "I've never space walked. I don't even like space travel."

"It's easy," Jax replied.

"Why can't Naomi do it?"

"Jeffry, stop being such a baby," Governor Singh chastised. "If Jax says it's safe, we can trust him."

"I need to help Skip test the equipment, and I can't..." She paused. Jeffry and Governor Singh did not know that she was an Interface. "...Do that from outside. I need to be at the console in engineering." Jax looked over and winked. She sighed and rolled her eyes.

"He said this piece of junk was safe," the administrative assistant protested, gesturing around the common deck.

"No offense taken," Skip deadpanned from the overhead speaker.

Jeffry groaned, "Fine."

Jax smiled. "That's the spirit. It won't take along." He pointed to the spiral staircase. "Let's go suit up."

The *Osprey* didn't have a large inventory of suits. The other reason Naomi made little sense as one of the space walkers was that none of the suits were her size—something Jax had to promise to remedy at the next opportunity. There were two rugged EVA suits in the storage locker at the forward section of the embarkation room at the lowest level of the ship, on the opposite side of the spiral staircase as the boarding ramp.

Jax pressed a control next to the boarding ramp, causing the thick metal plating to slide into place, cutting off the embarkation room from the rest of the ship. The spiral staircase that ran from that room to the flight deck had a break in it at each deck for seals to move into place. He turned to Jeffry. "Ready?"

"Not even a little," the other man replied from inside his suit. He reached up to his face, his gloved hand smacking into the faceplate. He frowned and lowered his hand.

Next to them was a toolbox and a piece of equipment that neither of them recognized or really understood, fresh off the industrial fabricator. Jax pressed another control, causing the air in the small space to evacuate. Another button soundlessly lowered the boarding ramp. Jax clipped a tether from his belt to a ring just inside the opening of the ramp. Before Jeffry could take a step, Jax reached out and grabbed his tether and attached it, as well. Jax picked up the replacement part that Skip had manufactured in engineering. He nodded to the toolbox. "You get that."

In the common area, Naomi looked at the governor. "I was thinking chicken tikka masala for dinner."

The older woman, sitting on the sofa, turned to look at the kitchen area where Naomi was standing. "I would like that. I'll help." She stood and joined Naomi in the small kitchenette space. She opened one of the cupboards, seeing the fruits of Naomi's earlier shopping excursion. "I like you." She smiled.

BACK ON TRACK

"No! No, not that one!" Jax shouted over the comms. Skip piped the two men's comms into the ship so Naomi and the governor could keep tabs on the progress of the repairs. Naomi looked at the governor, eyebrow raised. The older woman shrugged.

"Don't snap at me!" Jeffry replied. "Here."

There was a pause. "Thanks. Sorry," from Jax.

Rudy rolled over to the two women. "Need any help?"

Governor Singh looked down at the rust-colored navigation droid. "You can chop the garlic and the pepper." She offered a cutting board and a knife.

Rudy took the board but waved away the knife. "I have my own."

Both of the governor's eyes opened wide. She looked at Naomi, then back to Rudy as he rolled over to the small dining table to work. A hatch on his side opened, revealing a glistening eight-inch-long knife.

Naomi turned to look. "He picked up a new hobby back on Themura."

"Cooking?"

Naomi turned back to her work. "Stabbing and cutting."

At the table, Rudy's gun metal gray arm was a blur as he diced the garlic and chopped the pepper.

From the overhead speakers, Jax shouted, "No! Damnit, are you trying to kill us?"

"Don't yell at me," Jeffry replied.

"Then pay attention," Jax snapped. "Hand me the number four spanner." After a moment, "Thank you."

Naomi looked at the governor. "Should we lay odds on whether both of them make it back inside?"

The small framed Indian woman looked up. "He'd better not hurt Jeffry. That boy is a wonder in the office."

Naomi chuckled. "How long has he worked for you?"

The governor thought for a moment. "Three years now. He came on board after my last assistant retired." She grinned. "I decided to try a younger one this time, get more out of him."

Naomi shook her head. "Kinda diabolical."

The older woman winked. "I plan to be in office a while."

"We're done. Naomi, can you and Skip confirm?" Jax asked over the ceiling speakers.

Naomi put down the bowl she was holding and went to the stairwell. She looked at the ceiling. "One second."

"No rush. We're just hanging out here being blasted by cosmic radiation," Jax quipped.

"What?!" Jeffry exclaimed.

"I'm kidding, calm down," Jax replied.

As Naomi entered the engineering space, she called out, "Skip, ready?"

"I am," the overhead speaker answered. The primary display on the reactor control panel came to life at the same time. A wireframe of the *Osprey* was rotating slowly. A section of the ship was blinking yellow, the newly installed temporary fix to the damaged alluvial damper.

As Naomi placed both hands on the control console, her blue sub-dermal bio-circuitry lit up. The blue lines along her arms pulsed, and the lines around her eyes glowed as data flowed to her optic nerves. "I'm in. The power control system seems happy."

"I agree. Are you able to access the wormhole generator? I can run a diagnostic, but that would take an hour."

"One second." She closed her eyes for a moment. "Okay, yeah, the generator is getting positive control connections from the new hardware. I'm having it run a self-test routine now."

"I have a positive data stream," the ship's SI announced.

Naomi looked up; her bio-circuitry faded. "Jax, we're good here. You two can come back in."

"Thank God!" Jeffry said.

Jax chuckled. "We're heading in."

Naomi looked around. "Skip, you good?"

"I am. You may go back to your cooking," the SI replied.

Even with the hatch separating the cargo and engineering deck from the embarkation room closed, she could hear the clanking and jostling of the two space suited men returning.

By the time Jax and Jeffry made it up to the common deck, dinner was ready and waiting.

Jax nudged Jeffry. "See, this was worth it, right?"

The younger man clucked, "I'm pretty sure I'd be eating chicken tikka masala whether I went out there," he motioned to the nearest bulkhead and deep space beyond it, "or not."

NOW ARRIVING

The temporary fix to the alluvial damper held all the way to New Terra. Only once during the rest of the trip did Jax prank Jeffry by running down the stairs, screaming about an impending explosion. Jeffry didn't stop screaming for five minutes.

The *Osprey* dropped out of the purple and green swirl of disrupted space-time. Right into the middle of four Imperial Warhammer class cruisers.

"Uh," Jax said.

"We're in the outer system. Four Warhammer class cruisers, all in weapons range," Skip announced. "We're being targeted," the ship's SI added.

"And hailed," Rudy said.

Jax reached for the communication controls as Governor Singh came up the stairs. "What's going on?"

Jax looked over his shoulder and tilted his head so she could see his tactical screen. "This is independent transport *Osprey*. We're transporting a VIP to some kind of summit or something on New Terra."

"*Osprey*, we're sending a nav plot to you now. Proceed

to the indicated coordinates and power down to await customs inspection," an anonymous voice came from the speakers. It added, "Any deviation from the nav plot will result in the loss of your starship operator's license."

"Uh, okay, but we're kind of in a hurry. Our VIP needs to be at her meeting—"

The voice interrupted, "You will proceed to the designated coordinates." The comm system beeped. Channel closed.

"Fucking Imperials," Governor Singh hissed as she descended the stairs.

"Imperial corvette inbound," Skip announced. "It is on course for the rendezvous they gave us."

Jax stood. "Time to prep for visitors."

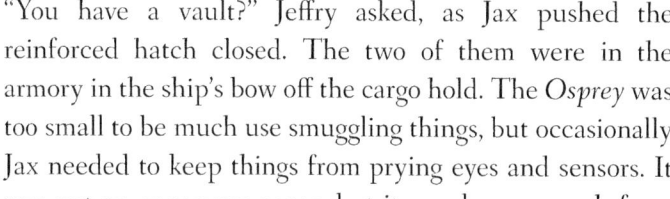

"You have a vault?" Jeffry asked, as Jax pushed the reinforced hatch closed. The two of them were in the armory in the ship's bow off the cargo hold. The *Osprey* was too small to be much use smuggling things, but occasionally Jax needed to keep things from prying eyes and sensors. It was not an enormous space, but it was large enough for a combat droid.

Jax winked. "Just for special stuff." He turned, gesturing for Jeffry to leave the room with wall-to-wall weapons and equipment. "Be good in there."

"Just get rid of them," Baxter complained from inside the vault, over comms.

"There wasn't a vault in the *Osprey* when your parents had her," Governor Singh said, arms crossed, as Jax joined everyone else in the cargo hold.

Jax looked at the ceiling. "Uh, just a little something I

added once I started flying her." His adopted aunt growled. He held up both hands. "It's not like I'm running guns or drugs, just the occasional contraband." He made air quotes at the end.

There was a clang from the port cargo door. A light over the personnel hatch in the larger cargo door blinked from red to orange, then settled on green.

Jax nodded toward the personnel hatch. "Company's here." He moved over to the hatch and pressed the release. He stepped back as the heavy hatch swung open.

YOU COULD AT LEAST BY ME A DRINK

Six matte gray armored Shock Troopers stomped into the cargo bay. They fanned out, three to a side, taking position on both sides of the personnel hatch. During the war, the Shock Troops' armor went through several design revisions until it was settled that they be as physically imposing as possible. The thick armor could deflect weapons fire from pistols. Micro musculature threads running through every piece of the armor doubled the wearer's strength.

An officer, a man in his fifties, by Jax's estimate, walked in. His crimson uniform was pressed and covered in medals. He looked around, steel-blue eyes locking on Jax. "Captain Burns?"

Governor Singh turned to her adopted nephew, eyebrows raised. He coughed. "Oh, sorry, that's an old record. Caruso, Jackson Caruso."

The officer nodded. "I'm Commander McGarry. I'll be conducting your customs inspection. Anything else you want to tell me before we start?"

Governor Singh stepped forward. "Hello, Commander.

I'm Governor Neeti Singh of Kelso station. We're expected at the Imperial Palace. If we could—"

McGarry cut her off. "This will take as long as it takes. I'm sure the emperor will understand, especially if we find contraband." He turned back to Jax. "Anything you tell me now will be looked at more favorably than if we find it ourselves."

Jax put his hands on his chest. "I run a clean ship, sir. Just ferrying this nice lady to the Capitol."

Commander McGarry harrumphed, then turned to his troops. "Two here, two on the deck above." He turned to Jax once more, pointing to the opening in the stairwell leading down to the embarkation room. "Your boarding room?" Jax nodded. He turned back to his troops. "One there, one up on the bridge." The Shock Troopers nodded as one and split up to their various assignments. Commander McGarry followed, heading up the staircase.

Jax looked at the others and shrugged. "Good times." He headed for the stairs. Everyone else fell in behind him.

Jeffry leaned down to his boss. "Burns?" The older Indian woman shrugged.

When Jax and the others arrived on the common deck, Commander McGarry looked at them. "You have a droid." It wasn't a question. Rudy was next to the main entertainment screen, plugged into his charging base.

Jax nodded slowly. "A nav droid, yes."

"You didn't mention it earlier."

"You're right. I also have a refrigerator. Droids aren't illegal," Jax replied, standing taller, his chest puffed up a bit. "The ship has an SI, as well."

The commander stared at Jax a moment, then turned and headed for the living quarters. Over his shoulder, he said, "When you land, keep your droid aboard the ship. It

ONE

isn't welcome on New Terra." He nodded to a Shock Trooper that was standing at the first of three doors to the living quarters, the room Jax and Jeffry were sharing.

Governor Singh placed a hand on Jax's arm once all of the Imperials on the common deck were out of sight. "Burns?"

Naomi whistled softly, looking at the ceiling. Jax shook his head. "These assholes don't need to know who I am." When he saw the confusion on both the governor's and Jeffry's faces, he continued, "Besides the other modifications post-mom and -dad owning the ship, I hacked the identity module so Skip could update it on the fly. They'd need a top flight hacker to even notice the hack," he whispered. "Any time we encounter Imperials, it's under a unique name."

"I appreciate you not playing that game this time," Jax's adoptive aunt said. "They know who I am, so it would have caused us unnecessary drama."

"What about your gPhone identity?" Jeffry asked, holding up a finger.

Each gPhone contained a secure enclave chip that held health and identity records for its owner. Presumed to be nearly unhackable, gPhones were universally used for personal identification and data storage.

Jax smiled. "Hacked, as well. Whenever Skip updates his identity core, it propagates to my phone." He wiggled his eyebrows in satisfaction. "We encrypted my actual records on the device. I can access them when needed."

Commander McGarry leaned out of the quarters that were normally Jax's. "Captain?"

Jax took a deep breath. "Coming, Commander."

"What is this?" the Commander asked. He and one of the Shock Troopers were in Jax's quarters, which, despite being larger than the other two, didn't leave a lot of room for Jax to join them.

"What's what?" Jax asked, trying to see past the Shock Trooper. The hulking gray armor took up a lot of space.

Commander McGarry held up a locked box. A very rugged looking locked box.

"Porn," Jax replied without a second thought.

"Porn?" The commander dropped the safe on the bed. He turned to Jax. "You keep your pornography in a personal safe?"

"My desires are...unconventional," Jax replied, straight faced. The Imperial officer's eyes went wide. The Shock Trooper standing next to Jax shuffled slightly to the side, away from Jax.

INTERESTING TASTES

"What are you doing?" Skip asked the Shock Trooper who was poking at Jax's command console. The trooper had a portable data console connected to the flight controls.

"Shut up," the trooper said. He continued to work, using his console to dig through flight records, Jax's personal logs, and more.

The bridge went dark. The trooper stood up. "Don't make me call my commander, you stupid droid."

The speakers crackled. "Excuse me. I am not a droid. I am a mark three Sapient Intelligence. I can process more data in a second than your feeble human brain will process in your lifetime."

"I have a job to do," the trooper retorted. "I'm going to do it."

The lights on the bridge flickered, changing color and intensity, causing the trooper to turn in a circle looking for a threat. The portable console screen went dark, then came back to life. Startled, the trooper turned back to his work and stumbled backwards. "What the hell is that?"

"Jax calls it tentacle porn," Skip replied cheerfully.

"Well, stop it!" the trooper said.

"No," Skip replied.

The trooper turned to his console and immediately turned away again. He put a hand to the side of his helmet. "Commander."

Jax's answer about the lock box drove the Imperial commander from the main berth to Naomi's room.

"This place is a mess," the haughty Imperial said, looking around.

Jax opened his mouth but said nothing as the commander put his finger to his ear, no doubt the ear with a commset in it. He nodded along as someone said something. Turning to Jax, "We're done here." He looked at the trooper and motioned them out of the room.

As the last of the troopers filed out of the personnel hatch to the Imperial corvette connected to the *Osprey,* the commander looked at Jax, Naomi, and the others. "Welcome to New Terra. Remember what I said about the droid." He didn't wait for an acknowledgement, turning and walking down the boarding tube connecting the two ships. The commander stopped and looked at Jax as the Shock Troopers continued into the corvette. "You need to find religion." He continued into his ship.

Jax rushed over and slammed the hatch shut, pressing the control next to the larger cargo door to lock it. A second later, a loud clunk sounded from the opposite side of the cargo door as the docking tube disengaged and retracted back to the Imperial vessel.

"What did he want in your quarters?" Naomi asked as the group moved up the staircase.

"They found my lock box," Jax replied, not looking back.

"The one under your bed?" Governor Singh asked.

ONE

That time, Jax turned as they all came out on the common deck, and he took a few steps up to be out of their way. "You been snoopin', Auntie?"

The old woman shrugged. "It's what we do. What's in it?"

Jax continued climbing the stairs. "None of your business." He whistled tunelessly as he continued up the stairs to the bridge.

"We're cleared to continue on to New Terra," Skip said from the overhead speakers as Jax arrived on the flight deck.

Jax nodded. "Any trouble up here?"

"None. The trooper was trying to snoop until I showed him your more exotic pornography."

"What?"

"The tentacle stuff," the ship's SI explained.

"Oh." Jax made a pained expression as he sat down. "That's not really what I'm—"

"I accessed your more recent acquisition."

"Yeah, okay. That's enough tentacle talk. Thanks." He brought the sub-light engines online and throttled up.

From the deck below, three loud bangs echoed.

"Could someone let Baxter out, please!" Jax shouted as he guided the *Osprey* toward her destination.

CHAPTER FIVE

PLANET FALL

After departing the company of the Imperial corvette, the *Osprey* burned hard down the gravity well toward New Terra to make up time, passing dozens of ships heading in and out of the system. New Terra was by far the busiest star system in the Empire. Hundreds of ships moved in and out of the system every hour.

In most star systems in the Empire, you could just drop out of a wormhole near the colony world you were heading for. Because New Terra was the seat of power, the entire system was ringed with interdiction field generators. There were four approved entry points into the system based in the outer system just beyond the orbit of Heathcliff, the outermost planet in the system. A ship entering from any other direction would be immediately chased down.

The Bellerophon system, previously known as the 51 Pegasi system to Earth astronomers three hundred years prior, was the second extrasolar colony that the people of Earth established. The first, in Epsilon Eridani, was destroyed when the colonists tried to secede from Earth's control. That planet was still uninhabitable.

The discovery of wormhole generator technology opened up systems near and far, allowing humans to leave their homeworld in droves. And they did. After Epsilon Eridani, the governments of Earth realized they couldn't control all of those new worlds. The Independent Systems Alliance was born.

New Terra was one of those one-in-a-million finds. Earthlike in every way meaningful to humans, lacking any native sentient species, the planet was perfect for establishing a colony. Plants and animals native to Earth took to the planet with ease. The population of New Terra exploded as emigration was open to all of Earth's countries.

The orbit over New Terra was one of the most congested that Jax had ever seen. Thousands of ships were sitting in parking orbits strung between almost a dozen orbital stations, most the size of Kelso station or larger.

One in particular was coming around the planet. "Gateway station," Jax said aloud.

Naomi whistled. "I always forget how massive that thing is."

Gateway station was the first thing built in the system. Meant to provide housing and logistical support for the earliest colonists, its purpose since then had shifted over the decades, as had its mass. The government had built upon it time and time again. Most recently, it was home to the Imperial Naval Command. Docked on either side of the massive station were two massive Warhammer class cruisers.

"Incoming call," Skip announced.

"Inbound transport *Osprey*, please maintain your course," a voice said over the speakers.

"Such a welcoming bunch," Jax groused. He busied himself with confirming system statuses and staring out the

ONE

window. He snapped his fingers. "Oh, hey. Rudy, find us a mechanic, will you?"

From his station behind Jax's, the navigation droid answered, "Will do. I won't have anything else to do."

Jax looked over his shoulder. "Hey, don't blame—"

"Independent transport *Osprey*, I am transmitting your flight path now. You are cleared through to Titan City Spaceport Alpha. Do not deviate from your assigned path."

Jax tapped the communications control. "Or you'll destroy us. We get it." He accepted the incoming data packed with their assigned flight path. He looked over his shoulder. "Want to get Auntie and Jeffry ready?"

Naomi stood up. "Chief Purser Himura is on it." She mock saluted.

Jax clucked, turning back to the flight controls.

Gateway station slid past as the *Osprey* entered the upper atmosphere of New Terra, directly into a raging storm. "Great," he said, tightening his grip on the flight controls. He tapped the intercom. "Hold on to your butts. There's a storm over the capitol."

"Looks like it is over half the continent," Rudy said. Jax nodded.

A bolt of lightning ripped across the sky ahead of the *Osprey*. Jax banked to avoid it, causing the nav console to beep angrily.

As the *Osprey* descended through the clouds, Jax could see the Imperial grounds and the Alpha spaceport of Titan City, capitol of the planet and the Empire. Wind and rain were buffeting the ship, and he could see that several streets in the older sections of the city were submerged. He reached for the comms. "Titan City Space Control. How long has this storm been raging? Is Spaceport Alpha safe and secure?"

"*Osprey*, the storm started last week. Rest assured, the spaceport is nice and dry. So long as you don't crash."

"Copy that, I think I'll be okay," he said, closing the channel. He tapped the intercom. "We'll be on the ground in ten more minutes. It's gonna be bumpy the entire way. Make sure to grab something that's bolted down."

Down in the common area, Baxter was moving luggage around. "Did you even use any of this?" he asked, turning his matte black face to Governor Singh. The ship lurched, forcing him to drop one of the bags to catch the governor as she lost her footing.

The old woman clucked as she straightened up, bracing herself on the magnetically affixed combat droid. "Oh no, most of this is for the summit."

Naomi frowned. "How many saris do you own?"

Jeffry made a face from the kitchenette. "Don't ask."

The boarding ramp hit the duracrete with a thud, splashing water. Jax was the first down. The *Osprey* was sitting in a ring of lights on landing pad D9, in the executive landing area of the Alpha spaceport, the largest spaceport serving Titan City. Rain was falling everywhere. It ran in rivulets from the wing roots as the ship acted as cover, funneling the rain into thick waterfalls.

Governor Singh and Jeffry came down, followed by Naomi. All three had luggage in hand and under arm. From up above, safely inside the ship, Baxter said, "Have fun." The boarding ramp folded as it rose.

A hover car arrived. Once it came to a stop, two well-dressed women got out, each opening an umbrella. "Governor Singh," the shorter of the two said, coming forward.

ONE

Governor Singh bowed her head. The taller of the two opened the car door. "This way, ma'am."

As everyone filed into the car, Jeffry asked, "Uh, our luggage?" They had left it piled under the ship out of the rain.

"Another car is on its way. We'll make sure your luggage gets delivered to your rooms," the shorter of the two said as she closed the door, sealing the four of them in the back of the luxury vehicle.

The car lurched slightly as it sped away from the landing pad on a cushion of its grav field. Jax opened a small compartment. He turned to the others, smiling. "Booze."

THIS IS FANCY

The hover car dropped them off at the Imperial Guest House, a building with a very misleading name. The Imperial Guest House was closer to a six-star hotel on the five-star rating system. It was how the emperor showed off his power and largess to visitors.

"Damn," Jax whispered, helping his adopted aunt out of the hover car. "You always stay here?"

The older woman looked around, then grunted. "Last time I was here, this place was being renovated. The emperor had us all stay in the palace."

Naomi looked around. "Hard to believe this is the consolation prize." As the porters came out to greet them, she turned to Jax. "I'm gonna go check out the city, look around."

The luxury car pulled away silently.

Jax raised an eyebrow but said nothing. She nodded, snatching an umbrella from a valet's hand, and walked off toward the bustling metroplex that was Titan City.

Jax turned to Governor Singh and Jeffry. "Okay, let's check this fancy joint out."

ONE

"Jackson, I've been here before, remember?" the governor said as the trio entered the lobby.

The lobby of the Imperial Guest House was enormous, not just figuratively. It was at least three times bigger than the widest deck on Kelso station. Admittedly, that said little, but it was still impressive. There was a restaurant off to one side, concierge on the other, and several rental desks for all manner of tourist excursions. While the guest house was the height of luxury, it apparently still had its share of wealthy tourists and their children.

The check-in desk was all dark marbled wood and what looked to Jax like solid gold accents. "Hello, are you checking in?" the young, dark-skinned woman behind the counter said as Governor Singh approached.

"Governor Neeti Singh, Kelso station." She gestured to Jax and Jeffry. "And party."

The woman consulted her display screen. She looked up. "Welcome back, Governor." She looked at the two men. "And welcome, gentlemen." Jax opened his mouth but slammed it shut when Jeffry elbowed him. The check-in clerk busied herself at her terminal for a bit, then looked up again. "You're all set. I've sent your access credentials to your gPhones." On cue, all three devices chimed.

Jax looked at his device. "Cool, high floor. Hope we're not near the ice machine." He picked up his duffel bag and walked off toward the bank of elevators. The governor and Jeffry followed, the latter carrying two small carry bags, the former carrying none.

"Naomi and I are in the suite across the hall," Jax said as he opened the door to the suite assigned to Jeffry and his aunt.

"What's the plan?" The two filed in. Their luggage somehow was already in the room. Jax assumed his and Naomi's were in their room, as well.

The governor moved into the spacious suite. She walked to a central sitting area, dropping a tablet she was looking at down on the table next to her. "The summit begins tomorrow. There is a dinner tonight." She moved to one of her suitcases, pulling out a sari of deep green satin.

Jax nodded. "Okay, need us for any of that?"

Governor Singh shook her head. "No, Jeffry and I will be fine. The summit ends in three days, and there's a reception the final evening. You and Naomi should come to that. I can show you off to my friends." She smiled.

Jax nodded. "Okay, cool." He looked from her to Jeffry. "Holler if you need me, or us." He left, letting the door quietly close behind him.

The suite that Naomi and he had been assigned was a twin of the one Auntie and Jeffry were in. Two rooms, a central sitting and entertainment area. Small kitchenette space with dining table off to the side.

WALK ABOUT

The downtown district of Titan City had changed little since Naomi was last there. Back then she had had little time to sightsee as she was running for her life, having escaped the Imperial Academy of Sciences complex, home to the Interface program. She was also barely fifteen at the time.

She caught a cab from the capital complex, shortening the five-kilometer distance considerably. Spending so much time on Kelso and the outer colony worlds, it had surprised her to see an actual human driving the cab. The emperor had very strict views on non-human life. Things like cabs, which would normally be managed by cheap-to-make Rudimentary Intelligences, were still the domain of human cab drivers.

"Where to?" the cabbie asked.

"The entertainment district," she answered. That wasn't her destination, but it was close enough, and it would leave no obvious record.

The trip was short. The cabbie was professional enough that he didn't make small talk after his initial *where are you from* was met with *not here*. She paid her fare and exited the cab into the busy entertainment district. Memories came flooding back of a decade past. Running through the wide streets, ducking into stores and behind food carts. Trying to not attract attention as best she could. While it wasn't unusual to see unattended children her age running around the entertainment district, a lone child was a bit odd. She had regretted splitting up from the others almost immediately, but they had agreed that they would be harder to track and capture if each went a separate way. The storm did not appear to be dampening tourists' or locals' spirits in the slightest.

She walked until she found a coffee shop that looked to be more of a local flavor than the crowded chain a half block away. Almost more importantly, it was dry. The smell of fresh brewed coffee, something not easily attained on Kelso or any of the outer colonies, embraced her as she opened the door, a bell jingling on the frame. She inhaled deeply as she shook her umbrella dry.

"You look like a woman who will appreciate a good cup of coffee," someone said.

Naomi shook her head a little, breaking her reverie. She looked around; her gaze settled on the man behind the counter. He was at least ten years her senior, athletic build, sandy blond hair.

She walked up to the counter. "I'll take the largest cup you've got."

The man smiled. "Of?"

"Dealer's choice," she replied, smiling. She paid and took a seat at a table near the front of the small shop, next to the floor-to-ceiling window looking out on the bustling thoroughfare outside. The storm had not let up since she left the

ONE

guest house. Puddles lined the wide pedestrian boulevard; awnings were creating waterfalls.

A few minutes later, the man from behind the counter placed a steaming cup in front of her. He also took a seat opposite her. "Mind some company? I've got a few minutes' break." He gestured around the small space. Everyone had drinks and no one was waiting at the counter. His smile was broad. He ran a hand through his light blond hair. Naomi smiled and made a welcoming gesture.

Naomi smiled and took a sip of her coffee. She held the cup in both hands, letting the warmth make her fingers tingle. "I don't. I'm...Stacy." She shifted her grip on her coffee to reach into her pocket. She found her gPhone and felt the bio-circuits in her hand activate as she accessed her identity core and updated it, pushing her Naomi Himura identity into an encrypted archive, just in case.

"Michael." He offered his hand. Releasing her gPhone, she shook his hand. "Here on business or pleasure?"

"What makes you think I'm not a local?" Naomi replied.

"I'd have noticed you," he replied, smiling.

"Smooth," she replied, leaning in, inclining her head. "Business," she added.

"You didn't look the tourist, but you never know." He nodded to her umbrella. "Plus, I noticed the Imperial Guest House logo." He smiled. He inclined his head, eyes on her coffee. "Like?"

She smiled. "I do. What is it?"

His shoulders went back as his chin raised a bit. "A new varietal. They've been exploring hybridizing beans from Earth to do better in the soil here in the high desert regions. A hybrid of Pache Comum from somewhere, I forget where, in South America and SL54 out of Kenya." His pride was obvious.

"Well, it's good," Naomi replied, taking a sip, not breaking eye contact. She looked around. "It's been a while since I've been in Titan City. I can't believe downtown has grown so much." She waved toward nothing in particular beyond the window. "Is the Academy of Sciences still over there somewhere?"

Michael's gaze lingered on Naomi for a heartbeat, then he turned to look out the window. "Yeah, it's just two blocks over." He pointed. He turned back to look at her. "They've been busy. The emperor has put a lot of effort into Titan City. You probably saw the development on your way down when you arrived." He continued, "They've been building towers as fast as possible and replacing entire neighborhoods."

Naomi nodded. "No argument, he's been busy." She turned her attention fully back to Michael. "I've got some errands to run. When do you get off work?"

Michael beamed. "I'm just covering for one of my employees. She had to leave early, sick. My other employee is on his way." Taking a chance, he added, "I live a few blocks west."

Naomi raised an eyebrow. "Do you now?" She took a sip of her coffee and stood, taking her gPhone out of her pants pocket. "I'll message you." She held her phone up and pressed the icon to exchange contact details. Michael's gPhone beeped, and he pressed something on the screen.

He stood and walked her to the door. "I look forward to hearing from you, Stacy."

She put a hand on his arm as she exited. "I look forward to messaging you." She winked. With a snap, she opened her umbrella and stepped back out into the torrential downpour.

As she crossed the street, she placed a call. "Hi, yes, I'd like to arrange a tour. I'm only here a few days, not sure how busy you are." She sipped her coffee as she walked toward the Academy of Sciences. "Yes, that would be wonderful. Thank you." She disconnected.

She rounded a corner, coming face to face with the blocky gray square that was the Academy of Sciences complex. The principal building reached up fifty or more floors, surrounded by several smaller outbuildings, all surrounded by a twelve-foot-high wall, complete with Shock Troops scattered along the top.

NIGHTLIFE

"Where are you?" Jax asked, staring out the window of the suite they had assigned him and Naomi. He had moved their luggage to the two bedrooms and dug through his bag for something more comfortable. Now his room looked like his cabin on the *Osprey* usually did. Clothes were on the bed, the floor, everywhere.

His gPhone was sitting on the dining table behind him. Over his earpiece, Naomi said, "I'll fill you in over breakfast. Don't wait up for me." The phone beeped to show that she had disconnected.

"Guess I'm on my own tonight," Jax said out loud to the empty suite. He turned and looked around. "Computer?" Nothing. He frowned. "Room?" Again, nothing. He inhaled, "Fucking backwards ass..." He trailed off as he looked at the coffee table in the sitting area. On it were several brochures and a central comm terminal. He looked at the device and headed for the door to the suite.

ONE

"Good evening, sir. How can I help you?" a staff member behind the concierge stand said as Jax approached.

"I'm looking for someplace to get drunk," Jax said.

The other man, dressed in the finest suit with tailcoat that Jax had ever seen, the accoutrements all Imperial colors, nodded sagely. "Indeed." He looked Jax up and down, appraising him. "I think I know just the place." He withdrew a tablet from an interior pocket of his coat. After a minute of tapping and swiping he looked up. "Here you go." He swiped towards Jax, causing Jax's gPhone to beep in his hand.

Jax looked down. "The Rusty Swordfish?" He looked up, grinning. "Sounds fun."

"You look like someone who might enjoy a bit of an edge to his evening. The Swordfish is not overly dangerous but resides near the Old Town section. A rougher part of town than many are comfortable with," the man said.

"I'm definitely not afraid of a little rough edge here and there." Jax grinned.

"Shall I summon a cab for you?" the finely dressed concierge asked, offering Jax a collapsed umbrella similar to the one Naomi had grabbed when she left earlier. He nodded, accepting the umbrella.

According to the cab driver, the news net said the storm currently drenching the city and everything near it was a *once in two hundred years* kind of thing.

The cab dropped Jax off outside the Rusty Swordfish. There was a crowd standing around outside the establishment, huddled under shared umbrellas. The venue didn't actually have a visible name, but had what had to be a ten-foot bronze swordfish mounted to the building.

Jax walked through the crowd of patrons into the dimly lit building. Inside was everything he hoped for. The concierge had read Jax expertly. "Just like home," he murmured.

Jax found a seat at the bar between a man Jax's age and his older friend and two women. "Okay to grab this seat?"

Both parties nodded. The two men immediately turned back to their conversation. The two women smiled. The nearer, a brunette, smiled and said, "By all means." She turned back to her friend, the two laughing to each other lightly.

Jax flagged the bartender down. "What's on tap?"

"Beer," the bartender, a heavyset man, replied, not slowing down on his way to a group at the far end of the bar.

Jax waited until the man came by again, but never got the chance as the bartender continued on to a group of three women and a man at the opposite end of the bar.

When the bartender came near again, the woman next to Jax shouted, "New Terra Lager." The bartender nodded, not slowing down. She turned, smiling. "He's more attentive to women. Might as well use the sexism." She offered a hand. "Julie." As Jax took her hand, she added, "My friend, Maggie."

Jax took the dark-skinned woman's hand, as well. "Maggie." As they released hands, he said, "I'm Jackson."

The bartender deposited a tall glass of beer and a data chip with the bill.

Jax grabbed the glass and the credit chip. "Thanks!" he shouted to the man's back. He turned to the two women. "Cheers." They both raised their drinks.

Jax chatted with Julie and Maggie until the two had to depart. As they paid their bill and said their goodbyes, bemoaning having to be at work the next morning, Maggie held her gPhone out, swiping her contact details to Jax. "If

ONE

you're in town for a bit, call me." She flashed a bright, toothy smile. The two women walked away, waving.

Before the two vacated stools could cool off, two men dropped into them. The one next to Jax nodded. "Hey." Both were in suits, likely working downtown in finance, Jax guessed. He decided they were definitely bankers.

Jax nodded back, saying nothing, his attention to his beer. He couldn't quite remember if it was his fourth or sixth. He wasn't overly concerned either way.

The first time the man next to him excitedly bumped into Jax, he turned and mumbled an apology. A third man had joined the first two and was standing next to them.

By the fourth excited bump, the apologies had stopped. Jax turned. "Dude, can you cut that shit out?"

The man frowned. "Sorry, man, don't be such a baby." He beamed. "We're celebrating Uni Day." He turned back to his friends when Jax put a hand on his shoulder.

"That's not for two more days," Jax pointed out.

The man shrugged his shoulder out of Jax's grip. "Fuck off." He turned to his friends. "Little asshole, probably some spacer Indie loser."

Jax inhaled, then tapped the man's shoulder. When the man turned, face red and angry, Jax punched him, instantly busting his nose.

The two other men stared for a few heartbeats as their friend fell to the floor screaming as blood flowed from his nose, then pounced on Jax.

The bartender, who had finally started to give Jax his attention, sighed.

CHAPTER SIX

CHANGES IN DIRECTION

The three bankers were clearly not fighters. Half of their punches lacked any sort of power or simply failed to do anything but glance off Jax's defenses. He sent one of them into the crowd of bar patrons with a roundhouse that left the man spinning, knocking over a table, and sending the occupants scattering. Those occupants launched into the fight, tackling the banker who knocked over their table, while the next table over attacked the first table's occupants over spilled beer.

Things escalated quickly from there, turning the entire bar into a knot of flying fists and beer bottles.

A meaty paw landed on Jax's shoulder. The owner pulled, spinning Jax around, right into a cross he was certain was going to leave him with a black eye.

Jax hit the ground, rolling away from his attacker. When he got back to his feet and looked around, whoever had slugged him wasn't pressing their attack.

The brawl spilled out onto the rainy street outside the Rusty Swordfish. Jax had completely lost track of the trio he initially was fighting, but more than a few dozen others had

had no problem stepping in for them. To his surprise, he wasn't the only Indie, or at least Indie-sympathetic, patron in the bar.

After being knocked to the rain covered ground and rolling away from a kick, Jax looked around, surprised to see that in the fighting's course, he had retreated out the door into the street. The rain was still pounding the sidewalk. He cursed, realizing that his umbrella was likely still leaning against the bar under where he had been sitting.

He stood and looked around, dodging a pair of men slugging it out, oblivious to their surroundings.

Jax was about to head back into the bar when the bartender stepped out into the rain, a plasma rifle in his arms. He raised the weapon and fired a single shot into the air. "All right, you assholes!" he shouted.

When the crowd didn't immediately settle, the bartender fired another round into the air. "Next one goes into one of you!" That got everyone's attention.

One of the brawlers pushed past Jax. "What the hell, Waldo?"

"Waldo?" Jax sneered. The armed bartender looked at him, shifting his grip on the rifle. Jax raised both hands. "Sorry."

The bartender said, "I just got off the comms. Old Town is flooding, people are going to be trapped in their homes!" He looked around the crowd. "Since you all swarmed out into the street, technically leaving your tabs, I have your details on file. If you don't want me sending it to the authorities, you'll march your asses over to the old commons." He looked around the crowd. "Now!"

There was a lot of grumbling until the armed bartender, Waldo, let everyone hear the rifle charging.

Jax rubbed his face and fell in with a crowd of over a

hundred people. How had there been that many in the bar before the fight started?

He sidled up to Waldo, still holding his rifle. "I don't understand."

The surly bartender looked at him. "Old Town is the original colony landing site. It's mostly empty now, save for the poor and homeless and those who can't afford to live in the glass towers, of course. Slums, shanties, and everything in between." Jax remembered the concierge's words regarding the location of the Rusty Swordfish.

"But why us?" Jax gestured to the ragged, waterlogged crowd marching down the road.

"The civil authorities will probably show up. If they do, it'll be hours. People will die."

That was all Jax needed to hear. He nodded. "Got it. Let's go." The crowd angled off the road and ended up in a sodden field with the remains of a gazebo or something in the center.

"Okay, everyone, listen up!" someone with a voice amplifier shouted. "The senior center and the shelter are our first priorities!" Jax looked around, wiping his hair from his eyes. He had lost track of Waldo. The voice continued, "After that we need to go door to door!"

Jax found a group that was heading off and joined them. "I'm new here. How can I help?"

A man at least twice Jax's age said, "Come with us. We're gonna start door to door. Another group is already on their way to the shelter and senior center." He pointed. The old colony area had far fewer functional street lights than Titan City proper. "We're hitting Garrison Street first."

Jax and two others took one side of the street, as the older man and three others took the other side of the street. Jax pounded on a door that was welded into the side of a shipping container. The sound echoed into the night as he pounded on the door one more time. There were no windows. He had no way of knowing if anyone was home.

The door swung in to reveal a scrawny man in a ratty robe. "What?" he shouted to be heard over the wail of the wind and rain.

Jax hitched a thumb over his shoulder. "This area flooding, you gotta get out of here!" The man looked over Jax's shoulder and nodded. Jax didn't wait. He moved toward the next building, another structure made of cargo containers. This one was three of them, two on the bottom and one making a second floor. He looked up the street. His two associates were several doors down.

WRONG DOOR

Two hours later, Jax was still banging on doors. If it was possible to be more soaked than he was when he started this adventure, that was his current state. The storm was still raging, and lightning was dancing across the sky accompanied by earsplitting cracks of thunder. As far as he could tell, it had not let up even the slightest since they arrived on the planet.

The door opened into a brightly lit living space. The blinding light framed a ruggedly built man, a very naked ruggedly built man. "What?"

Jax backed up. "Uh, dude." He found something to look at in the sky, squinting against the rain drops pummeling his eyes. "You gotta get out of here. The storm ain't letting up, this entire area is gonna be underwater." He glanced down, eyebrow raising. "Put on pants."

At the end of the street, a flatbed hover truck slid into view, already half full of people who had fled their homes.

A pair of men came towards Jax. "Come on, man, they need some help on the next block." He fell in with them.

As they slogged through the mostly muddy street, Jax asked, "What's the deal here?" Water was up to his shins.

The Asian man to his left said, "When you can't afford one of those," he gestured through the rain to the glittering towers of downtown Titan City, "you end up off-world, if you're lucky, or here."

The other man added, "Old Town takes everyone." Jax shuddered, not because of the cold, though he was freezing. It had to be well past midnight.

When they reached their destination, the Asian man divvied up sections of the block for them all to tackle. A hover truck was rumbling nearby, likely waiting for residents. This section of Old Town was a significantly lower elevation than the block he had just been working. Water was pooling everywhere and in most places was up to Jax's knees even in the street.

He waded to toward his first house. Like most of Old Town, it was made of colonial cargo containers welded together. This one was made up of two large metal rectangles with one sitting atop. A luxury dwelling by the standards of Old Town.

He pounded on the door; it echoed a deep rattle, metal against metal. The door opened and the barrel of a blaster rifle stuck out, stopping inches from Jax's face. A hand reached out and grabbed the front of his soaking wet T-shirt, yanking him into the dwelling. Lightning arced across the sky, followed by thunderous booms.

THIS IS UNEXPECTED

"Woah," Jax said as the hand dragged him into the structure. He hit the ground, splashing into the standing water that filled the room. Getting to his knees, he looked around; several men and women surrounded him, all armed.

One woman leaned down, putting a blaster pistol under Jax's nose. "Who are you? What're you doing here?"

Jax's eyes darted around the room. Lots of guns. "I'm just here helping evacuate Old Town." He splashed one hand. "Kinda flooding."

"What do we do with him?" one man asked, looking out a narrow window at the raging storm outside. "It's getting bad out there." Lightning lit up the sky.

"We can't stay here," a woman said, entering the room. "Not if they're evacuating everyone. We'll draw attention."

"Look guys, I'm not from here. I don't know what the hell all this is, and honestly, I don't care," Jax tried to explain. "I was just trying to help folks." He looked around. "You see, I was in this bar fight. Some knucklehead Imperial sympathizers were celebrating Uni Day early, and well…"

He smiled. "One thing led to another, and it was a brawl. A really good one, if I'm being honest. Then all of a sudden—"

"Shut up!" the woman with the pistol shouted. She turned to the others. "Tie him up and bring him along. We'll let the commander decide what to do with him."

One of the other women reached for Jax's wrists. She produced a plastic zip tie and bound his wrists behind his back. She guided him to a sofa and pushed him down. The sodden material squished. "Stay."

While he sat there, the storm raged outside. Thunder rumbled across the sky, shaking the metal container home. He watched the occupants move quickly through the rooms, kicking water up. Several brought large crates down from the upstairs area.

"What is this?" he asked out loud before thinking better of it.

A pair of men in worn fatigues were moving a box that looked suspiciously like the box that one might keep rifles in. They looked over. One of the two men said, "The more questions you ask, the more likely you are to not live through this." Thunder cracked outside.

Jax closed his eyes and leaned back on the sofa. It made a soggy, squishing sound.

Jax sat on the sofa for what felt like forever but was probably an hour, until the woman who had bound his wrists came into the room. "Come on, Boy Scout." She reached out and grabbed his shirt, helping him up and stretching the fabric, and wringing rain out of it. She let go, but the sodden fabric did not bounce back.

"Guess I'll get a new shirt later," he said, looking down at the stretched-out neck. He followed her out of the living room into a back room with a large roll-up door. All the boxes he had seen the group moving around were now stacked along the walls.

The large roll-up door opened, revealing a water-logged alley that looked like a river. A wheeled transport vehicle was standing in water now almost up to the middle of the wheels. Water rushed into the garage space. The assorted men and women began loading the crates into the transport, splashing water as they worked. Jax watched until they were done and the woman from before pushed him toward the transport.

Jax took a deep breath and stepped into the rain between the building and the vehicle. Two men in the transport lifted him up into the vehicle. He looked around. People and cargo crates filled the transport. "You guys all from around here, or...?" No reply. He shrugged. "Anyone got the time?" Still no reply.

A man across from him leaned forward, causing Jax to lean forward to hear what he was about to say. Instead, a meaty fist struck him in the temple, knocking him out cold.

MANHUNT

The door to the suite opened. "Oh, good morning, Naomi," Jeffry said. He stepped aside to allow her entry into the suite the hotel had assigned him and Governor Singh.

She walked in and looked around. "Jax isn't here?" Jeffry shook his head.

Governor Singh walked out of one of the bedrooms. "Oh, good morning, dear."

"Morning, Governor. Have you seen or heard from Jax?" Naomi asked. She walked over to the window. "Great view."

Jeffry helped the governor assemble her large handbag, adding several tablets from the dining room table. He looked up at Naomi. "We've been here working, haven't seen him." He gestured to the table, room service containers still sitting out. "We ordered in after the reception—horrible food."

"The worst," Governor Singh agreed.

Naomi tapped the glass. "When I got in this morning, he wasn't in the suite, and it didn't look like he'd slept in his bed."

ONE

"When you got in this morning?" the governor repeated. "So, your bed hasn't been slept in, either?"

Naomi blushed. "Well..." Suddenly the ceiling was very interesting.

"I'm just giving you a hard time. You and Jax are grown adults." The small Indian woman chuckled as she shrugged her purse onto her shoulder. She paused, then slipped it off and handed it to Jeffry. She turned to Naomi. "He probably found a different bed to sleep in. I'm sure he'll turn up. He always does."

"Yeah, maybe," Naomi admitted. She headed for the door. "Okay, thanks. You two have fun at your summit."

The governor clucked, "Oh yes, eight hours of the emperor making sure we know how big his dick is. Can't wait." She turned to her assistant. "Let's go, Jeffry. We don't want to be late."

The young man nodded to Naomi as he and the governor left the suite.

Naomi pulled her gPhone out of her pocket. "Hey, Skip?" She left the suite, headed for the elevators.

"Yes, Naomi?" the Sapient Intelligence of the *Osprey* replied.

"Have you guys heard from Jax? He didn't come home last night."

"Negative. We haven't heard from the Captain since you all departed. How is everything going? His missing, notwithstanding."

Naomi smiled, knowing that the ship loved hearing from Rudy and Baxter about the outside world during jobs. This time the other two bots were stuck aboard the ship with him. "So far, so good. You get your wormhole generator fixed?"

"The engineering team is coming today," the ship's SI

replied. "I'm not thrilled about strangers crawling around inside me, but what are you going to do?"

She nodded, stepping into the elevator. "That's a disturbing image. Good to hear. Oh, can you ping his gPhone?"

This time it was Rudy who answered, "One second."

The lift doors parted, and she walked into the lobby of the Imperial Guest House. Outside, the storm was still raging. Lightning lit up the sky.

"Naomi, it looks like he's someplace called Old Town," Rudy said. He added, "His last stop was a bar called the Rusty Swordfish. Need me to send you map data?"

She shook her head. "No, I'm good. Thanks, I'll see what I can find. Thanks, guys. Have fun with the engineering team. Don't get into trouble." She hung up. She had the concierge hail her a cab and was on her way to the Rusty Swordfish within minutes.

The cabbie looked over his shoulder. "Mind if I ask why you want to go to Old Town? Especially now? This storm's got to have most of it hip deep in water now."

Naomi was looking out the windows at the rain slashing the cab and pooling in every low spot on the street. She turned forward. "I can't find my friend, and his last known location was the bar, before his signal went into Old Town."

The man shrugged. "Good luck."

As the cab drove, cinderblock buildings and what looked like hundreds of years old prefab colonial construction replaced the glitter of downtown and its entertainment districts and commercial towers. The cab came to a stop in front of a nondescript building with a large rusting fish sculpture mounted on the exterior. "We're here," the cabbie said.

Naomi looked around. "This is it?"

ONE

The man nodded. "Yeah." He pointed. "That's the Rusty Swordfish. If your friend was here last night, they may know what happened to him." He pointed off into the warren of decrepit buildings. "That's Old Town."

She thanked and paid the cabbie. The door to the bar was locked. She banged on it, hoping someone was around. She huddled under her umbrella until the sound of a locking bar disengaging rang out and the heavy ten-foot-tall door opened a crack. "We open at five."

"I'm looking for a friend," Naomi said. She held up her gPhone with a picture of Jax eating a hotdog in an immensely unflattering way.

"Oh, that asshole. He started a fight with a bunch of local tool bags," the face in the door's gap replied.

Naomi nodded. "Sounds right. Do you know where he went or what happened?" Lightning cracked behind her, near enough that she jumped.

The face—a man, she was pretty sure—said, "Yeah, we got a call that the flooding in Old Town had gotten bad. I roped the brawlers into a work gang." A hand jutted out, pointing. "I didn't see him after we all got to the field."

Naomi looked down the road, then back to the door. "Okay, thank you." The man on the other side of the door said nothing, closing and re-locking the door.

She pulled her gPhone out of her pocket. "Skip? Can you send me the locator data on Jax's phone?"

"Of course. Do you mind if I ask what for?" the *Osprey*'s SI asked.

"I can reprogram my phone to ping his and help me narrow down his location," Naomi said.

"Good idea," the SI replied. Her phone beeped, announcing the incoming data packet.

CHAPTER SEVEN

STRANGERS

They're here, Skip announced over the ship's network. Rudy and Baxter were in the middle of the cargo hold.

Baxter turned and walked to the forward section into the armory. *I'll be hiding in the vault.*

Footsteps echoed on the staircase coming up from the boarding room. "Hello?" a female voice said.

"Greetings." Rudy rolled over to the stairs. "I am...uh, Artoo Detoo."

A heavyset woman came into view. "Not a very original name." She looked around. Two more people were coming up the stairs behind her. "Your owner a big fan of old vids, huh?"

Smooth, Skip beamed.

Rudy rolled in a circle. "Indeed. Welcome aboard the *Osprey*."

A lanky, middle-aged man looked around. "Just you, droid?"

Rudy fumed, but simply replied, "Indeed. Our alluvial damper failed. My...owner...was able to make repairs, but we require a new one."

The team lead nodded her head, her beaded hair swaying, clacking as intricately carved beads of many colors collided. "Okay, we'll need access to your engineering space. One of my men, Gregory, will run diagnostics while the rest of us will be on the hull." She produced a band from a pocket and set about capturing her beaded locks into a single mass behind her.

Rudy nodded with his fist and rolled towards engineering. "Please follow me."

Gregory followed while the team lead and the other man went back down the stairs to climb onto the hull. As they entered the engineering space, Gregory, the lanky middle-aged man said, "Tidy." He moved to the main engineering display, currently showing a full system status.

Gregory turned to Rudy, who was still standing in the hatchway. "Lot of things need fixin'. Sure your owner doesn't want us to get this bucket ship shape?"

Bucket! Skip beamed over the network.

Rudy spun his squat, cylindrical head in a full circle. "I am unable to authorize additional work."

The tall man shrugged, rubbing a hand over his shiny, hairless pate. "Whatever." He tapped his ear. "Gina, you ready up there?" He nodded along, tapping the control screen, making adjustments. "Yeah, I see it. You're good to go, all connections de-energized."

Gregory made a slow circle, taking in the space again. He pointed to Baxter's charging dock. "What's that?"

Rudy made a noncommittal noise. "Came with the ship."

The lanky human turned to Rudy. "Go get me a drink." When Rudy remained where he was, the man frowned. "Please?"

Rudy said nothing, rolling away.

ONE

When they're done, I could kill him. No one would find him, Baxter sent over the shared network connection. He was once again hiding in the hidden vault in the forward section.

I'm pretty sure the captain would frown on that, Skip replied.

Rudy reached the kitchenette and retrieved and bottle of water. *This will be over soon.* He rolled back to the staircase as loud thumps echoed through the ship as the humans on the outer hull effected repairs.

MEET NEW PEOPLE

Jax was enjoying a really pleasant dream. The woman from the bar, Maggie, featured heavily in it. Then he woke up when water splashed his face. His eyes snapped open and crossed as they focused on the business end of a spray bottle.

"Hello," a deep baritone said. Jax's eyes uncrossed and focused on the holder of the spray bottle: an older man, salt and pepper hair and a well-groomed, close-trimmed beard.

"Hi," Jax said, trying to adjust his position in the chair someone had dropped him into while he was unconscious. He looked around. They were in a warehouse. Where it was, he couldn't tell, but he could hear the rain battering the corrugated metal roof, so still near Titan City, at least. He was in a small room, probably an office of some sort. There was a single grimy window behind spray bottle man. Jax wasn't sure, but it looked like grime was holding the glass pane in the frame more than grout.

"So...who are you?" the man with the spray bottle asked, his hand lowering, the spray bottle resting in his lap. The room was about three meters square, empty except for the two currently occupied chairs. No table or anything else.

"No one," Jax replied.

The other man cocked his head. "No one? That's not good. Nobody misses no ones when they don't come home."

Jax nodded. "Fair enough. My name is Michael Keaton. I'm—" He didn't finish because a stream of water hit him in the face.

"We have your gPhone," spray bottle man reminded Jax, withdrawing the device from his jacket with his free hand.

Jax thought hard about the ident he had last used. He was sure it wasn't his real one. "Fine, fine. My name is Leonard McGarry."

"From?" The other man made a *go on* motion.

"Here. I live down—" More water. Jax rubbed his face. "Cut that out!"

"You're not a local," the other man said.

Jax inhaled. "Fine. I'm from Jericho station. I'm here ferrying a VIP to a summit the emperor is hosting."

Spray bottle man nodded slowly. "What kind of summit?"

Jax opened his mouth to answer but stopped when a stream of water hit his face. "Hey, what was that for?" He shook his head to get rid of some of the water running down his face.

The other man smirked. "Preemptive." He waited a moment. "Go on."

"It's the emperor's Independent Colony and Station Summit. He brings everyone here to show off and remind them of their place in the galaxy," Jax said.

Spray bottle man nodded slowly. He was about to say

something when the door to the small office opened. A woman came in. Jax was pretty sure she was at the house, whenever it was that he had been at that house. He wasn't sure what time it was. He looked up at the grimy window. Not very bright out, but with the storm, that wasn't saying much. It could have been midnight or high noon. The woman leaned down, whispering in spray bottle man's ear.

Jax only caught the odd word but was pretty sure something was happening soon, something that the emperor wouldn't like. "You're the Rebellion?" Jax asked out loud.

Spray bottle man, probably the commander he had heard about earlier, looked past the woman to meet Jax's eyes. He nodded to his underling and waved her away, saying, "Tell Oden to prep the two ground cars." She nodded and closed the door behind her.

"You're the commander," Jax said.

The commander nodded. "I'm not sure it's good that you put it together, but yes to both."

Jax grunted. "Cool."

"Cool?" the commander repeated. "That's not the reaction we usually get."

Jax tried to shrug, but the binders keeping his wrists in place behind him made that difficult. "I mean, I'm glad you all exist and all. I'm no fan of the Empire or anything, but I'm kinda preoccupied with not getting killed right now. Have you heard of the Cri—" Thunder boomed outside the warehouse, cutting him off. Jax looked up. "This storm, right?"

The commander smiled. "I like you." He looked at the ceiling. "Ever thought about getting involved?"

"In the Rebellion?" Jax asked. "Thought about? No. Interested? Also no. I have my hands full out in the outer colonies, criminal syndicates trying to kill me and stuff. Keeps one busy." He tilted his head. "Sorry."

The man smiled. "Yeah, I like you." He stood. "I'll be back. I've got some things to take care of." He opened the door and turned to Jax. "Need some time to think about your fate."

BUSTIN' OUT

"Take your time." Jax smiled as the door closed. A lock clacked into place.

Outside the door, he could hear people talking to the commander and each other. He only ever picked up a few words here and there. From what he could gather, the rebels were planning something. What it was, he wasn't sure.

Someone brought in an Imperial Navy ration pack and sat it on his lap. He looked at the man. "My sex life would be awesome if I were that flexible, but..." He let the innuendo hang there awkwardly. Finally, he said, "My wrists."

"Oh!" the man said as his cheeks burned crimson. He produced a switchblade and extended the blade with a *snikt* sound. He leaned over to reach behind Jax and cut the binders. "No funny business," he warned as Jax moved his arms and rotated his wrists in front of him to get his circulation back.

"Promise," Jax said, taking turns rubbing each wrist.

The man produced a new set of binders and secured Jax's ankles. "Just in case."

ONE

Jax pulled open the foil top of the ration pack. "Of course." He nodded to the meal. "Thanks."

The man grunted and closed the door behind him.

As Jax finished his meal, something landed on the roof with a clang.

Jax looked up, but heard nothing further. He looked down at his ration pack and brought it up to his face to lick up the last scraps of not-even-sort-of-tasty meat-like substance.

"Are you licking the ration pack?" a voice asked. A familiar voice.

Jax lowered the ration pack. "Naomi?" he asked out loud. "Where are you?" He looked around.

There was a knock on the window before it opened, swinging out and away. The sound of the storm outside increased, and a gust of wind blew in.

Naomi's head popped down from the top of the frame. "You're not easy to find."

"You're a sight for sore eyes. Get me out of here," Jax said, wiggling his feet.

Naomi shimmied in the through the window. "What's going on? Who are these guys? Why do they have you tied up?" She knelt down and cut the bindings around Jax's ankles.

"The freaking Rebellion," he answered.

She stood up. "The what? Rebellion? Against what?" Jax made a face. "Oh." Understanding spread across her face. "Against him, the emperor. Wow. That's big."

"Yeah," Jax said. He moved to the window. "Ready?" She nodded, joining him at the window. He knelt down, cupping his hands.

"Excuse me?" a deep voice asked.

Jax turned in time to get a stream of water to the face.

"Hey!" He dropped Naomi, who grunted as she hit the floor.

"What's wrong with you?" she said from the ground, then turned to get her own blast of water, which caused her to splutter.

"We have a front door. It's a bit bigger than that." The commander pointed to the window. He walked over to Naomi. "Hi." He offered his hand.

Naomi's cheeks burned. "Hello."

Jax sighed. "Can't blame us for trying?"

The other man met his gaze, then turned to Naomi. "I'm curious how you found him, and us."

Naomi smiled. "I had Skip, er… a friend of ours, send me the locator signature for his gPhone. I tweaked the network antennas in mine to ping against his. Sort of like a range finder." She added, "Not an exact science, but out here there aren't a lot of likely places." She grinned. "Even less that have active network connections."

"How did you—" the commander began.

"She's a talented hacker," Jax offered. The commander quirked an eyebrow.

Naomi broke the silence. "So…Rebellion, huh?" The commander looked at Jax, who shrugged. Naomi continued, "Have you looked at the Academy of Sciences complex?"

"Looked at it for what?" the commander asked, then raised a hand. "Why don't we move this conversation out of this room?" He opened the door, extending an arm.

Naomi and Jax exited what had been his cell into a bustling command center.

"Woah."

MAKIN' PLANS

"So, explain," the commander said, pointing to a large conference table littered with food containers and data tablets.

"I booked Jax and I a tour at the Academy of Sciences for tomorrow."

"Jax?" the commander asked.

Jax made a face. "Nickname."

"For Leonard?"

Naomi looked from each man to the other and back, her head tilted to the side a bit.

"Middle name is Jackson. Leonard Jackson McGarry." Jax smiled, biting his lip.

"I've been on it. Boring," the commander said.

"It would be if we were taking the tour." Naomi grinned. "But we're not gonna be on the tour. We're gonna be robbing them."

"So, you're thieves?" the commander said, seeming unimpressed.

"You make it sound so dirty," Jax quipped, crossing his arms.

Naomi clucked, "We're not you. It's just the two of us. We're not trying to take down the Empire or anything like that." She took a breath, then added, "This isn't about *robbing* them, per se. It's about getting a little payback."

The commander made a face. "Payback? For what?"

Naomi looked at Jax, who inclined his head. "Your call."

She held up a hand. The bio-circuitry glowed. A tracery of circuitry around her left eye lit up, as well.

The commander leaned forward. "Interesting." He looked Naomi in the eye. "What are you?" He reached out to poke her cheek where a line of blue was glowing under the skin, only to have his hand swatted away.

Naomi explained the Interface program, including how she entered it and how the Imperial scientists treated the children in the program, and ended with her escape.

"I just want to bloody the emperor's nose."

"And maybe make some money," Jax amended.

The commander rubbed his chin. "I had heard rumors about something like this toward the end of the war. Nothing solid ever materialized." He looked Naomi up and down. "Huh."

Naomi looked at Jax out of the corner of her eye. "We can get into the tower. So, if that helps you..." She let the offer hang in the air.

The commander looked over his shoulder. "Mara." A young woman came over. "We still have two operatives in the Academy of Sciences building, right?"

The young rebel thought for a moment. "Yes, sir. Brandon and Monica. They're not very well placed. Neither has clearance above the first ten floors, that I recall."

"Thank you," he said. His underling departed.

The commander thought for a moment, then looked at

ONE

his guests. "How about this? I can arrange for a few surprises to be left in the building. With the storm going, I suspect a lot of the researchers are working from home these days. You get in, do what you're going to do, move my surprises up to the secure levels."

Jax shrugged. "Sure." He held up a finger. "So long as we can still get off the planet. I wasn't kidding about not getting involved."

The commander inclined his head. "Fair."

They worked out the details for another hour. It surprised Jax to learn how well organized the Rebellion was, and that it was not just on New Terra, as he had originally thought. The Imperial news outlets had done an amazing job at downplaying the Rebellion's relevance.

The commander, it turned out, was an ex-military, hence the name, but what surprised Jax was that he fought on the side of unification. It was only after the war, the years of the emperor consolidating his power and placing those he most trusted in positions of authority throughout the government, that the commander realized his error. By then, it was far too late, at least officially. The Indies had long since surrendered and gone into hiding.

As they left the warehouse, Jax groaned, "I was finally dry." It was still pouring.

After walking a few blocks huddled under Naomi's umbrella, she said, "I think we're we far enough. I'll see if a cab will come out here." Jax nodded. She tapped her phone a few times, then slid it into a pocket.

Ten minutes later, a cab pulled up a few hundred meters from where they were standing, the nearest piece of non-submerged road.

While they walked to the cab, Jax said, "By the way, thanks." He smiled. "Partner."

As they slid into the backseat of the cab, the cabbie looked over his shoulder. "Where to?"

"The Imperial Guest House," Naomi replied. The driver's eyebrows rose as he looked at the two wet, bedraggled people in his back seat asking to be taken to one of the nicest places in the city.

Jax looked at his phone. "So gross. They got sticky goo on my phone." He groaned as he wiped the device on his pant leg. "I had plans for…I guess earlier tonight. She was smokin', too. I can't believe it's already evening."

Naomi clucked, "You got in a bar fight—"

Jax stopped her by holding up a finger. "Started it, actually."

She nodded. "Started a bar fight, helped save a bunch of folks from the flooding, then somehow stumbled," she leaned closer, lowering her voice, "into the hands of the Rebellion, and you're thinking about sex?"

He looked at her. "I'm also starving."

When they reached the Imperial Guest House, the in-house restaurant was already closed, so Naomi convinced Jax to eat a protein bar and get some sleep. He tried to swing by the still open bar, citing the likelihood of the availability of pub mix. Naomi none too gently guided him toward the elevator bay. They had a big day ahead of them. They agreed to sync up in the morning.

BREAKFAST OF CHAMPIONS

Jax's adventures the previous day and night had drained him more than either he or Naomi had expected. He slept until around eleven o'clock. When the door to his room finally opened, Naomi looked up from whatever she was doing on her gPhone. She grinned up. "You look rough."

"Think they're still serving breakfast?" He ran a hand through his hair.

She stood. "Only one way to find out. Our tour is at 1:15. We better get a move on." She slid her gPhone into a pocket on her cargo pants and walked to the door of their suite.

She grabbed two disposable coffee cups from the coffee table, offering one to Jax. "Here."

He took a sip. "Okay, this is good."

She nodded. "My new friend gave me a bag when I left his place."

"Now you're just rubbing it in," he groused, holding open the door to their suite.

The hostess at the in-house restaurant, called the

Emperor's Table, gave them a look. "It's pretty late for breakfast."

Naomi pointed at Jax. "He's been craving the Emperor's Breakfast since we checked in."

The young woman smiled, leaning forward a bit. "It is quite good," she admitted conspiratorially. After looking around, she said, "This way."

Sliding into the booth, Jax groaned, "So hungry." He yawned. "So tired." He took another sip of his coffee.

An older woman appeared. "Take your order?"

Jax looked up. "Emperor's Breakfast."

"Two," Naomi added. The woman nodded, tapping on her tablet. She walked off without another word. Naomi turned to Jax. "So, our tour of the Academy of Sciences building is in a few hours."

"I know," he replied, taking another sip of coffee. "This is really good."

The server returned with two large plates. "Two Emperor's Breakfasts." She put the plates down. "Anything else?"

Jax looked up. "I'm sorry, I meant to ask for toast."

She nodded. "Be right back."

Once the server was out of earshot, Jax turned back to Naomi. "How we gonna do this? We've got no prep, no intel. It's been what? A decade since you were here?"

She clenched her jaw. "Well, we'd have had all day yesterday if you hadn't played hero." She waved his reply away. "It's been a while, yeah, but I'll never forget the layout of that place."

"You gonna be okay?" He took a bite of his breakfast, savoring the flavor. "Damn."

"I'll be fine," she snapped. She thought for a moment.

ONE

"As long as the commander's people do their thing, it'll be fine. I know—"

"Toast," the server said as she walked up.

Jax looked up, smiling. "Thank you so much." As the woman walked away, he looked at Naomi. "It's weird, right? Human concierges, hostesses, cab drivers..."

Naomi nodded. "Yeah, the coffee shop I stopped at, owned by man, run by people." Under her breath she added, "A hot man."

"What was that?" Jax asked around a mouthful of toast.

"Nothing." She waved him off.

They ate in silence for a few minutes until Jax said, "So, like, we just go in, download whatever we can, and get out?" He cocked his head. "Sounds too easy."

"I never said it would be easy," Naomi corrected. She took another bite of her pancakes. "Outside the public areas, the place is a fortress." Jax made a *go on* motion. "Once inside, we can break off from the tour group." She held up a hand, the bio-circuitry glowing. "I do my thing to get into the secure areas. We get up to the data center, find what looks like the most valuable data we can, get it, and get out."

"When you put it that way," Jax replied. He took a bite of toast, then washed it down with the coffee Naomi had brought. "This really is good. Let's stock up before leaving the planet. Think your boyfriend can do big orders?" He grinned.

"He's got 'big' handled." She winked.

Jax paused, then laughed loud enough to draw stares from other diners. He ducked his head in apology. He looked at Naomi. "Okay, so what do we need? We can't use the boys. They're trapped on the *Osprey*."

"You've got your gPhone. It's loaded with plenty of

intrusion apps and such. I've got myself." She grinned. "We need to pick up a data storage module." She took a sip of her own coffee. "We can grab one on the way. There are dozens of tech shops in the entertainment district."

Jax slid his plate to the edge of the table. "Okay, so you have a tour booked. You mostly know your way around." He shrugged. "Let's go rob the Empire. What's the worst that can happen?"

Naomi raised an eyebrow.

CHAPTER EIGHT

AND WE'RE WALKING...

The tech shop worker smiled. "Good morning, folks! How are you this morning?" He looked to be eighteen years old. These tech shops were all over the Empire. There was one on Kelso station, but Jax avoided it. Too pricey. On New Terra, this one served the right purpose. Downtown was a mix of corporate drones bustling to and from the various high rises and tourists from around the Empire taking in the sights. A cheaper option did not exist.

Jax shook his head as he closed his umbrella. "Hi. We need a portable data storage unit." The storm was still raging outside, but the sky was lighter and the rain had moved from monsoon to downpour.

The young man nodded and pointed to the back of the store. "Back there. Larger capacity are near the top shelves."

Jax nodded. "Thanks."

"Holler if you need any help," the young man said as Jax and Naomi headed to the rear of the small shop.

When he and Naomi reached the back of the shop, he gestured to the assorted data storage units. "Take your pick."

Naomi looked up and down the shelves, tapping her chin. She plucked one from the shelves near the top. "This should have plenty of space." She held the package up so Jax could see it.

He shrugged. "Cool." He turned to walk back to the middle of the shop, where the payment stations were set up on a circular counter top. The friendly staff member was waiting.

As they exited the tech shop, Jax opened the package and removed the data storage unit, throwing the packaging away in a recycler on the corner of the nearby intersection. He handed Naomi the slim device, all sleek aluminum with a pointless but decorative strip of glittery paint around the edge. "What now?"

Naomi pointed. "That way, couple blocks." She was holding the umbrella over the two of them, offering it to Jax.

The public entrance to the Imperial Academy of Sciences extended out beyond the wall that surrounded the compound. They set large glass doors into a duracrete tunnel. Shock Troopers on either side welcomed people. "Very inviting," Jax said as they passed through the massive entry. Propaganda highlighting the achievements of the science academy lined the walls of the tunnel.

"Good afternoon. Welcome to the Imperial Academy of Sciences," the smiling security guard said from behind an imposing reception desk. "Here for a tour?"

"We are," Naomi said. She pulled her gPhone out. "Uh, group F." She held up her phone to show the man the screen.

The guard nodded and pointed to a small group of people. "Right over there. Those folks are in your group." Jax and Naomi nodded and moved to join the group.

ONE

The group was a good size, almost a dozen people. Jax looked around, whispering, "Lotta tourists."

Naomi nodded. "Did you think the locals took this tour?" He made a face.

They stood around for a bit, making awkward small talk with the other tourists. Jax particularly enjoyed messing with the couple from New Toledo, explaining some of his romantic escapades in vivid detail.

Eventually, a young woman with close-cropped blonde hair came out from a side door, her dark skin gleaming. "Hello, everyone." She found a young boy in the crowd. "Junior scientists." Jax looked at the ceiling, groaned. Naomi elbowed him. The tour guide continued, "I'm Melissa, an intern here at the academy. I'll be your guide. If at any time you have a question, just shout my name." She smiled so broadly, Jax was certain he saw her wince from the strain. She opened the door she had come in from. "Off we go."

The mass of tourists began filing through the door, Jax and Naomi letting themselves fall to the rear. Naomi adjusted her ponytail, pulling her jet-black hair tighter. "We need to wait until we're on or near the twentieth floor or so."

Jax sighed. "Gonna be a long day."

An hour into the tour, Naomi elbowed Jax. "Pay attention. We're nearing the floor we want."

Over the last hour and a half, the tour group had first explored the lower levels of the main tower, then moved to higher floors. The Empire restricted most of the research on the upper floors, but almost all floors had a public lobby for tours. The emperor didn't want to miss out on an opportunity to show off.

He jerked and made a croaking noise. "I didn't know that I could walk while asleep," he quipped.

Their group was moving to the elevators, having finished watching clean-suit-clad scientists doing who knows what in a clean room.

Naomi gave him a look, then took his arm as the tour group was rounding a corner up ahead. As they approached the corner, there was a door with a label on it, Security Station 7-B. Naomi pressed her hand to the security badge reader. The door unlocked in under two seconds. The two of them ducked inside.

"Guess our friends came through," Jax said as Naomi quickly moved to a console set in a rack of processing units. Next to the processing cores were several ruggedized cases about the size of a shoebox.

She looked over her shoulder as she rested both hands on the nearest processing core. "Smart of them. There's one of these substations on each floor in case of an issue. They're not manned and not really checked or anything."

Jax nodded absently, looking around the room. "So what now?"

Naomi shook her head. "We need to get up to 42. For now, though, we wait."

"Yay," Jax drawled. He looked around, eyes settling on the cases. "Did they pack us a meal?" Naomi shook her head.

ROBBING

It was one thing to get into the security substation; it was an unguarded closet. Being able to walk around the complex freely was a horse of a different color, as Jax's memaw used to say. The plan was to wait until after most of the building's occupants left for the day. The commander had been right. With the storm raging, that number was lower than a normal work day but still numbered in the thousands. The risk of discovery while wondering the corridors was too high.

"Your move," Jax said, inclining his head to Naomi's own device. She held it up. "You're not very good at this." She tapped the screen of her phone, and Jax's beeped a sad tone. He swore. Laughing, she suggested, "Maybe something other than chess?"

"Go?" Jax offered.

Naomi smirked. "I think you're picking games in the wrong direction. How about Yahtzee?"

He frowned. "How about Scrabble?"

She shrugged. "Sure." He started up a game, then initiated local area competitive play.

A couple of hours later Jax said, "So, uh..." He blushed.

"What?" Naomi asked, looking up. They had grown tired of games an hour or so earlier. Jax tried to nap, and Naomi continued reading a book she had started a few days prior.

"I have to pee."

She closed the reading app and looked at the time. "Then this will have to do." She stood and walked to the processing cores. As she placed her hands on the nearest computer, they pulsed with blue light. A few seconds later, the glow of her bio-circuitry faded. "Okay, I just configured the security system to not see us."

Jax nodded appreciatively. "You go. They won't notice your hack?"

She wiggled a hand. "Not tonight, at least. Someone will notice in the morning for sure. I'll try to undo it on our way out, to be safe." He nodded his agreement.

Naomi added, "I mean, we should try not to get seen by people. We're only invisible to the cameras. Someone remembering us, whether on camera or not, will be an issue."

"That'd be cool, though." He reached down, picking up one of the rugged cases. "We good?"

She nodded, picking up her own case. "Elevator is to the right at the intersection."

"I remember," Jax said. "It wasn't that long ago."

As they exited the elevator on the forty-second floor, Naomi took the lead. "The Interface program was the floor below this, mostly. We came up here sometimes for practice sessions."

"Practice?"

She nodded. "Intrusion, counter-intrusion. Since the data cores are here, and all."

ONE

"Fun childhood," Jax replied sadly.

"That doesn't even include the weeks of surgeries to install the bio-circuitry, then the data storage nodes. It was a hoot," she deadpanned. After looking around, "This way, quietly."

They crept along hallways between glass enclosed data centers and laboratories for a few minutes. Jax watched as they crept past research labs full of things he couldn't identify and people working on them. None of the researchers seemed to notice the two civilians walking past their labs.

"Here?" Jax pointed at a glass enclosed data center, full of racks and racks of servers, covered in blinking lights. The space looked deserted.

Naomi pointed to a label over the door, Life Sciences. "I don't think we'll get much of value." She pointed further down the corridor. "I'm thinking Industrial Engineering." She continued toward her destination, adding, "Or Starship Engineering?" He looked over her shoulder. "Probably some nifty toys we could add to the *Osprey*."

Jax rubbed his hands together. "You have my interest."

The entire floor was a grid of labs and server farms. Jax couldn't imagine growing up surrounded by such a stark environment. Even Kelso station had a warmer feel to it. "Your entire childhood was," he gestured to the white floors and ceiling and similarly white wall paneling, "this?"

She nodded. "Yeah. The floor they raised us on was a little homier than this, but not by much." She stopped. "Well, hello." She pointed at a door ahead of them. "That's new."

Before he looked up, Jax said, "Well, it's been a few years." He looked up. "Oh, that sounds lucrative." The label over the door read Special Projects. He turned to her, both eyebrows arched. "Yeah?"

She nodded. "Probably some goodies on those servers." She reached for the access control panel, the bio-circuitry in her hand glowing. She rested her hand on the panel, and her circuitry tattoos pulsed. She frowned.

MEMORIES

"What?" Jax asked, then looked around. They had encountered no security, and all the scientists they had seen were in labs working. He turned back to look at Naomi, who was still standing at the access control panel. The tattoos lining her hand and arm were glowing brightly, pulsing. More than Jax had ever seen before. "You okay?" he whispered, turning to look up and down the corridor again.

The access panel beeped, finally. She dropped her hand as the door slid open. Turning to Jax, she said, "That was way more difficult than it should have been." Jax followed her in.

"What does that mean?" he asked.

She shrugged. "I don't know. It was almost like they designed the security system to counter Interface abilities, or something."

"Or something? Like, there's one of you around here?" he pressed.

"One of me?" She put a hand on her hip. "What does that mean?"

Jax waved her off. "Never mind. Now what?"

She walked over to a rack of processing cores. She set the portable data storage module on a small slide-out keyboard tray, resting one hand on the storage unit while she pressed one against the processing unit. Both hands glowed blue, light pulsing from the hand on the processing core to the hand on the storage module. The bio-circuits around her eyes pulsed as if she were watching the data move from one device to another.

"Neat," Jax said as he watched. He turned and walked further into the server room, exploring.

He set his case down, opening it. "Oh, this is interesting."

"Jax?" Naomi whispered. "Where'd you go?"

"Back here," Jax answered.

"Is that?" she asked, joining him.

"Yup," he said, looking at the case and the device inside.

She ran a hand through her hair. "That's gonna leave a mark."

Jax nodded. "Yeah. You still good with this?"

She knelt down to inspect the device. Her hand lit up as she touched it. "Huh." She looked up. "Yeah. This will really make the Imps cranky." She looked past Jax. "Worst case, we can make sure any stragglers aren't still in the building."

Jax frowned. "How?"

She pointed to the door to the server room, and on the wall next to it, a fire alarm system. Jax shrugged one shoulder. "Cool."

They exited the server room, Jax holding the second ruggedized case. They nestled the first between two large processing core arrays. Anyone that came into the room would have to be standing almost on top of it to see the case.

ONE

The hallways were lit at fifty percent illumination. By that time, almost everyone had gone home for the day.

Jax's stomach rumbled. He held up the second case. "Where does this bad boy go?"

Naomi thought about it as they moved down the corridor, passing server rooms and research labs. "Do you remember what floor the city's network management hub was on?"

Jax made a face. "Mmm, no?"

Naomi turned to him. "Is that a question? It was on the tour."

He shrugged. "Like I said, I tuned out." He used his free hand to rub his chin. "I want to say 30?"

Naomi squinted a bit as they walked. "I think so, yeah. Either way, should be close enough even if we're a floor or two off." Jax nodded his agreement as the elevator doors slid apart.

Naomi slipped the portable data unit into a thigh pocket of her pants as the lift moved.

The thirtieth floor was a lot like the forty-second, as far as its layout.

"Looks familiar," Jax said as they walked around. "This what the levels you lived on were like?"

Naomi looked at him. "The floors we were on were a little more residential than this." She waved to the nearest server room. "Not by much, though." She pointed to a different bank of servers behind a glass wall. "That would be the overseer's office." Her hand moved a few degrees. "The training area." She turned around. "The bunks would be there. Just me and forty-odd of my closest friends. Random kids from all over the Alliance. Tormented by angry adults that scolded us and worse whenever we got out of line, or failed a test."

She held out her hand. Jax handed her the second device that the commander had arranged for them to find. She walked to the middle of the floor, putting the case down. After opening the case and pressing a few buttons, she looked at Jax. "Let's get the hell out of here."

As the two walked back to the elevators, the device they had just walked away from wirelessly connected to its mate several floors up. Once the two devices connected to each other and synchronized, they called home.

Jax looked at Naomi. "I'm so freaking hungry."

She was about to reply when the elevator doors slid open to reveal a security guard. "Oh," was all she said.

"Wha?" the guard stammered.

Naomi leapt into the elevator car, tackling the guard.

"Wha?" Jax gaped. A moment later, his wits returned. He rushed into the lift car as Naomi and the guard wrestled. She had one of his hands pinned, knocking his gPhone aside.

Jax saw the stunner a moment before the guard jammed it into Naomi's thigh. The sound of energy discharging from the high-volume capacitor into his business partner filled the small space.

Naomi didn't jerk about as one would when thousands of volts dumped into them. Jax tilted his head. Instead, she swore and punched the man in the face. "No, no, no!" she hissed. The thigh pocket of her pants had a scorch mark. She snatched the portable data storage module out of her damaged pocket. It, too, had a scorch mark on the casing. "Damnit!" she added. The painted-on stripe had melted and peeled away. The unit's status lights were blinking erratically.

"What the hell?" Jax asked, kneeling.

ONE

Naomi didn't say a word. She placed both hands on the device, bio-circuits pulsing with blue light. Jax watched in silence.

WRINKLES

Naomi stood up, kicking the sparking data storage unit away.

"Now what?" Jax asked, looking around. The guard was still out cold on the floor, his hand still clutching the stunner. "You okay?"

Naomi looked at the guard, kicking the stunner away from his hand. "I don't know." Naomi rubbed her temple. "Yeah, I'm okay. Let's get back to the guest house. Your aunt is expecting us to accompany her to the closing ceremony thing." She pulled her gPhone out of her pocket. "Soon."

Jax shook his head. "Are you sure you're okay? Did you just copy all of that data into your spleen or whatever?"

Naomi nodded. "Yeah. I didn't know what else to do. If we lost the data, this was all for nothing." She made a face. "And it's not in my spleen. The bio-storage units are all over my body, but not in organs."

"Do you know what the data is?" Jax asked, stepping closer to her.

She shook her head. "No, it's encrypted." She rubbed

her temple again, then pressed the button for floor 18. "We'll drop him off there, a storage room or something." The lift car started its descent.

Jax pulled his gPhone from a pocket, looking at the screen. He entered a series of numbers, the onetime address that the commander's underling had given him. His finger hovering over the *send* button, he looked at Naomi, who nodded once. He pressed the button. He did not know that the devices on the floors above had already called the commander and were hard at work doing the job they had been designed to do.

"Are you going to be okay?" He put a hand on her shoulder.

She shook her head. "I don't know. This is more data than I've ever carried. They didn't build us to be couriers. The bio-storage modules were meant to keep the odd secret file or small database, not petabytes of data. Not for very long." She groaned and tried to smile. "I'm now an edge case."

"Can you get rid of it? Cut our losses?" Jax pressed. The elevator doors slid apart. He leaned out, looking left and right. No one was around. They dragged the guard to a storage closet and tied his hands and feet. Naomi found a handkerchief and jammed it into the man's mouth.

"Sorry, man. Someone will find you, eventually," Jax said to the unconscious man.

They made their way back down to the ground floor of the massive science complex. The elevator made no stops, and they saw no other guards.

The elevator doors slid apart, and Jax leaned out. A pair of lab technicians were walking away from them, animatedly arguing something. The pair rounded a corner down the hallway a moment before the entire building shook. The lights in the hallway blinked several times before the hallways went dark. Two seconds later, red emergency lighting came on. An automated message started playing from the overhead speakers, encouraging people to exit the building in an orderly fashion.

Jax looked at his partner. "I kinda expected more."

Naomi shook her head. "Come on." She nodded once and took the lead, heading in the opposite direction the lab techs had gone. Looking over her shoulder, she said, "Oh, and no, I can't delete it. I should be able to purge the storage modules, but something is wrong. Maybe there's too much, I don't know. I didn't think to grab an instruction manual when I fled this place the first time."

"What about your nanites?" Jax asked, his head moving back and forth, looking for threats.

"They're doing what they can," she replied. She thought back to the day she and her classmates, as the scientists called them, learned of their impending fate. The researchers and military overseers all thought that they had built the perfect enclosure for their charges; no wireless signals, no data ports, no wires in the walls. They failed to consider the ingenuity of curious children. Intelligent, curious children.

Martin, one of the older boys in the group, had sensed a data pathway under the floor of their bunkroom. In the corner, under the floor panel, there was a junction box that fed the room next to theirs but was just reachable if your arm was long enough. Martin's was.

At night the Interfaces formed a chain, holding hands and sharing data that Martin pulled from the building's network. It wasn't much. They fire walled the entire building off from the greater planetary network, except for very specific and hard-wired access points.

Unfortunately, the researchers had chosen to keep the order to terminate the Interface project, with prejudice, on a server in the building—one the children could access. Once they saw the order, the children were divided on what to do. Many, including Naomi, were in favor of escape. She wasn't the only one to have been conscripted against her will. The rest, convinced that the order meant they'd be returned to their homes anyway, wanted to do nothing.

When the men came to the children's bunkroom, they found the children as expected, half of them. Having access to the building network, Martin and those who wished to leave, including Naomi, had snuck out, much the same way Jax and Naomi were doing now.

Naomi eased open a door, the same door she had fled through all those years ago. This time, with the fire warning still droning, exterior doors had all unlocked to allow for the safe exiting of the building. The storm outside had lessened, the rain more of a drizzle. "This way," she whispered through clenched teeth.

Jax looked up at the sky. It was dark, well after sundown, but he could tell that the cloud cover wasn't the same uniform blanket it had been since their arrival. He hoped the storm was finally abating.

They emerged into a small alley between the tall main Academy building and the wall that surrounded the campus. Jax looked around. "Now where?" Naomi said nothing, pointing off toward the wall and a delivery door set in it. Jax nodded.

Above them, two floors of the building had burst into flames, leaving the floors above and below completely dark. The devices had wirelessly interfaced with as many processing cores as possible, corrupting the Imperial network. Then they exploded.

Jax pushed the delivery door open and looked around, sighing. "We're clear." He held the door for Naomi. They walked as quickly and casually as they could down the street until Jax spotted a cab.

TWO

CHAPTER NINE

NO REST

The cab ride back to the Imperial Guest House passed quietly. Naomi sat with her eyes closed, rubbing the side of her head. Jax watched the city pass by outside the window. The storm was definitely winding down. Here and there he could see stars. The cabbie, thankfully, remained silent for the drive. Jax couldn't tell if the storm had finally blown itself out or if the eye had moved over Titan City.

The cab pulled to a stop in front of the Imperial Guest House, the passenger doors sliding open. Jax paid the fare and followed Naomi into the lobby. By that point, she seemed to be feeling better. Jax pressed the button to summon the elevator. "You look like you're doing better."

Naomi nodded. "I am. I think the nanites finally got a handle on things." The elevator doors opened, and she stepped in, followed by Jax. "I still have to figure out how to get rid of the data, but at least I don't feel like my insides are on fire."

Jax swore, "We shoulda stopped and bought a new data storage module." The elevator arrived at their floor.

Naomi shrugged. "We can grab one tomorrow. I'll take

something for the headache, but I think I'm good. For now, at least." They reached the door to their suite as the door to Governor Singh and Jeffry's slid open.

"Hello, you two," the diminutive Indian woman said. She eyed them both up and down. "You look like shit."

Jax grimaced. "Thanks, Auntie." He held the door open so Naomi could enter. When he spied his adopted aunt still standing there, he asked, "Something else?"

She clucked, "You forgot? The closing reception for the summit." She consulted her gPhone. "It's tonight, in thirty minutes, to be specific."

Jax rubbed his face. "Would it be—" he started.

Governor Singh cut him off. "I will ring the buzzer in thirty minutes, so we can arrive fashionably late." She held up a finger. "But not too late." She didn't wait for his reply, stepping back into her suite, letting the door slide closed.

"How did she even know we were out here?" Jax wondered aloud as he entered the suite, letting the door slide closed behind him.

Inside the suite, the door to Naomi's room was closed. Jax looked around, muttering, "Beer or shower?" He tapped his chin as he thought, then moved to the kitchenette space, grabbing a beer from the refrigerator. "Shower beer." He headed for his room.

Thirty minutes later, almost to the second, the announcement chime rang. A display set next to the door came to life. On it, Governor Singh and Jeffry were waiting outside, both dressed in their finest.

Jax opened the door. "That's a lovely sari, Auntie."

Naomi appeared behind him. "It really is."

The old woman made a face. "Don't try to sweet talk me." She hitched a thumb toward the lifts. "Let's go."

TWO

Jax and Naomi were in the nicest clothes they had brought to New Terra.

The reception was being held at the palace, which meant a cab ride. Despite the name, the Imperial Guest House was not that close to the Imperial Palace, or even on the palace grounds.

By the time their cab arrived, they were appropriately late.

"Mind your manners while we're here. These people are my peers, and my friends," the governor scolded as she stepped out of the cab. She looked at Jax. "Also, if you act up, the Imperials will kill you." Jax inclined his head, holding his hands up, palms out.

The Imperial Palace wasn't a repurposed governmental building. When the war ended, the newly crowned emperor razed the Independent Systems Alliance grand council chamber. He called it a symbol of dysfunction. In order for humanity to claim its place in the galaxy, a building that reflected the shared strength of purpose was needed. That the project created jobs for several years helped wipe away most objections.

Made to resemble castles of old, the palace had several towers that reached dozens of stories into the sky. The main tower dwarfed them all, reaching into the clouds. If you ignored what it stood for, and who lived in it, it was a beautiful building.

As the group approached the main doors, two immaculately dressed Imperial guards opened the massive doors to the palace. Jax put on his best innocent expression. "Would I—?" He looked at Naomi. "—We, embarrass you?" The look the elderly woman gave him would burn through titanium.

The palace's grand foyer was fifty meters wide and

easily two hundred long. The emperor had lined it with banners and artifacts from around the Empire. Between the banners, on marble pedestals, sat models of starships, fighters, and power armor used during the war. Spaced along the walls between trinkets were doors leading off to meeting rooms, supply rooms, and who knew what else. At the far end of the foyer, off to the left, was the door that led to the hallway that led to the elevator that led to the throne room. It was the only way up to that ultra-secure space. Jax had heard that the views from the throne room on a clear day were magnificent.

A voice over the loudspeaker said, "Governor Neeti Singh, Kelso station, and entourage."

"Yes. Yes, you most certainly would." Governor Singh looked at Naomi. "Not you, dear. Just him. He's trouble." She looked at Jeffry. "Why don't you and Naomi mingle? I'd like Jackson to meet a few of the others."

"Entourage?" Jax looked around, frowning.

Jeffry offered his arm to Naomi. "Shall we?" She took his arm.

The governor looked at Jax. "Come, Jackson." He groaned.

PARTY TIME

"Barbara, Steven," Governor Singh said as she approached a pair of well-dressed older people.

The woman, around Governor Singh's age, with white hair and a long black skirt, turned. "Neeti." She looked at Jax. "This must be your nephew." Jax reached out, taking her offered hand. "I'm Barbara Rosales, Governor of Durango station."

"Nice to meet you, ma'am," Jax replied.

The woman looked at Neeti. "He's cute." She turned to Jax and winked.

"Oh, Barbara, stop messing with the boy," the man she was with, Steven, said. The dark skin crinkled around his eyes as he grinned, his hairless pate shining in the flickering mock candlelight of the room. "Jackson, pleased to meet you. Steven Tesfaye, Konso station." He offered his hand.

Jax shook the offered hand. "I've been to Konso a few times. Great station, amazing food." Jax grinned. "Oh, and that club in the industrial…" He trailed off when he saw the look of interest on Governor Tesfaye's face. "Never mind."

Barbara chuckled and leaned in, which forced everyone else to follow suit. "Did you hear?"

Governor Tesfaye shook his head. "Hear what?"

Governor Singh nodded. "What?"

"Someone attacked the Imperial science academy building. Blew it up," Rosales whispered.

"Not all of it," Jax mumbled under his breath.

"What?" Singh said. "What do you mean? How is that even possible?" She straightened, looking around. "Why isn't the city in lock down?"

Governor Tesfaye nodded. "Yeah, that seems like something they'd lock everything down for."

Rosales continued, "I heard from a contact in the palace's administrative pool that there are rumblings of a rebel faction, based right here on New Terra."

"No way," Tesfaye said. He ran a hand over his bold head as his eyes darted around the space.

Governor Singh looked at Jax, who had been standing off to the side of the trio of governors. "Jackson, had you heard anything about this?"

"Who? Me?" He put a hand on his chest. "Why would I have heard anything about it?"

His adopted aunt's brow crinkled as she studied him. "You were out somewhere before we came here," she replied, her eyes boring a hole into his soul.

"Oh, yeah. Right." Jax's cheeks flushed. "Yeah, no, we didn't hear anything about it. We definitely weren't anywhere near the science academy." Governor Singh's eyes narrowed as she scrutinized him.

A server came by with a tray of stuffed mushroom caps, forcing the trio of conspiratorial governors to change topics.

At the bar halfway along the length of the grand foyer, Naomi and Jeffry were clinking wine glasses.

TWO

"Cheers," the young man said.

Naomi smiled. "So how was the summit?" She took a sip, enjoying what must have been a several-hundred-credit glass of wine. "Oh, this is good," she purred.

Jeffry ran a hand through his light brown hair, exhaling. "Mind numbing."

Naomi took a sip of her drink, her headache finally subsiding. "What goes on? I'd kind of expect it to take longer than a few days."

Jeffry took his own sip. "A lot of posturing from the Imperials, mostly. The governors break out into working groups, going over supply chains and cargo routes." He took another sip. "They formed some working groups to discuss trade and other things. Nothing will come of them." He sighed.

"That sounds…horrible," Naomi admitted.

Jeffry smiled. "The whole almost-dying-on-our-way-here thing really should have had a better payoff than two days of meetings and Imperial posturing." Naomi raised her glass in agreement.

"Jackson, this is Marcus Johansson. He's the governor of Humbolt colony."

Jax and the man shook hands. "Nice to meet you," the former said, inclining his head.

Before the heavyset man could return the pleasantry, the overhead speaker announced, "Ladies and gentleman, Emperor Justin Abernathy Stenson of the Grand Human Empire."

Conversations around the large space immediately wrapped up as everyone turned toward the large doors at the end of the foyer as they swung open. Imperial guards in their finery marched out. While dressed in what Jax considered puffery, each guard was an expert in many types of hand-to-hand fighting skills, and under their frilly coats were likely many guns and, probably, knives. Almost certainly knives.

The emperor came out after his guard had fanned out. "Greetings, everyone," he boomed, his voice carried by the overhead speakers. He took the five steps up to the small stage. There was no lectern, just a flat surface that raised him above all others.

"Thank you all for joining me on this last night of our time together. It's been a wonderful two days. I wish we had more time together. I'm sure you all will return to your stations and colonies energized to work hard and make our Empire ever stronger."

The emperor continued, "Our Empire is as strong as she's ever been. Together we'll continue to show the human settled galaxy that our strength is in our unity. Humanity is destined for greatness, and we'll get there together, as one—Imperial colonies and stations, hand in hand with our fringe brothers and sisters."

Governor Singh made a noise, causing Jax to look down at her. She waved him off.

The emperor continued talking, his gaze roving across the faces of those gathered, making sure everyone was paying attention. Jeffry and Naomi were still standing near the bar. They had been talking to the governor of Anker colony when the emperor took the stage. As the trio turned to watch him give his address, Naomi found her wine glass more and more interesting, unable to look upon the man who had issued the order for her and many other children's deaths.

Naomi slowly became aware that the room had gotten a little quieter. She looked up to find the emperor staring right at her. He caught himself, continuing what he had

TWO

been saying, but his eyes stayed on Naomi for a bit longer. When the ruler of most of human controlled space moved his attention elsewhere, Jeffry leaned over. "Uh, what was that?"

Naomi shrugged. "No idea." She shuddered and put both hands on her wineglass to keep it from sloshing.

"No idea? Do you know the emperor? His gaze certainly gave the impression he knows you."

Naomi noticed that several other attendees of the reception were looking at her—some openly, others out of the corner of their eye, trying to be discreet. "I don't feel well. I'm going to head back to the guest house."

Jeffry stared for a moment, then got his wits about him. "I'll go with you."

THIS PART TOOK A TURN...

"You're not looking so hot," Jeffry said as he and Naomi walked out of the palace, into the night. A line of cabs was waiting for the other reception attendees. The night was clear, stars dotting the sky. The storm had finally, fully blown itself out.

Naomi shook her head. "I'm not feeling so hot. I think I'll go to the ship and see the auto-doc."

"Couldn't you visit a med center here? I'm sure there are several public wellness centers downtown. They'd be a hell of a lot closer." He pointed off toward the glittering skyscrapers in the distance. The palace sat at the edge of downtown, putting the towers, monorail stations, and government buildings between it and the spaceport.

"I could, but I trust our auto-doc more, and it's not tied to the Imperial medical database."

Jeffry stared for a long minute. "Okay." He leaned forward, tapping the seat. "Change of plans. Can you take us to the spaceport?" He turned to Naomi then back to the driver. "Alpha."

"Sure thing," the driver replied, adjusting her course.

TWO

The cab made a turn and angled away from the Imperial Guest House and towards Spaceport Alpha.

Twenty minutes later, Jeffry and Naomi were walking between two medium freighters towards the waiting *Osprey*.

Naomi reached into her pocket and handed Jeffry her gPhone after tapping on the screen. He took the device looking at it, then put it to his ear. "Uh, hello?"

"Hello, Jeffry," the voice of the ship's SI said.

"Oh, uh...Skip, hi. Naomi and I are coming back. We're almost to you."

"Is everything okay? Is the captain with you?" Rudy cut in.

"No, he's not with us. I think he's okay, but Naomi isn't. She doesn't look good," Jeffry said as Naomi put more of her weight on him. He grunted. "She's pretty messed up. I don't know what's wrong. She's also heavy."

"I'll meet you at the ramp. Hurry up." That time it was Baxter.

The duracrete of the spaceport was still wet, puddles scattered here and there. The *Osprey*'s boarding ramp lowered, unfolding as it did. It hit the wet ground with a thud. A matte black droid crept down the ramp.

I'm not detecting anyone in the vicinity except Jeffry and Naomi, Skip beamed to Baxter. *I think you can go get them.*

Baxter turned in the direction the two were coming from and dashed off. *On my way.*

A few minutes later, Baxter was easing Naomi onto the bio-bed in the *Osprey*'s small med bay. He turned his swishing optic sensor to Jeffry. "What happened?"

The young gubernatorial assistant shrugged. "No idea. We were at the emperor's closing reception thing, and she just started looking bad." He stepped back from the bed as the auto-doc lowered from the ceiling. "She insisted we come here instead of a med center downtown."

The auto-doc, a shiny white oval on an articulated arm, possessed a specialized Rudimentary Intelligence packed with medical procedures, drug facts and interactions, and basic surgical skills. While the main processor of the auto-doc was the foot-long oval, the entire med bay was its body. Segmented arms mounted to the wall nearest the bio-bed deployed, some with scanners, some with medical implements. Baxter and Jeffry scurried out of the way as the shiny white ovoid got to work.

"Governor Singh," the emperor said as he reached the governor and Jax. Two imposing Imperial guard troopers were keeping a respectful distance behind him.

"Emperor." She inclined her head respectfully. Jax looked around, then followed suit, his eyes never leaving the two guards.

"Emperor Stenson, this is my nephew, Jackson..." She chewed on the rest, "Caruso."

The emperor's eyebrows crept up his face. "Caruso?"

Jackson blushed. The emperor smiled. "The past is the past. It's a pleasure to meet you, young man." He extended his hand.

It was easy for the emperor to be so blasé about the past; he was the emperor. Jackson's parents were both dead, along with thousands of other Indies.

Jax looked at the offered hand, his mouth a compressed line. Governor Singh elbowed him in the hip. "You shake it," she hissed. Jax shook his head and shook the emperor's hand.

"Your parents were good people. Misguided in their views on how humanity should progress in the galaxy, but good people," the emperor said.

"Uh...thank you," Jax stammered.

The emperor turned to the governor. "Governor Singh, during my speech, I spied a young woman standing next to your assistant. She looked incredibly familiar. Who is she?" Regal privilege replaced his previous friendliness.

Governor Singh opened her mouth, but Jax cut her off. "No idea...uh, sir. She didn't come with us." The emperor turned his attention back to Jax.

The emperor looked from Jax to the governor. "Where did your assistant go?"

Governor Singh looked around. "I... I don't know." She turned to Jax. "Did you see Jeffry leave?"

Jax shook his head. "No. He must have gotten tired, turned in early." He glanced at the emperor, still addressing his adopted aunt, "You know how much he hates space travel. Maybe he wanted one more good night's sleep before our trip home."

The small Indian woman shrugged, then looked at the emperor. "He's a baby about space travel."

The emperor frowned. "Interesting." He looked around. "Excuse me." He turned and walked towards the bar Jeffry and Naomi had camped out at, his guards falling in line. One of them watched Jax out of the corner of his eye as he passed.

Jax pulled his phone out of his pocket. He tapped the screen a few times. "Weird, they're at the spaceport, aboard the *Osprey*." He looked at his aunt to see that she wasn't listening to anything he had just said.

Governor Singh had her own phone out. "Jeffry, where are you?" Jax could not hear the reply. "Why are you there?" She turned to look at Jax, who showed her his gPhone screen, with the locator dot for Naomi aboard the *Osprey*. "What's wrong with her?" Jax frowned. "What do you mean, you don't know?"

Jax tapped her shoulder. "We should go."

The diminutive Indian woman said, "We'll be there shortly." She did not wait for Jeffry to reply. She tapped the screen and deposited the phone in her handbag. "Let's go."

AWKWARD CAB RIDES

As the cab pulled away from the palace, the governor leaned closer to her nephew. "What did you do?"

"What do you mean?" he asked.

She shifted in the seat, her sari rustling. "Don't you *what do you mean* me. First, I hear that there was an attack on the Imperial science academy building, then there was that bit with the emperor? Why did he think he knew Naomi?" She reached over and pinched Jax's midsection. "You better not be mixed up in whatever happened downtown."

Jax flinched. "Ouch! Why did you...?" He looked at the cab driver, who was doing her best to ignore the domestic squabble taking place in the back seat. "Not here," he hissed. He asked the cabbie, "What's going on downtown? We heard there was an explosion."

The governor harrumphed but did not press the conversation. Her expression made it clear to Jax that he was enjoying only a temporary reprieve.

The cabbie looked in the mirror at her passengers. "No

idea. They're saying a power cell exploded or something. It was one of the tall government buildings."

Jax looked at Governor Singh, his face saying, *See, it wasn't me*. Her face replied, *I do not for one second believe you*. He pulled his gPhone out of a pocket and started tapping the screen. The local news net seemed more preoccupied with the emperor's summit wrapping up and some press release that indicated the station and colony governors had once again committed themselves to the peace and prosperity of the Empire.

He had to scroll a bit to find mention of the Academy of Sciences explosion, barely two paragraphs. An experimental power cell, one that would eventually revolutionize power generation, exploded. There were no fatalities and only minor injuries because of the storm and time of the explosion, well after most employees left for the day.

The Imperial Guest House at that hour was a ghost town. There was only one bored looking bellhop leaning against a pillar when the cab pulled up to a stop. The young man opened the cab door for Governor Singh. "Welcome back, ma'am."

She nodded to the man and said, "We'll be checking out. Please send a cart to suite 809 and 806." She headed into the lobby.

Jax paid the cab driver, and as the vehicle departed, said, "We'll need a ride to Spaceport Alpha in about thirty minutes." The bellhop nodded.

TIME TO GO

An anxious half hour later, Jax and Governor Singh were back in a cab on the way to the spaceport. "They had better not damage anything," Governor Singh groused. Their luggage, hers mostly, was in another vehicle, as the cab they were in had insufficient cargo space.

Jax turned from looking out the window. "I'm sure it'll be fine." It was nearing midnight. Outside the window was mostly pitch black, except for the towers of downtown. Noticeably absent was the Academy of Sciences building. It was completely dark. He had hoped that the commander would stay true to his word, but it hadn't surprised him when the devices went off before he and Naomi had even left the building. Even more stars were visible above. The clouds seemed to have exhausted themselves, finally, and the storm was nowhere to be seen.

For a moment, Jax's thoughts wandered to Old Town and its residents. He hoped the people he had met and worked with were okay.

At that time of night, the spaceport was largely deserted, with only a minimal night watch on duty at the main entrance. As the cab pulled away, a woman in a spaceport control uniform came out. "Can I help you folks?"

Governor Singh nodded, hitching a thumb to the cab full of luggage, pulling in as their cab departed. "You can get us someone to help with all this."

The woman's mouth fell open as the cab driver got out, opening all the vehicle's doors to reveal the suitcases piled inside. "Oh, my."

"You've no idea," Jax said. He added, "We're parked at D9." He moved through the entry to make his way through the security checkpoint, Governor Singh following. The spaceport woman watched as the cab driver kept piling suitcases up. Sighing, she waved to one of her colleagues.

One upside of returning to the spaceport in the middle of the night was that the security line was nonexistent. Jax and Governor Singh were through in a matter of minutes. The governor scolded several employees to be careful with her luggage and hurry and get it to the ship. Jax had tried to calm her down, but after a series of open-handed slaps to his shoulder, he realized she was tired, and he was okay with the spaceport employees being the focus of her attention. They caught a small ground car from the spaceport entrance to the pad D9.

Jeffry was waiting for them at the foot of the *Osprey*'s boarding ramp. He was nervously shuffling from one foot to another. When Governor Singh approached, the young man rushed over. "Sorry for leaving so suddenly, ma'am."

She waved him away, moving up the ramp. "Water under the bridge." She looked over her shoulder. "See to our luggage."

Jeffry looked at Jax, who just pointed to the approaching cargo vehicle. "Good luck." He followed his adopted aunt into the ship.

TWO

Once on the cargo deck, Jax moved quickly to the small medical bay just forward of the engineering space. Naomi occupied the sole bed. The auto-doc had tucked itself up near the ceiling. It had done everything it could.

"You look like shit," Jax quipped.

Naomi opened an eye. "You suck." She closed her eye, then opened them both. "I don't know what's going on, but it ain't good." A hand trailing an IV line moved to her torso. "There's too much in here."

Jax looked at her. "I knew it was your spleen." He grinned. She made a rude gesture.

Naomi nodded toward the dormant auto-doc. "It couldn't really make heads or tails of what's going on inside me other than to point out that the data storage modules that are tucked into my nooks and crannies seem to be failing or overloading." She closed her eyes. "Or something." She grinned. "It did give me some outstanding drugs, though."

Jax looked at the ceiling for a moment. "What do we do?" He ran a hand through his hair. "Can you upload it all into Skip?"

Naomi shook her head. "It's stuck. I don't know why. I don't know if it's corrupted or just too much." Her eyes closed and Jax thought she was unconscious until she said, "Columbiana," in a whisper that trailed off. Jax's heart nearly leapt from his chest until he glanced at the bio-monitor. That time she was asleep.

When Jax came up the stairs onto the common deck, Rudy was waiting. "I hate this place. I can't even begin to explain how boring it is being cooped up on this thing." The squat droid's head made a full rotation as he rolled up to Jax.

"This thing has a name," Skip said sourly.

Rudy waved both of his thin arms. "You know what I mean." There was a pause. "I take it things went sideways?"

Jax ignored them. "Auntie and Jeffry turn in?"

There was a crash from below. Rudy said, "That would be Jeffry struggling with the luggage still. The governor is in her quarters."

"My quarters," Jax mumbled, then said, "Hey, Baxter, can you help Jeffry? I'd like to get off this rock."

"On it."

Jax headed for the flight deck. "Skip, let's get ready to go."

"Copy that," the ship's SI replied. Before Jax reached the flight deck, the low rumble of the reactor spinning up vibrated through the deck plating.

Dropping into his command seat, with Rudy clipping into his station, Jax toggled the comm system. "Titan City Space Control, this the *Osprey*. Requesting departure clearance."

There was a static filled moment. "*Osprey*, departure in the middle of the night is uncommon."

"But allowed?" Jax pressed.

Another pause, the hiss of the open channel filling the flight deck. "That is correct, *Osprey*. One moment."

Jax looked over his shoulder. "Plot us a course to Columbiana station."

The droid made a noise. "Columbiana? You're not taking the governor home?"

Jax nodded. "I mean, eventually, yes. Naomi needs something or someone on Columbiana. Hopefully she'll tell us who or what once we're on the way." He turned back to face the wide, clear forward viewscreen. "Auntie is just gonna have to tag along." He heard Rudy whisper something about not cleaning up the blood.

CHAPTER TEN

WE'VE BEEN ROBBED

"Dr. Sorensen." A technician turned from a rack of processing cores on the fifty-third level of the primary building of the Imperial science academy. The explosions had not damaged the structure of the building but had done significant damage to the two floors where the devices had been placed. While the physical damage was relatively minor, all things considered, the non-physical damage was extensive. An electromagnetic pulse had scrambled processing cores up and down the building. Add that to the virus that the mystery devices had injected into every open system they found. Researchers would be working to undo the damage for months.

"Yes?" a middle-aged man said, walking over. He was wearing a rumpled suit, clearly having gotten dressed in a hurry in the middle of the night.

"I've been trying to piece together some of the log files from this server farm."

"And?" the senior researcher and department head asked.

The young technician stammered, "Well, sir. As you of

course know, the pulse heavily damaged most of the processing cores." Dr. Sorensen made a *go on* motion with his hand. "I found a spike." The technician wiped his brow. "Someone copied several petabytes from one of the processing cores on level 42, the special projects servers." He added, "Before the explosions."

"Well, it wouldn't have happened after, would it?" Sorensen said. He pushed the technician aside, looking over the data. "What the hell?" He turned to the technician. "Can you identify the files that were copied?" Sorenson stepped back to make room for the technician. With the technician working on pulling up the data he requested, the doctor tapped his earpiece. "Send in the security chief, please."

When the chief arrived and Dr. Sorensen explained the situation, the heavily muscled security man asked, "So, which files?"

The technician handed him a tablet. "I can't be certain this is a complete list, given the damage," the man apologized.

As the chief scrolled through the list of project files, he tapped his ear. "Ensign Topher, go through the entire building's logs. Someone broke in. Find them." He looked at Dr. Sorenson, handing him the tablet. "This is big." He ran a hand through his black hair. "I'm going to have to include Intelligence."

Sorensen paled. "Surely, you don't need to include Imperial Intelligence, Chief."

The security chief shook his head. "This was too well executed to be anything other than the Rebellion. That's out of my league, doctor." He reached out and pointed at the screen, his finger resting on a project name that gave him and everyone else in the room a shudder.

TWO

Two hours later, a trio of men in bespoke suits was standing in the special projects' server room, most of the processing cores silent. One or two, those furthest from the blast, were whirring away in the background. With the trio was Chief of Security Santos and Dr. Sorensen. The darker skinned of the pair was holding a data tablet.

One of the trio had walked over to the tower of still functional processing cores, running his hand along it. One of the other men said, "Did your review of the building's security logs reveal anything?"

Chief Santos wiggled a hand. "Sort of."

The shortest of the suited men said, "Sort of? Show us."

Santos gestured to a wall mounted display. It came to life. He swiped up on the tablet, sending a data stream to the display. The first image was a tour group from earlier in the previous day. "These are the tour groups from yesterday. There are a few each day."

The third of the trio of suited men came over. The tallest of three, he leaned in to look at the group, squinting. He turned to Chief Santos. "One of them? We don't screen tour groups?"

Santos shook his head. "They're tourists." The look the agent gave him made Santos' cheeks warm. He continued, "Uh, no, tour groups aren't screened. Despite what goes on up here, the tours never get anywhere near these levels." The chief pointed to the grid of images. He pointed to the lower left. "This is the 1:15 group." He pointed to another image in the grid. "And this is them leaving."

The tallest of the trio leaned in again to look at the still. "Two are missing."

Santos nodded. "Yes." He brought up the first image again. "These two."

The tallest of the well-dressed trio leaned in to look at the screen. "Hmmm."

Santos nodded to the screen. "We have them starting the tour, then that's it. We don't know where they went."

"And you didn't see anyone walking around the floor in any of the feeds?" the middle-height man of the trio asked. Santos shook his head. "That seems… implausible." His colleagues nodded.

The tallest turned back to the towers of processing cores. "Whoever they are, they're probably not locals. We should check all the incoming traffic from the last few days."

"That's gonna be a lot of ships," the shortest man said. Nods all around.

The tallest man rested his hands on one of the towers. He looked over his shoulder at his colleagues, who ushered Dr. Sorensen and Chief Santos out of the room.

The tallest man's hands began to glow blue.

TRANSIT

The flight controller eventually came back with departure clearance. Jax thanked them and throttled the lift engines up to full power. As the *Osprey* rose over the ring wall of the spaceport, Jax spotted the darkened science academy tower. *Hope it was worth it*, he thought to himself as he guided the lithe Interceptor out of New Terra's atmosphere. By then, the horizon was brightening.

Not nearly enough hours later, the hatch to the berth Jax was sharing with Jeffry opened with a bang.

"What do you mean, we're not going right home?" Governor Singh demanded from the doorway.

"Good morning," Jax groaned, sitting up on his elbows. It seemed Jeffry was plenty worn out from all the recent excitement. He made a weird noise and rolled over, putting his back to the hatch.

"Do not 'good morning' me," the angry Indian woman scolded. She was wearing what Jax had taken to calling her travel sari.

Jax sat all the way up. "I'm going to get up now, and I'm

naked. It's your call if you stay or not." Governor Singh harrumphed and let the hatch swing closed.

"You're not actually naked, right?" Jeffry said from his bunk, back still to the room.

"You wish," Jax said, standing and walking over to the small duffel bag he'd shoved clothes in when his adopted aunt had kicked him out of his quarters. He was in his boxer shorts. Jeffry muttered something about being thankful.

Since he knew he wouldn't make it to the shared head in the forward section of the ship, Jax dressed for the day. When he walked into the common area, his aunt was sitting at the small dining table, tablet in front of her cup of something steaming in one hand. He moved to the coffeemaker. Empty. As he set about getting the machine running, he said, "I'm sorry about the detour. Naomi isn't doing great, and she said someone, or something, on Columbiana could help her."

"What did you two do?" The governor had calmed a bit in the few minutes between her storming in to Jax and Jeffry's quarters and Jax coming out.

"What do you mean?" Jax asked as innocently as he could, pretty sure she saw right through it. She always did. She cast a sideways glance over her shoulder but said nothing. "Fine. We boosted some information from the Imperial Academy of Sciences."

"You did what? The Imperial Academy of Sciences? The one that exploded?" The small woman spun and was out of her seat in the span between two heartbeats. She slapped at Jax until he could move her back to the table.

"Auntie! Stop it!" When she calmed down, he said, "Yes, that Academy of Sciences. No one was hurt, that I know of, and no one knows we were there." He added under his breath, "Except that guard."

TWO

"You blew it up. I think they know someone was there, Jackson!"

"We didn't blow it up!" Jax defended. The coffee maker beeped. He went about preparing his cup. "We didn't know what the devices the rebels gave us would do."

"The rebels?" his aunt repeated. She sighed. "I know I raised you better than that. Not being caught does not make crime okay." She shook her head slowly. "Now you're throwing in with rebels?"

Jax sat down across from her, his own cup of coffee steaming. "I know that, Auntie, I really do." He put his free hand on hers. "After last night, the way the emperor reacted to me, do you really think we were in the wrong?"

"He's a turd, yes. That doesn't excuse robbery," she retorted.

"Technically, we just copied the data." The look Jax got made it clear that was not a distinction his adopted aunt cared for. "The odds are good we're gonna lose it all to make Naomi better. I know that doesn't excuse anything, but it is what it is. We need to get to Columbiana as fast as we can. We'll pop in, get Naomi patched up, and get on our way back to Kelso. In and out, lickity split." He smiled. She frowned.

Columbiana was one of the truly self-sufficient and sovereign territories. The station had fiercely fought off Unity and Indie forces alike. All were welcome at Columbiana, so long as their purpose was trade. Any ship or force that tried to bring Columbiana into the fold on their side had always been met with a formidable defensive capability. Even the big Imperial ships kept their distance now, just in case.

REVIEWING THE TAPES

"Uh, excuse me...uh, agent?" a nervous looking space control operator said. The tallest of the three well-dressed men turned. He was alone this time.

"You can call me Agent Two."

"Oh, okay, great. Thanks. I think."

When the operator didn't continue, the agent said, "Yes?"

"I've compiled the report you asked for." He offered a tablet.

The agent scanned the report, tapping his thumb on the casing. "Do you have the footage from last night? The security checkpoint."

The operator looked around. "Oh, uh...yes, one moment." He set about working on the console next to him. The agent continued to review the traffic data. The emperor's summit of governors had just ended. Almost half of the delegations had already departed; the rest were preparing to depart.

"Here you are, sir." The operator gestured to his screen.

TWO

On it was a still image of two people at the security checkpoint leading into the spaceport. A woman of Asian descent, her jet-black hair pulled back in a single ponytail. She was with a man, younger than the one from the tour group footage.

"Which ship did they board?"

"Oh, uh. One—"

"Moment. Yeah, I got that." The agent made a *go on* motion with his hand. While the operator went through the records, he watched the security footage again, then with his finger dragged the tracking blip forward, scrubbing the video forward until another group arrived, just over two hours later. An older woman in a sari and a man that looked exactly like the Asian woman's friend from the tour group.

"Sir?"

The agent looked up to see an image on the operator's monitor: a Valerian Coop Interceptor. He handed the tablet to the operator. "They went to the same ship, yes?"

The operator took the tablet, looking at it. He went to work on this console, then said, "Yes, sir. The *Osprey*." He looked up at the man standing over him.

"Did they file a flight plan?"

More tapping at the console. "No, sir, I'm afraid not." He looked up. "Oh, uh...however, we do know where they came in from." He looked down at one of his displays. "Kelso station."

"Thank you. Excellent work." The agent turned and left the space control center. He tapped his ear, opening a channel. "I'm going to need a ship. A fast one." He listened to the other party. "I don't know yet. Possibly Kelso station. Just get me a ship."

Agent Two left the administrative section of Spaceport

Alpha. He had missed breakfast, leaving the Imperial science academy building and heading straight for the spaceport, assuming his mystery pair wouldn't stick around. He was right but had underestimated how quickly they'd leave the planet. Kelso station was interesting.

CHAPTER ELEVEN

RED TURTLE SHELL POWER

"How are you doing, dear?" Governor Singh asked. She was standing next to the bio-bed in the small med bay.

Naomi smiled. "My head doesn't feel like someone is trying to get out of it with ice picks. That's a plus."

Governor Singh grinned. "I'd imagine. The auto-doc pumped you full of analgesics." The old woman consulted the bio-monitor. "It couldn't make heads or tails of whatever's going on inside you." She smiled, tapping an image of Naomi's thoracic region, full of mysterious shapes with question marks on them. "Jax said you'd explain it." When she saw Naomi's expression, she held up a hand, adding, "When you're ready."

Naomi nodded. "That's fair. Are we en route to Columbiana?"

The aged Indian woman nodded. "What's a few more days away from Kelso? Work can wait." She smiled a tight-lipped smile.

Naomi nodded. "Thanks." She looked around, then met the governor's eyes. "And sorry."

The governor pulled a stool out from under the small

workstation set against the wall opposite from the bio-bed. "I gave Jackson a ration of shit, but to be honest, it's fine. I called ahead and arranged a meeting with the station governor. If nothing else, it gives you all some cover, but I wouldn't mind catching up with Ivanka. It's been a while. She doesn't get invited to the emperor's dick wagging summits since they seceded." When Naomi smiled, the older woman added, "Don't get me wrong. I'm still pissed, at the both of you." She sighed. "But that ship has sailed. Now it's time to make the best of things."

Naomi nodded, her smile thin. The pain wasn't gone, but it was far less than it was on New Terra.

The older woman met her eyes again. "So. Tell me what you are."

"What happened to 'when I'm ready'"?

"I'm old. I don't have forever."

Naomi sighed. "Okay."

Upstairs, Jeffry and Jax were sitting in front of the large bulkhead-mounted entertainment screen, playing a game where each player controlled an animated vehicle driven by a cartoon character.

"Hey, cut it out!" Jeffry shouted as Jax's cartoon vehicle nudged Jeffry's into a turtle creature, causing it to spin and eject a bunch of the gold coins he had collected.

"All's fair in love and Mario Kart!" Jax replied. His kart, driven by a green lizard creature, zipped ahead.

Jeffry's driver, a mushroom person, recovered. His kart began accelerating, passing a computer-controlled vehicle driven by a shabby man in red coveralls.

As Jeffry's kart was gaining on another, driven by a

TWO

woman in a pink ball gown, she turned and hurled a red turtle shell at him. "Oh, come on!" He shouted as his kart flipped over in an explosion of coins.

"Sorry," Skip said. The pink gowned woman waved as her kart pulled away.

Jax grinned. "In our defense, we've been playing this game for a long time."

"I've never heard of it," th,e other man said, leaning bodily into a turn, holding his controller at an angle.

"I had Skip look the company up when I found the archive with all these ROMs on it. They merged with another game company two hundred odd years ago, then eventually merged with another, and then finally that company went out of business."

"Pity," Jeffry said. He glanced over his shoulder. "Hey, Rudy, could you get me another beer?"

The rust-colored nav droid was plugged into his charger base nearby. "Oh, sure, I'm just sitting here not doing anything. Just charging so that I can, you know, remain alive." With a click, he disengaged from the charger and rolled to the kitchenette.

"Me too, pal," Jax said.

Rudy was placing the two beers on the coffee table when Jax threw his arms in the air. "Boom!" His racer had crossed the finish line and was doing a dance as the kart continued on.

Jax and Jeffry were picking new racers when Naomi and the governor came upstairs. Jax turned and set his controller down. "Good to see you up and around!" He got up and joined the two of them, ushering Naomi toward the sole chair in the lounge space. "How are you doing?"

She nodded. "Not bad. Not out of the woods, I don't

think, but I'm least up and around." She dropped into the plush chair.

"That's something," Jax agreed.

Governor Singh moved to the kitchenette and started preparing a meal. Naomi watched her. "What time is it? How long was I out?"

Jax smiled. "You were out most of the day. We'll be at Columbiana tomorrow afternoon."

She looked shocked. "Damn. I guess holding all this," she tapped her head, "really took it out of me."

Jeffry raised an eyebrow but was ignored by everyone else.

WELCOME TO COLUMBIANA

The *Osprey* clanked and rattled as she sat down on the landing pad. Columbiana station was a design Jax had seen used only a few times. The station was built into an asteroid half a kilometer in diameter and almost five tall. They had built the space dock facility outside of the rocky primary station. Two kilometers of what looked like the skeletal remains of a Christmas tree were hanging from the bottom of the potato-shaped rock. Landing bays on arms of various lengths jutted out like spokes. Some arms nearer to the station were over a kilometer long and ended in large airlocks. They were designed to accommodate larger bulk freighters, keeping them from crowding the docking area. Smaller bays like the one Jax had just set the *Osprey* down in were half spheres: flat on the bottom, the dome overhead large enough to handle a ship nearly four times the size of the Valerian Coop Interceptor. When closed, each half sphere made an enclosed space, perfect for transactions one didn't want anyone else witnessing.

Columbiana station orbited a gas giant that had started out with hundreds of moons, moonlets, and large asteroids the giant's gravity had snagged over the millennia. Mining had reduced that number to closer to a hundred or two, making moving about the planetary orbit a lot safer in some ways. While the years of mining had reduced the number of orbital hazards, the lethality of those left behind was considerable. No one but those in command of Columbiana knew exactly how many, but the rumor was that most of the remaining asteroids were weapons platforms. Missile batteries, plasma cannons, railguns, and likely a bunch more things that no one knew about, made any unauthorized approach to Columbiana a suicide mission. This was something at least two bold Imperial admirals had discovered during the war. Each thought they could turn Columbiana's substantial Helium-3 and other mining industries to Imperial ends. Each was wrong.

The gas giant provided a nearly endless supply of rare elements like Helium-3 and other elements. The moons and moonlets provided the raw materials to build the station both inside the asteroid and out.

An indicator on the flight console turned green. Jax toggled the intercom. "We're green. Meet me at the embarkation room."

He turned in his chair, looking at Rudy. "At least you get to stretch your...roll your ball."

"That sounds disgusting. Never say it again," the droid said, disconnecting from his navigation console and rolling toward the spiral staircase that connected all the decks of the *Osprey*.

When Jax reached the common deck, he spied his aunt sitting on the couch, cup of tea in one hand, tablet in the other. "You staying here?"

She looked up. "Is there a reason I need to come with?"

"No. Should be pretty straightforward, I hope," Jax

replied. His aunt nodded, turning her attention back to what she was reading on her tablet.

Naomi was already waiting in the embarkation room, leaning on Jeffry. Rudy was there, as well.

The ramp lowered and unfolded to clang against the metal of the landing platform. Jax looked at Naomi, who was back to looking like death warmed over. Her earlier recovery the night before had been short-lived. "So, your friend? Leonard, you said? How do we find him?"

Naomi was leaning heavily on Jeffry. "He keeps an office on level 23." She stopped, breathing deep. "Abernathy Brokerage is the name."

Jax nodded, then looked at Rudy. "Plot us a course." The droid bobbed one small metal fist, *yes*, and rolled off ahead of them.

They moved slowly. Naomi could barely maintain a shuffle, and a fast walk was out of the question. Jeffry had suggested having Baxter come along to carry her, but Jax was always leery of having the combat droid walk around an unfamiliar space station, especially one he hadn't visited before.

Space control had assigned them a docking bay near the midpoint of the two-kilometer length of the space dock facility. The lift stopped a half dozen times, spacers mostly, coming and going from one section of the space dock to the other. Most barely even glanced at Naomi: pale, her eyes sunk in. When they finally cleared the space dock section, the lift went straight to level 23.

"This way," Rudy said, rolling off down the corridor. It took half an hour to navigate the warren of corridors that made up level 23. Clearly, this section of the commercial zone was the low-rent district, most businesses taking up a space smaller than Jax's berth on the *Osprey*. They passed prospecting equipment rentals, loan brokers, immigration lawyers, and more.

When they arrived at Abernathy Brokerage, they found the door locked. Jax pressed the call button repeatedly. Nothing. He looked at Jeffry and Naomi. The ex-Imperial Interface was not looking good. Her jet-black hair was limp and sweat soaked, hanging in front of her face. Jax slammed his fist on the door.

"Go away. We're closed for the day," a voice said from the intercom unit above the call button.

"Open up. We need your help," Jax said, leaning down to the intercom. It had a camera pickup, as well.

"We don't do helping people. We're a brokerage."

Jax opened his mouth, but Naomi spoke first. "Leonard, it's Naomi."

Jax waited to see what would happen. When nothing did, he raised his fist to slam on the door again, but it slid open. Standing inside was a lanky Asian man. "Come in," he urged.

Jax and Jeffry rushed inside, followed by Rudy.

The interior of Abernathy Brokerage was not what Jax expected. It was more university dorm than business; food and carbonated beverage containers were everywhere, sometimes not completely empty.

"Well, this is disgusting," Jeffry complained.

Their host moved to stand in front of them. "Keep your judgment to yourself, preppy." Jeffry looked at Jax, eyebrows up. The latter shrugged.

Leonard came around to look at Naomi. "You look like shit. What's wrong?" He looked up at Jeffry and Jax.

Leonard moved to a sofa that Jax wouldn't sit on if someone offered him money. After clearing food containers, tablets, and what might have been the packaging of a sex toy, he said, "Put her here."

Jax helped Jeffry lay Naomi down on the incredibly disgusting sofa.

Leonard looked at each of his guests before repeating, "So? What's wrong?"

Jax looked at his aunt's assistant. Naomi had come clean to her, but not Jeffry, and Jax wasn't thrilled about one more person being 'in the loop.' He cleared his throat as he thought. "She...uh, well, she took in a bunch of data. We meant to store it on a data storage unit, but it was damaged and she had to act fast, so she pulled it all off of the storage unit." He wiggled his fingers for emphasis. "She said it was too much, now it's hurting her." After a breath, "She tried to upload it to the ship's computer but couldn't."

Leonard looked from Jax to Naomi. "What kind of data? How much?"

"A couple of petabytes, and does it matter?" Jax retorted.

The lanky Asian man shrugged. "Kinda. I mean, it will affect how much I charge you." He quickly stepped back when Jax lunged for him. He wagged a finger. "Hey, muscles, I'm her only hope."

Jeffry looked at Jax appraisingly. "Muscles?" Jax gave him a look.

"Leonard," Naomi whispered, still hanging off Jeffry. "Just fucking do it."

Jax added, "I'll cut you in on twenty percent of what we get, when we sell it." He looked the other man in the eye. "Guessing that's more than your normal take."

Leonard made a noise like someone had just insulted his mother. "Forty."

"Twenty," Jax repeated.

"Thirty," Leonard countered.

"Twenty, and I don't punch you repeatedly," Jax said.

"Twenty, but you do something for me, as well," Leonard said.

Jax opened his mouth but closed it when Jeffry put a hand on his arm, then gestured to Naomi on the couch. "Fine."

"Fine," Leonard said.

Jax looked at Leonard. "So, can you transfer the data from her into a storage unit? Or something?"

Leonard looked around the cramped space. He turned to Jax. "Go to the commerce zone and get a storage module. I don't have any that are big enough."

"What level?" Jax asked.

"Level eighteen. The big shops are up there. There's a Spacer Tech that doesn't overcharge."

Jax nodded. "Okay." He turned to Jeffry. "Keep an eye on him."

The younger man looked aghast. "What am I going to do? Incapacitate him with paperwork?"

Jax frowned, looking from one man to the other. "He's a string bean. Blow on him." He didn't wait for a response. "Come on, Rudy. I'll need you to find this rabbit hole again." They left, the door sliding shut behind them.

Jeffry rocked on his heels. "So...brokerage, huh? What's that like?"

SHOPPING

"You know we can't trust that guy, right?" Rudy said, rolling along beside Jax as they made their way back to the central elevator bank that ran the entire length of the station.

"We don't have a choice. I'm guessing he's an Interface, like Naomi. It only makes sense. No one else would have a clue how to help her."

"That tracks," the droid agreed.

They reached the lifts and entered the first available upward bound car.

Level 18 was a marked difference from 23. The walkways were considerably wider, and the ceiling was at least four or five meters high instead of three. The shops on that level were mostly brands that Jax was familiar with, many having an outpost on Kelso station, as well.

Spacer Tech was near the outer hull of the asteroid-turned-space-station. The back wall of the space was brown and gray rock, carved into decorative patterns. Jax had Rudy wait by the door when he entered, moving quickly down the aisles to the data storage modules area.

Another droid, a newer model navigation droid, approached Rudy.

Hello, I am B7X-1900-G. My friends call me Gertie, it beamed wirelessly to Rudy.

I am Rudy, he replied, not bothering to share his original model or serial number.

Are you lost? That would be humorous, a navigation model, lost, the other droid pressed.

Rudy's head made a full rotation. *Of course I am not lost. I am waiting for my friend.*

Gertie was several generations newer than Rudy. Instead of a smart material roller ball, she hovered on a finely tuned grav-lift system. Her frame was spotless white, like polished ceramic. Her arms were folded into her body, blending almost seamlessly. She said, *They allow you inside. This station is Imperial adjacent; however, the authorities and most of the residents do not share the emperor's rather bigoted views on droids. At least mostly.*

Rudy rolled closer to the door. *I am aware. He asked me to wait here; we are in a hurry, and he does not need my help in shopping.*

Are you new to Columbiana? the other droid persisted.

We are just here on business, Rudy replied, adding, *I am afraid we will not be here long.*

Jax emerged. "Ready, pal?" He looked from Rudy to Gertie.

"I am," Rudy replied, rolling away. His head swiveled. *Goodbye, Gertie. It was nice to meet you.*

Goodbye, Rudy, Gertie beamed as Jax and Rudy rounded a corner.

"Making new friends?" Jax asked as they worked their way back to the central elevator stack.

TWO

The droid made a noise. "I can't focus on romance with Naomi at death's door."

Jax chuckled. "You're so melodramatic."

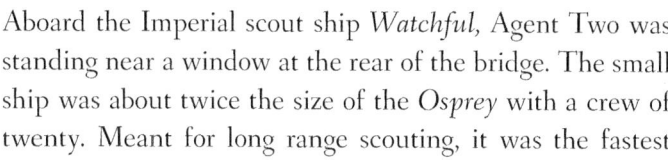

Aboard the Imperial scout ship *Watchful*, Agent Two was standing near a window at the rear of the bridge. The small ship was about twice the size of the *Osprey* with a crew of twenty. Meant for long range scouting, it was the fastest type of ship in the Imperial Navy.

For the most part, all ships traveled through wormholes at the same speed, but in recent years, Imperial physicists had discovered a means of shortening wormhole travel time by compressing the wormhole. It took an incredible amount of power that was directly proportional to the mass of the ship. For the time being, only scout ships and secure courier ships had this new technology installed. It was the first wormhole-related discovery since the initial discovery of the *Ganymede* ship.

A lieutenant approached the agent. "Sir, I've got something for you. I've been accessing station and colony space control systems since we departed, looking for anything that matches what you gave us." The *Watchful* was sitting in deep space a day out from New Terra.

"You've found something." It wasn't a question.

The young woman nodded. "A ship named the *Osprey* docked at Columbiana Station."

Agent Two nodded. "Please have the captain set a course, best speed." The lieutenant nodded and hurried forward to the bridge proper. Two turned and left the bridge.

Down in the cargo hold, he checked in on two of the enlisted crew members working on a project for him. "Remember, no data lines, anywhere within a meter. Even under the deck plating."

CHAPTER TWELVE

DATA TRANSFER

Walking into the pigsty that was Abernathy Brokerage, Jax handed Leonard the data storage module, the other man quickly unwrapping it.

Jax looked at Jeffry. "Any funny business?"

The younger man shrugged. "We had a lovely chat about his business."

Leonard shrugged. "Your boy Jeff has—"

"Jeffry," Jeffry corrected.

Leonard shrugged again. "—Has some solid business chops." Jeffry smiled. As Leonard unwrapped the device and checked its settings, he asked, "What can you tell me?"

"It's a lot of data, encrypted into a single, massive, archive," Jax answered.

"Imperial?"

"Does that matter?"

"Not particularly." Leonard kneeled down next to Naomi, putting a hand on her forehead, "It's good to see you again. Wish it was under better circumstances." His old friend nodded once, not opening her eyes.

Leonard moved his hand to Naomi's and put his other

on the data ports of the storage unit. He closed his eyes. Bio-circuits identical to Naomi's began to first glow, then pulse, slowly as data moved from Naomi through Leonard into the storage unit. Lights on the device blinked. Leonard's and Naomi's bio-circuit tattoos pulsed together synchronously.

Jeffry's eyes bugged out. "What the hell is that?" He pointed first at Naomi, then Leonard. "What is that? What's happening?"

Jax put a hand on the other man's shoulder. "It's a long story. It's okay. That's normal... -ish...for them."

It took Leonard thirty minutes to complete the data transfer. By the time he took his hand off of Naomi's, he was sweating and breathing heavily.

"Done?" Jax asked.

"I'm fine, thank you," Leonard replied. He stood slowly, a hand on the sofa. "Yeah, it's done. The data is on the portable." He turned to Jax. "I had to go slow and guide her nanites as I extracted the data to make sure the bio-storage modules didn't leak into her bloodstream." He took a breath. "That's some hot stuff, by the way."

"You decrypted it?" Jax asked, suddenly nervous.

"No, but I know that encryption scheme," the lanky Asian man said. He continued, "I know a fence that might be able to help move it, too."

"Not you?" Jax asked.

"Hell no. I hide porn and money trails. Whatever that is," he pointed to the data storage module in Jax's hand, "is out of my league."

Jeffry said, "It's that kind of thinking that's limiting you." Jax cleared his throat. "Sorry." Jeffry blushed.

"Who's this fence?" Jax asked.

Naomi groaned and sat up. After looking around, mostly at the sofa she was on, she bolted upright. "Gross!"

TWO

She turned her glare to Jax, who shrugged and pointed to Leonard.

"Man, you live like a slob," she scolded.

The lanky Interface shrugged. "You're welcome. It was my pleasure to save your life, taking that rapidly degrading data out of you before it killed you."

"Degrading?" Jax asked.

Naomi sighed. "Fine. Thank you, Leonard. You still live like a slob." She smiled. "I knew you'd help."

"For twenty percent," Jeffry added.

"Degrading?" Jax asked again.

Leonard turned to him. "Oh, it's fine. Another day or two and she'd be dead and the data would have been completely unrecoverable. You lucked out in coming to me now."

"Twenty percent?" Naomi asked.

"So lucky," Rudy said, low enough that no one seemed to hear.

"About that fence?" Jax pressed.

Leonard snapped his fingers. "Oh, right. Yeah, I can make an introduction. It'll take a few hours. Probably not until tomorrow morning."

Jax looked at Naomi, then to Leonard. "I don't know. We're kind of on a tight schedule."

"I'm sure he'll make it worth your while," Leonard insisted.

"Your aunt won't be—" Jeffry started.

"Okay, that'll give us time for your errand, I guess. What is it?" He looked down at Naomi. "She can stay here and rest."

Leonard nodded. "So there's this woman."

The data broker explained the details and what he needed Jax to do, and why. Jax fumed but agreed—or rather, did not renege on his earlier agreement. He and Jeffry stopped at the *Osprey* to break the news to Governor Singh.

"What do you mean *we aren't leaving yet?*" She looked from Jax to Jeffry. "Where is Naomi?" She leaned to the side to peer past the two men.

Jax sighed. "Auntie, it'll just be a few more hours. Rudy will keep you company. Jeffry and I have an errand to run. Go to bed. When you wake up, we'll be on our way." Her expression darkened, so Jax rushed ahead, "Look at it this way. If we can get rid of the data here, nothing has to happen on Kelso." He shrugged. "That's a win, right?"

His aunt's expression lightened slightly. "That's something, I suppose." She turned to Jeffry, then Rudy. "You can help me while he's gone. Let's get to some of the paperwork I had sent from Kelso. No reason to return to thousands of messages waiting for us." The navigation droid turned his flattened cylinder head to Jax, making a sad sound. Governor Singh looked back to Rudy. "Oh, and see if you can reach Columbiana's governor's office. Get me an appointment."

After Jax, Jeffry, and the droid left, while Naomi rested on the couch, Leonard went to his room and made a call. Setting up the meeting with the fence was easier than Leonard had made it sound. The fence, a man named Joe, was eager to meet Naomi and Jax and would have met them immediately. Leonard told him they were busy until much later that evening. Once that meeting was set up, he made another call.

After twenty minutes of nervously waiting by his gPhone, he got a call back. "Yes? Okay, yeah, I told the fence three hours. I can call them now and let them know. Okay, I will. No, I haven't forgotten." He hung up and called Jax, giving him the details of the meeting he had set up with Joe.

He walked back to the small front office space. Naomi was still asleep. He sighed. "Sorry."

SIDE QUESTS

Jax and Jeffry departed the *Osprey*. The younger man, Governor Singh's assistant of several years, said, "Why did you bring me along?"

"In case there's shooting, two targets are better than one." He glanced over and saw Jeffry's face. "I'm kidding." He added, "Mostly," under his breath. In a normal tone, he said, "I don't know what the deal with this woman is. I might need help."

Jeffry stared at him. "Uh, I'm still not sure how I add value."

Jax shrugged. "Like I said, worst case, cannon fodder." He didn't wait for Jeffry to reply.

The woman they were looking for kept an office in the old section of the station, the asteroid mining facility outside the rocky exterior of the station. Bare metal walls and floors mixed with rough-hewn rock still bore the scars of excavation equipment.

The lift doors opened. Both men recoiled. "Oh God, that's not right," Jax said, holding his nose. He pointed to a plaque bolted to the rocky wall. "That way, looks like." He headed off, Jeffry trailing after him.

"I can't believe you agreed to this," the younger man complained, falling in behind Jax. He ran his hand along the rough-hewn rock of the asteroid. It was damp from the humidity in that section. The atmospheric processors of the station interior kept humidity at just the right levels. The exterior sections had no such balance. That particular exterior section was an older and unused auxiliary facility for one of the massive gun batteries that kept Columbiana sovereign. In Jax's opinion, it was a good spot for illicit activity. He nodded to himself approvingly.

Ahead of Jeffry, Jax shrugged. "We've got time to kill, and Naomi needed to rest." He looked over his shoulder. "Besides, this could be fun." Jeffry's expression made it clear what he thought of that.

According to Leonard, the woman they were looking for was a finder. The lanky Interface had given them a coin and said that trading it to her would get them a package that Leonard had been waiting for. The shady-on-a-good-day data broker had been dodgy on why he couldn't just do this job himself.

"Fun? The reason Leonard isn't doing this on his own is because this section is dangerous." Several overhead light panels were missing, or destroyed. It was hard to tell which.

"Meh." Jax waved his hand. "Dangerous for beanpole losers, maybe." No sooner had the words left Jax's mouth than three men stepped into the corridor ahead of them. Jax glanced over his shoulder to see that two more had stepped into the corridor behind them.

Jeffry leaned forward, whispering, "You were saying?"

Jax ignored his companion, raising a hand. "Hi, we're looking for Meredith."

One of the trio in front of them stepped forward. "We're not guides. We're toll collectors." The man leaned against the rock wall, making it clear he wasn't going anywhere.

"Okay..." Jax replied. "What's the toll?" He looked over his shoulder. "Can you take those two?" he whispered, tilting his head toward the two thugs blocking the corridor behind them.

Jeffry's mouth opened, then closed, then opened again. Finally, it closed as his shoulders bunched. He said, "Not even a little. I file paperwork. I take a stern tone with waste management middle managers when they slack off and cause the governor problems with complaints."

Jax shrugged and ran right for the three goons in front of him. He closed the gap before any of them could react, leaping into the air to tackle the man who had spoken. As Jax and the man fell to the ground, Jax pummeled him fast with two quick jabs to the face. The leader of the group was out cold by the time he and Jax hit the ground.

The two other men broke out of their stupor just as Jax stood and lunged for the nearest of the two, grabbing his shirt and pulling him into a headbutt that made Jeffry, down the corridor, wince.

Jeffry turned to see the two goons blocking the other end of the corridor move towards him. "Look guys, I can pay the toll. Whatever it is," he said, backing up, hands up in front of him. Behind him he could hear Jax and the remaining man fighting, grunts and the sounds of fists hitting faces.

Jeffry backed up until he stumbled over the unconscious form of the leader of the goons. As he hit the floor, his hand landed on something, the grip of a pistol. His eyes bulged as he pulled the weapon from the waistband of the man he was still half sitting on. He pointed the gun, closed his eyes tight, and started pulling the trigger. He pulled the trigger again and again.

Jax and the remaining goon he was trading punches and kicks with, stopped and turned, mouths hanging open.

"The fuck, dude?" Jax said in a low voice.

Jeffry was sitting where he had fallen, energy pistol smoking. The corridor beyond him was a scorched ruin. The bodies of the two men who had blocked the back of the corridor were smoking messes crumpled on the floor.

The man next to Jax did not say a word. He looked at his compatriots nearest him, then back to those Jeffry had just killed. He turned and ran up the corridor, vanishing around a bend. Jax reached out to help Jeffry up. "You are full of surprises." Jeffry, pale as a sheet, nodded numbly.

SMALL PACKAGES

Meredith turned out to have an office space a level up from where Jax and Jeffry encountered the toughs acting as toll collectors. They had called in an anonymous complaint about the bodies once they were a safe distance away from the crime scene.

Jax pressed the button on the announcer panel next to the hatch to her space. "What do you want?" a voice demanded. Jax looked at the panel, then up to the frame of the hatch and embedded camera pickup. He held up the coin Leonard had given him. The hatch slid open.

The space inside was brightly lit and, despite being built into the rocky shell of the asteroid, spotless. Someone had polished the rock to a dull reddish gray gleam. Meredith, it turned out, was an older woman, her gray hair pulled tight into a ponytail. She had a gun belt on her hip. *I guess I'm the only one following the rules here,* Jax thought as his hand brushed where he would normally keep his pistol. She was sitting behind a large wooden desk. Shelves lined the walls on both sides, packed with boxes and crates of various sizes. An older model personal assistant droid stood in the corner behind her.

The droid was one of the bipedal models, popular before the war. It had likely been gold plated earlier in its life. Now a patina of grime and oxidation covered it, making it more green-and-rust-colored than gold.

She looked at her two guests. "So?"

Jax stepped forward, offering the coin. The older woman took the coin, holding it up inches from her face. She squinted at the coin, then Jax. "How'd you get this?"

Jax rocked on his heels. "Well, we're doing a favor for a friend."

"*Friend* feels a little strong," Jeffry offered.

Jax looked at his companion. "A guy we just met." He looked at Jeffry. "Better?" The other man nodded. He turned to Meredith. "Leonard."

The woman clucked, "That giant chicken." She turned in her chair to look at the shelving on her left. "Grabby, come here."

Jax looked at Jeffry, who shrugged. "Do you mean—"

She glared at Jax. "I mean the droid."

The assistant droid shuffled out of its corner. "Pardon me," it said, moving past Jax.

Jeffry looked at the woman. "Grabby?"

She stared at him, arms crossed. "He grabs things." She looked at the droid. "Shelf seven, section thirteen."

The droid moved to the designated section. As it raised its arms, a seam at the forearm appeared, then separated as the arms extended. The box was near the top of the set of shelves, and as the droid's arms retracted, something inside the box shuddered. The droid turned to its master as its forearms clicked, locking back into place. It offered the box. "Here you are, ma'am."

The surly old woman stood up and Jax saw why she had a droid to get things off shelves. She couldn't have been more than a meter and a half tall. Jeffry opened his mouth but closed it when Jax gave him a look.

The droid deposited the box in Meredith's hands, then ambled back to its corner. She held the box at arm's length and shook it. Something inside hissed. The two men on the opposite side of her desk reared back a bit.

"What the hell is that?" Jax asked.

The old woman shrugged. "Beats me. I'm paid to bring 'em in, not ask questions."

"That's not at all reassuring," Jeffry said under his breath.

Jax tentatively reached for the box. As his fingers brushed it, Meredith shook it, causing it to hiss again. When Jax jumped back, she chuckled. "Pussy."

Jax scowled and snatched the box from her outstretched hands. He looked at the box, then her. "You suck." He looked at Jeffry. "Let's go."

The small woman cleared her throat. She had a hand out, fingers wiggling. Jax handed the box to Jeffry as he tossed the coin to her. Jeffry immediately thrust the angry sounding box back to Jax.

The walk from Meredith's workspace to the lift banks was uneventful. Jax took a path that didn't include the corridor they used on their way in, in case Jeffry's handiwork was still lying there.

"Oh man, thanks!" Leonard said, taking the box from Jax. He gave it a gentle shake, eliciting a hiss. Jax and Jeffry both took a step back.

TWO

Leonard looked at them and laughed. "Relax, just New Egyptian hissing lizards." He reached up and pushed a takeout food container aside on a shelf to make room for the box.

Naomi was sitting on the couch. Jax looked over. "Ready to go?"

She nodded, then turned to Leonard. "Remember what I said." He nodded.

WON'T BE HERE LONG

As Agent Two descended the boarding ramp of the *Watchful*, he looked around the docking pad dome the ship was parked in. Two Imperial naval officers were at the base of the ramp, acting as sentry.

He turned to the two men. "I'll be in touch. Have your captain keep the reactors on standby." The senior-most of the two nodded, saying nothing.

Agent Two skirted the customs station with a flash of his gPhone screen showing a credential that told any who saw it, *This person can come and go as they please and has the full authority of the emperor.*

After narrowing his search to Columbiana Station, it had not been hard to get a feel for the illicit trades and where they were in the station. Narrowing his search to data brokers further refined the decks of the station he needed to focus on. Criminals tended to group together.

Walking through a corridor, he encountered a droid. "You, droid. Come here."

"Yes, sir?"

Agent Two placed a hand on the droid's chest. His

Two

hand pulsed, blue bio-circuitry tattoos lighting up. A few seconds later, the droid was following him back to the space dock facility.

Naomi walked in from the ship's head as Jax was setting his gPhone down. He looked at her. "How you doing? You look a lot better."

She nodded. "Good. The headache is mostly gone. The pains in weird places have all faded." She walked to the refrigerator, grabbing a beer. "Where's Jeffry?"

Jax pointed at her beer. "He hit the sack. How about we see the sights?" Naomi put the bottle back.

Jax looked at Rudy. "You wanna come with? We can track down that lady bot that was interested in you."

Rudy was motionless, off to the side of the lounge space. His head rotated to focus on Jax, but the droid remained silent.

"So moody," Jax joked. He looked at the ceiling. "Skip, if Auntie or Jeffry asks, let them know where we went, please."

"Sure thing," the ship's SI replied.

Jax pointed to the staircase. "Shall we?" Naomi nodded.

As they reached the embarkation room, the boarding ramp was unfolding as it lowered. Skip kept the ramp up when possible as a security protocol.

They found a bar that reminded Jax of the Angry Spacer, with a clientele that made him and Naomi feel right at home. The bar was loud, the floor sticky, and the bartender, while not a cyborg like Lucas, was every bit as surly. He walked by, sliding two bottles of New Terra Lager in front of Naomi, who slid one over to Jax.

"This place is nice," she said, deadpan.

Jax turned, grinning. "Right? I found it on the directory. It had several one-star reviews."

Despite his earlier silence when invited, Rudy had left the *Osprey* with them, but broke off shortly after with nothing more than a wave. Jax was used to the small nav droid doing his own thing, so waved and said nothing as he and Naomi continued on.

Jax took a sip of his beer, then said, "So, Leonard. Another Interface?" He wiggled his fingers for emphasis.

Naomi nodded. "Yeah. When we escaped, we agreed that keeping in contact was a risky idea, but I bumped into Leonard a few years ago on New Dallas. He was hocking public food dispenser hacks."

Jax took a long sip of his beer. "So, he's always been shady?"

"Hello, pot, would you care to meet kettle?"

"Okay, okay, but still. He rubs me the wrong way."

Naomi nodded. "Yeah, even as a kid, he was the one we all kept an eye on."

"You trust him?" Jax asked. He reached for a small bowl of assorted nuts the bartender had dropped off.

"Not at all," she replied quickly, then thought a bit. "I mean, as much as anyone, I guess. He doesn't want to be outed any more than I do, so there's some mutually assured destruction built into our relationship. He knows if he did anything to screw me, I could easily screw him."

"And his fence?" Jax pressed. He had the portable storage unit tucked into the inside pocket of his jacket.

"Even less. My advice is, we get in, let him take a peek at the data, take what he offers, and get off this station as fast as we can."

TWO

They drank in companionable silence for a while after that, each lost in their own thoughts.

Rudy was rolling through the corridors of the main commercial district when another droid appeared up ahead. It was not the unit he had met earlier, Gertie. The droid ahead was bipedal, meant to mimic human physicality. It waved him over to a narrow side corridor. Someone had painted it bright blue with a yellow racing stripe on its left side from shoulder to foot.

After initiating a one-time data exchange, the other droid beamed, *Did you arrive aboard the ship called* Osprey?

I did, he replied. Unsure what was happening, Rudy dialed up the gain on his sensors as much as he could. Nothing seemed amiss. As a precaution, he also activated a secondary firewall.

I work in the space dock facility, the mysterious droid sent.

Very good. Thank you, Rudy sent back. He rolled away, stopping when the other droid reached out.

I have information I believe will be valuable to you. An Imperial ship docked recently.

Okay. That was interesting. Rudy didn't believe the Imperials visited the sovereign stations much. He rolled backward. *What type of Imperial vessel? What type of data?*

The other droid shook its vaguely human-looking head. *Not here. I will meet you at your ship.* The droid turned and departed. Whoever painted it had missed a few spots on the machine's backside.

Rudy watched it go.

CHAPTER THIRTEEN

TEA

"Neeti!" the elderly woman at the table said, standing.

"Ivanka! It's been too long!" Governor Singh replied, pulling her friend into a hug. As the two separated, and Governor Singh took a seat, she said, "It's good to see you. I'm glad you could make time to catch up." They were at a small cafe in the commerce district. Their table looked out into the open expanse of the sprawling retail jungle.

The other woman, somewhere around the same age as the governor of Kelso station, was in a nondescript light brown jumpsuit, the same as many station workers wore. She had added epaulettes to denote her role on the station. She smiled. "A chance to have tea with an old friend? I wouldn't miss it. I will admit to being surprised at your sudden appearance. I'd have thought you would have called ahead."

A waiter came over with two cups, porcelain by the look of them. Each was filled with steaming water. The young woman produced a small box of assorted teas, placing it at the end of the table.

Governor Singh dipped her head. "I apologize for the

short notice. My nephew and his business partner had a meeting here that I wasn't aware of." She selected a tea bag, dunking it several times until it settled. "We're supposed to be on our way home from New Terra." She shrugged. "But, apparently, we will be here a day or so."

Governor Ivanka Rostova smiled. "Well, I'm glad I get to see you." She held her own delicate cup up in salute. "How are things on New Terra? I'm guessing you got dragged out there for his majesty big dick's summit?" She chuckled at her joke.

Singh came close to spitting hot tea all over the table. "I'd be lying if I said I didn't contemplate throwing my lunch plate at him a few times." She shook her head. "How we ended up here, with that closed minded buffoon running all of human-occupied space, is beyond me."

"The good guys don't always win," the governor of Columbiana said into her cup.

Singh smoothed her hair back with her free hand. "Indeed. Now all we can do is ride it out."

Governor Rostova fiddled with one of her epaulettes. "And hope someone takes care of things, eventually." She met her friend's gaze. Both women nodded.

Governor Singh finally said, "Listen, Ivanka, I might need your help here soon."

Her friend leaned forward with a wolfish grin. "Do tell."

QUESTIONS AND ANSWERS

"I swear, I don't know!" a haggard man screamed. He had lost count of the number of times he had answered that question with the same answer. The man seated opposite him tilted his head, as if examining a peculiar animal.

"Joe, you're the most highly regarded fence on this station, specializing in exotic and expensive data," Agent Two repeated.

The man sagged in the chair. "How many times do I have to tell you, man? I haven't bought or sold any Imperial data in weeks."

Agent Two had a compact blaster in one hand, resting it on the table between them. The fence had a black eye and bloody nose from when he had tried to deny Agent Two entry to his workshop. Agent Two nodded. "I know they're on the station, which means they'd find their way to you."

The other man sobbed. "But they haven't," he pleaded. He looked around frantically. "I swear it!" Agent Two raised his blaster. "Wait! Wait!" Agent Two paused, eyebrows arched. "A friend of mine set up a meeting for me later today. I don't know who the sellers are, just that he, my friend, said it'd be worth my time. Maybe that's them?"

"Then, I guess I'm early." Agent Two said, firing a single bolt of energy into the other man's chest. The force of the blast sent the body tipping backwards in the chair. Joe the fence was dead before his body hit the ground.

Agent Two was settling in to wait for his prey when his gPhone buzzed. His involuntary droid operative had just completed its job, much sooner than he had expected. He swore at the timing, knowing that if he missed his opportunity to get aboard the *Osprey,* he'd never get another shot. Standing, he realized he'd have to work on apprehending his old friend and her lover, or whatever role the guy she traveled with served, later. He stood and left Joe the fence's workshop.

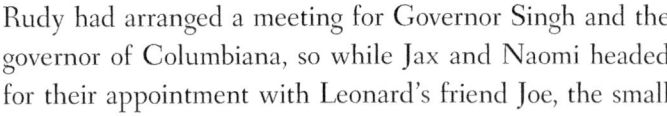

Rudy had arranged a meeting for Governor Singh and the governor of Columbiana, so while Jax and Naomi headed for their appointment with Leonard's friend Joe, the small Indian woman went about getting ready for her meeting.

"Jeffry, where is my dark blue sari?" she shouted as Jax and Naomi stepped off the *Osprey*'s boarding ramp.

"You know, she's gonna be pissed if her meeting ends and we're not ready to go," Naomi said as they walked to the hatch of their landing dome.

Jax shrugged. "Yeah, guessing two days' delay is the most we can hope for. I'm kinda surprised she hasn't gotten violent yet."

They rounded the corner on level 24 and spotted three men in bespoke black suits standing outside the door that Jax was pretty sure was their destination.

TWO

Jax put a hand out, stopping Naomi. "Uh, are those—"

She moved his hand down, then looked past him. "Crimson Orchid goons? Yeah, looks like," she finished. The largest of the trio had a distinct tattoo of an orchid peeking out over the collar of his shirt.

"How the hell did they get here?" Jax wondered, stepping back further around the corner.

"Leonard," Naomi hissed. "I knew they put a bulletin out on you but assumed he wouldn't get himself involved." She leaned to look around the corner. A fourth man exited the space they believed the fence, Joe something-or-other, worked out of. The man shook his head and touched his chest. The foursome conferred for a minute, then departed.

"I'll kill that asshole," Naomi hissed. She looked at Jax. "This doesn't look good for selling that data."

They crept toward the door to Joe the fence's space. It took Naomi less than a second to override the locking mechanism. The Orchid goons had done an admirable job of hacking the mechanism. It wasn't damaged or in any outward way violated. Inside, still lying on the floor, tied to the overturned chair he had died in, was Joe the fence. The burned hole in his chest had cooled, the blood coagulated into a brownish smudge.

Jax looked around. "We better go."

"I need to see Leonard," Naomi said.

Jax shook his head. "He sold us, and him," he pointed to the body, its single scorched wound in the chest, "out. I think it's time to cut our losses."

"Did he, though?" she pressed. "I mean, yeah, he sold us out, but didn't it look like the Orchids were as surprised as we are?" She pointed to the wound. "Plus, that's not fresh. I doubt the Orchids would hang around after killing him."

Jax looked down. "Good point. So, who killed this guy?"

Naomi shrugged. "I could try to find our mystery killer and ask, if you'd like." Her expression told him what she thought of that idea.

"Jax, Naomi?" Rudy said over both of their earpieces.

"Yeah, what's up?" Jax replied.

"A droid that works in the space dock just approached me with information. It wouldn't say what, just that it was important and related to the Empire. There's an Imperial ship here, just arrived."

"Why did it approach you?" Naomi wondered.

"An Imperial ship? Here?" Jax said.

Rudy ignored him, answering Naomi, "At any time in our association have you seen me exhibit the ability to read minds?" The droid didn't wait for her reply. "I have no idea. It said the Imperial ship arrived, which was odd, so it started to dig around, landing on us."

"Okay, well, that's a bit weird. Are you okay doing the meet?" Jax asked.

"Agreed, but seems like the smart play. I'm on my way back to the ship now," the nav droid replied.

Skip jumped into the call. "We'll keep an eye on things."

"You sure you'll be okay?" Naomi asked.

There was a sound like a cluck. "Skip can ensure nothing happens. Plus, you know, the combat droid will there, too."

"Damn right, I will be. I don't like strangers, droid or biological," the combat droid said.

"Plus, Rudy has his knives," Skip offered.

"I thought we talked about those," Jax said. No one answered. He sighed, "Keep us posted." He looked at Naomi. "What now?"

WELP

"I don't think this is a good idea," Jax said for the second, or maybe the third, time. They were on deck 22, almost to the door of Abernathy Brokerage.

The door was closed. Jax pressed the announcer button next to the door. Naomi looked around and rested her hand on the control panel. Her hand pulsed several times. She frowned.

"You okay?" Jax asked, looking at her hand on the control pad.

"Leonard rewrote the control system. Gimme a second. Okay, there." The door slid open. Several black-suited men turned to look at the newcomers. They were further inside the space, gathered around a seated Leonard, the latter looking terrified as his eyes settled on Jax.

"Oh, shit," Jax whispered.

The door slid shut. "You were right," Naomi said. "Bad idea." Several loud bangs came from the other side of the door. Jax looked down. Naomi's hand was still on the control panel. She smiled. "Now I rewrote the control software."

They turned and ran down the corridor.

Unsure how many Crimson Orchid operators might be on the station, or who the mysterious Imperial ship belonged to, they made their way back to the space dock quickly and quietly, avoiding using the comms, just in case.

When they reached the *Osprey*, Skip wasn't responding. Neither was Baxter or Rudy. The boarding ramp was down.

Jax looked at Naomi as they approached. "Not good." She nodded. Neither of them was armed. Columbiana, being a sovereign station, set its own rules, and citizens carrying guns was frowned on. Visitors carrying guns was explicitly forbidden. Only law enforcement officers could carry weapons. Jax was pretty sure he saw side arms on the Crimson Orchid goons, and someone definitely burned a hole through the fence.

They crept up the ramp, then up the spiral staircase into the cargo and engineering deck. Rudy was lying on the deck in the middle of the space. Jax rushed to the droid. "Buddy, hey?" He tapped on the droid's head. Naomi crept past them to the engineering space. The normally closed hatch was half open.

She pushed hatch all the way open. "Jax!" she hissed.

Jax came up beside her. "Holy hell. What is all this?"

Inside the engineering space was normally a tidy area, thanks to Baxter. Since his charging station was in engineering, he considered the entire space his, despite knowing almost nothing about starship engineering. Baxter was in the middle of the space, frozen mid-stride, held firmly in place by some type of foam that looked like it had come from a droid Jax did not recognize. The mystery droid had frozen mid-fall, only a few feet from Baxter. It looked as if the latter was charging the former when the foam erupted from the torso of the intruder. The foam seemed to have exploded outward as a mist or fog, then flashed into a hardened state.

Jax knocked on the hardened foam, solid. "Who the hell is that?" Jax asked, pointing.

Naomi shrugged. "Must be the droid Rudy mentioned." She tutted, "Certainly an elaborate trap."

Jax groaned. "Auntie!" He bolted for the staircase.

Naomi followed, then stopped, kneeling next to Rudy's inert form. She placed a hand on his head, her bio-circuit tattoos activating.

"GAH!" the droid shouted as indicators on his head and cylindrical torso lit up.

Naomi stood up. "Come on."

By the time Naomi made it up the stairs, Rudy zipping up the null gravity center column of the staircase, Jax was in the lounge space of the common deck, standing perfectly still.

"Jax?" his business partner said in a low voice.

"They're gone," he said. "My aunt and Jeffry, they're gone."

Naomi walked over and put a hand on his shoulder. "Jax..."

He shrugged her hand off and turned to face Rudy. "What the hell happened?"

The nav droid made a low keening sound. "I don't know, Jax. I wish I did. I got here just before that other droid, P-54X2, did. He insisted on coming aboard. The moment we got into the hold, he disabled me with a localized EMP." The squat droid rolled around in a circle. "He must have run into engineering to take out Baxter."

"And Skip?" Jax asked, looking at the ceiling.

Rudy bobbed up and down nervously. "The droid must

have fired off an EMP at the same time he immobilized Baxter."

Naomi looked down at Rudy, then headed for the stairs. "I'll try to get to the computer core and get Skip up and running."

Jax nodded. He turned to Rudy and sighed. "It's okay, bud. Something is going on, and we're still at the starting block."

A noise burst from the overhead speakers. Like gravel in a jar. "Watch out! Jackson! Governor Singh! Jeffry! AHHHHH."

"Skip!" Jax shouted, looking at the ceiling.

There was a moment of silence. Jax looked at Rudy, who said nothing. Finally, Skip said, "Jackson, I'm sorry. I failed."

Jax smiled. "It's okay, buddy."

"No, it's not," the ceiling retorted.

Naomi came back up the stairs. "I left Baxter offline for now. I couldn't even budge that foam stuff." She smiled. "I had to climb over it to get to the core."

Jax nodded. "He'd just wig out." He looked back to the ceiling. "What happened, Skip?"

NOW WHAT?

"That droid arrived, the one Rudy met," the ship's SI said. "Nothing seemed out of order at first. Then he whammied Rudy and rushed into engineering. I warned Baxter, but it was too little, too late. The droid exploded." A pause. "Then I was offline."

When Skip didn't continue for almost a minute, Jax said, "What happened then? An EMP shouldn't have completely knocked you out."

"I...I don't...I don't know," the ship replied. "You're right. Wait."

Jax looked at Naomi, who shrugged. Jax said, "Skip?"

"I found something." The bulkhead-mounted entertainment screen came to life. On it, a still image of a tall man in a bespoke suit entering the cargo hold. "I don't remember doing it, but I saved that snapshot in an encrypted comm buffer." A long pause. "I don't know who that is. I have no memory of him coming aboard. I don't even remember saving that still."

"I do," Naomi said. Jax looked at her. "Know him, that is. He's an Interface."

"You know him?" Jax pressed. "An Interface? Like you?"

She shook her head. "No. At least I don't think so. I don't recognize him. But only an Interface could get aboard and completely override Skip and shut Baxter down before they could get a warning to us." She took a deep breath. "Not to mention wiping Skip's memory so thoroughly."

"Damnit. What the hell is going on here?" Jax exhaled. "Why did he take my aunt and Jeffry?"

"I'm sorry, Captain, I don't have any other answers. He wiped everything," the Sapient Intelligence that managed the *Osprey*'s systems apologized.

Jax put his face in both hands. "If anything happens to her, I don't know what I'll do."

"And Jeffry?" Naomi asked.

Jax shrugged and looked up at her. "Sure, I guess. He's okay, too. Be a bummer if he died." He quirked a smile.

"Captain, I might have an idea," Skip offered. Jax looked at the ceiling. "Rudy's booby-trapped friend may not have been lying about why he was here. If I can infiltrate the space dock management computer, and find the ship that brought the Interface here, maybe I can find him on cameras and we can track him."

"And the Crimson Orchid?" Naomi wondered, not addressing anyone in particular.

Jax took a deep breath, rubbing his face. "Damn, yeah, we gotta address them, too. I know this time wasn't them following us or anything, but obviously they've got reach, even outside Imperial territories."

She nodded. "Why aren't they surrounding the ship? Those goons at Leonard's definitely recognized us."

This time it was Rudy who chimed in. "They probably can't. Columbiana doesn't mess around, as far as security

TWO

goes. Sneaking a few pistols in is one thing. Storming a docking dome would attract a lot of attention."

Jax nodded. "The fact they got side arms through security is impressive, and terrifying, but he's right. They can't just walk around flaunting them." He smiled. "That might be our one bonus right now. They have to follow the same rules we do." He shrugged, and added, "More or less."

Jax stood up. "Okay, let's get engineering cleaned up and Baxter online." He looked at Rudy. "And dispose of your friend."

Rudy spread his arms. "How could I know he was a Trojan horse?"

It took thirty minutes and a laser saw to free Baxter. The engineering space would need a significant amount of cleanup and a fresh coat of paint at some point down the road.

Naomi only needed a few minutes to unlock the combat droid's processing core and bring him back to full functionality. The other droid was a lost cause. The explosion of capture foam destroyed its processing core and most of its torso.

"I will rip someone apart," Baxter said, once Naomi got him back online.

Jax rested a hand on the matte black combat droid's chest. "You'll get your chance, buddy."

"Captain, I think I've got something," Skip said. Jax and Naomi looked up. The ship's SI continued, "Our bad guy—well, the non-organized-crime bad guy—is some type of Imperial agent. He arrived aboard a ship that made it from New Terra to here in almost a third of the time it took us."

"That's impossible," Rudy said.

Jax looked at the small droid, shrugging. He looked at the ceiling. "Anything else?"

"According to the space dock control computer, the ship's crew is still aboard, keeping the reactor running. I was able to access the security feeds for the space dock. I compared the image I captured of our intruder to the feeds, and found him. They are one and the same."

Jax headed for the staircase. "Okay, any chance he had a name tag on or anything?"

"I am afraid not," the ship replied.

On the common deck, Jax said, "I think it's time we looked at our treasure."

THIS IS BAD

The data storage module was sitting on the shelf in the vault, right where Jax had left it the day before. They were lucky that their Imperial visitor had not had time to ransack the ship and discover the vault. Jax placed the storage unit on the small dining table. He was on one side, Naomi on the other. Rudy and Baxter were standing nearby, watching.

Naomi had her eyes closed, both hands resting on the storage unit. Both hands were pulsing blue, slowly sometimes, then faster.

"Anything?" Jax leaned forward.

She opened one eye. "Concentrating."

He leaned back, hands up defensively. "Sorry." He turned to Rudy, shrugging.

She removed one hand from the storage module, placing it on a tablet lying on the table next to her. The device's screen immediately came to life. Lines of computer code scrolled down it.

Jax watched the process, his foot tapping the floor, until a look from Naomi stopped it.

Finally, she opened her eyes, the bio-circuitry lining her

arms and face fading until they were nearly invisible, then perfectly hidden. She picked up the tablet and looked it over, tapping and swiping the screen. "Oh, crap." The tablet lowered to the table. Naomi just stared at it.

Jax looked at the tablet, then back up at his partner's face. "What?" He reached for the tablet.

After a minute of browsing the files on the device, he whistled. "Improved grav-plating. Wormhole compression. Improved micro-controllers for synthetic limbs. Pulse cannons." He looked up. "Cool."

"Keep going," Naomi urged, rolling her hand for him to continue.

Jax scrolled to the next set of files. "What is this?" He opened file after file, finally looking up at his business partner. "Okay, this is bad."

"What?" Rudy demand, rolling sideways anxiously, then coming up next to the table.

Jax looked at the navigation droid, handing him the tablet.

Naomi looked at Rudy, then the ceiling. "Sorry, I disabled the wireless gear so no one can get into it."

Rudy browsed the files on the device while Baxter watched over his shoulder.

Baxter looked up. "The emperor certainly aims high, doesn't he?"

Jax nodded. "Do you understand any of it?" He looked at each of his team in turn.

Baxter shook his matte black head. "Something to do with harnessing or inverting gravity or something," the combat droid said, adding, "I'm better at killing than science."

"Thanks for that image," Jax said.

"Yeah," Naomi agreed.

Baxter made a motion as close to shrugging as his frame allowed.

Rudy offered, "I can't offer much, either, on the tech side, but the summary tells us more than enough. Planet-breaker, they call it."

"Okay, so what? We can't exactly take this," he gestured to the device on the table, "back and say we're sorry."

"And assuming those devices that the commander had us plant were as powerful as they looked, this is the only copy," Naomi said.

Jax groaned. "You know, I had forgotten those. Damnit."

She inclined her head. "This is so much bigger than anything I expected to get." She held out her hand to Rudy, who gave her back the tablet. She pointed to the droids. "The guy who did a number on them was an Interface, like me. I don't know what him being an agent means, but I can't imagine it's a good thing. Clearly, the Empire wants it back." She tapped a finger on the data storage module.

"I thought the emperor canceled the program. Killed all of your friends and stuff," Jax said.

She shrugged. "Version two? I honestly don't know."

Jax sighed. "How did you not look at the data when you copied it?"

She glared, holding up a finger. "One, they encrypted it." Another finger. "Two, we were kinda in a hurry." Another finger. "Three, I just looked for interesting sounding project and folder names. There was no way to know that one was a set of plans for a planet-killing super weapon. Who names a project like that Moonbeam?"

Jax tilted his head. "Fair." He looked around and leaned back in the chair. "We've got an undisclosed number of Crimson Orchid goons on the station out to get us and an

Imperial secret agent with the same whammy powers as Naomi. They all want us, to some degree or another, dead."

"Thank you for the summary," Baxter quipped. Jax made a rude gesture.

"I don't think there are degrees of death," Rudy pointed out.

"What if we call the Crimson Orchid, give them the tablet?" Skip offered from the ceiling. "Surely they have the means to sell it or make their own planet-buster?"

Jax looked at the ceiling speaker. "Oh yeah, that's a great idea. Let's give an organized crime syndicate the plans for a planet-killing super weapon, not to mention the rest of this stuff." He looked at the table. "Not to mention that doesn't get Auntie and Jeffry back."

THREE

CHAPTER FOURTEEN

I HAVE AN IDEA

"Captain, I've found something," Skip said.

Jax and Naomi were still sitting at the small kitchenette table, several empty beer bottles between them. With no further information, they hadn't been able to think of a next step. Jax voted for drinking and Naomi couldn't come up with a better alternative.

Jax looked up. "What is it?"

"I hacked into the station's computer and have been running our mystery Imperial through the security system," the ship's SI replied, a hint of pride in its voice.

Jax raised an eyebrow. "You made sure that no one can trace your intrusion back here, right?"

The overhead speaker made a rude noise. "Infiltrator is not just the space frame, you know." Before Jax could reply, Skip continued, "So, yes, no one will know I was in the system. My intrusion software is quite advanced, if you recall. If I can get back to my point, I've been able to track our friend. He left the space dock facility with your aunt and Jeffry. He seems to have set up shop in a security substation on the residential levels. It's not much more than an outpost for the security staff to have better response times."

Jax's head rocked back. "That's weird. Why a substation? Why not the main facility?"

Naomi shrugged. "If I had to guess, he's not supposed to attract a lot of attention. I can't imagine he has any actual jurisdiction here." She looked around. "He may very well be operating completely outside station management's notice."

Rudy chimed in, "She's probably right. The substation provides him a base of operations that is relatively secure."

"The substation personnel?" Jax wondered.

Skip said, "Before he arrived with Governor Singh and Jeffry, the security detail assigned to the station departed rather hastily. It looks like he tricked them into leaving by faking an environmental warning. Then he cleared the logs and has been rerouting personnel ever since."

Naomi whistled. "Damn, that's impressive. He gets a fully stocked security station, and no one notices."

"Bold move," Jax said. "What about actual calls for security?"

"It looks like he's routing them back to the nearest substation with a canned 'We're busy' request," the *Osprey*'s SI replied.

Jax thought this new information over. "Okay, we know where he is, but I still don't know how this helps us. We can't just knock on the door and propose a swap. The emperor isn't that forgiving." He leaned back in the chair. "Skip, are we locked down? Can we depart if we want?"

There was a pause as the ship's SI shifted gears to check their status. "As far as I can tell, there is no lockdown order for us. The only thing I can see is an alert setup to notify a

THREE

gPhone ident on any flight plans we file or changes in our docking status."

Naomi grunted. "Further evidence he's trying to keep station management out of this."

"Wonderful," Jax said. "So," he raised a hand to tick points on his fingers, "we need to get the Orchids off our ass. We need to get this Imperial agent guy off our ass. We need to get Auntie and Jeffry back." He dropped his hand, then raised it. "Oh, and I guess, clear our names." He ticked another finger, sighing, "And figure out what the hell to do with the data."

Naomi rubbed her hands together. "You know, I have the inklings of an idea. I think."

Jax leaned forward. "Do tell."

After Naomi outlined her rough thoughts on how they could extricate themselves from what Jax definitely considered a royally fucked up situation, he nodded. "I like that. What if we made it an auction?"

"An auction?" Naomi asked.

Jax nodded. "We break into the fence's database." He points to Naomi. "That's your job."

He continued, "We get his list of contacts and set up an auction, here on Columbiana."

Naomi nodded. "Okay, yeah. Bringing in every scumbag we can means that the Crimson Orchid can't move on us." She made a thoughtful face. "Okay, that's...that's not bad."

Jax held up a finger. "But wait, there's more." He grinned. "While all eyes are on us," he pointed to Baxter and Rudy, "they break into the security substation and bust Auntie and Jeffry out."

Naomi made the same face. "Okay, also not bad. Not

quick, though. It'll take at least a day or two to get all that set up."

Jax shrugged. "Yeah, that's gonna piss her off. Not much we can do about it, though. I hope mystery Imperial is treating them well." He looked at Naomi. "Oh, and sometime in the middle of all this, we frame our Imperial friend."

She smiled. "Let's go get this started."

"Who are you? Never mind. I don't care!" an irate Indian woman shouted from the holding cell she and her assistant were in. "Why did you break into our ship and kidnap us? I am the governor of Kelso station. I have diplomatic rights."

"Shut up, please," the tall, well-dressed man said from the desk he was sitting at. He was holding a tablet, reviewing something. Governor Singh couldn't see the screen.

The governor and Jeffry had been working at the small kitchen table when it sounded like all hell had broken loose in the cargo hold below. Skip had started to say something. Then, there was an explosion, and everything went quiet. The two had sat where they were, staring at each other, until they heard the footsteps.

A well-dressed man came up the stairs, pistol in hand. He told them they were under arrest and would come with him or be shot. They went with him, being led through station corridors until they arrived at the security substation. When they arrived, it was deserted, and no one had shown up since.

The pair had sat quietly for a time until the governor's patience had finally been depleted. "I will not!" she protested.

Jeffry put a hand on her shoulder. "Ma'am, I don't—"
She spun. "Don't make me fire you."

The man outside the cell sighed, removing a stun pistol from the desk drawer. He aimed it at the cell. "You can pass the time quietly or unconsciously. Your choice."

YOU'RE INVITED

The fence's office space was just as they had left it. Jax looked at the body. "Kinda surprised no one has reported this." He pinched his nose, looking around the room. He stopped. "That looks promising." He toed a food delivery box off of something with blinking lights, leaving a greasy smudge.

Naomi nodded, kneeling next to a processing core tucked into the lowest level on a floor-to-ceiling shelving unit packed with what looked to Jax to be mostly junk. She looked up. "It's still powered up." She placed a hand on the device, making a face.

Jax leaned through a doorway off to the side of the room. "Oh, damn."

Naomi looked up. "What?"

Jax made a *go on* motion. "Our pal." He looked at the body. "Did we know his name?" She shook her head. "Well, dead dude had some interesting taste in entertainments, and living alone, he doesn't keep that sort of thing under his bed, like a civilized person." He shuddered, looking down at the body. "You were a gross dude."

THREE

Naomi looked up again. "Then don't look at what's on this." She stood. "No contact list. Just porn. Lots and lots of porn." She wiped her hand on her pants.

Jax looked around the small office space. "If I were a criminal who made all his money connecting other criminals with each other for a cut, where would my contact list be?" He tapped his chin as he looked around the small space.

"His gPhone?" Naomi stood and moved to the body. She patted the body until she produced the phone. Her hand lit up its familiar blue. "Nothing on it. Well, more porn, but nothing that felt like a list of underworld contacts."

Jax turned back to the doorway to the bedroom. He took a deep breath and walked in.

"Oh, my," Naomi said as she followed Jax. "I don't...Is that?" She pointed to a poster stuck to the ceiling over the bed.

"Yeah," Jax said, not looking up from rooting around in the closet. After making a choked gagging sound, he said, "This guy was a deviant." Over his shoulder he said, "I'm no prude, but this is making my skin crawl." He stood. "Hey, think I got it." There was a tablet in his raised hand. It was old, covered in stickers: companies long gone, racing empires, and subculture icons.

Naomi took the device, her hand immediately pulsing with blue light. The tablet's scuffed screen came to life, lines of computer code flowing across it. She looked at Jax, smiling. "This is it." She walked back into the small sitting room. "Let's make the call from somewhere else. This place is really creepin' me out."

Jax nodded. "Yeah."

As they walked down the corridor, Jax took his gPhone

out of his pocket. "Yes, hello. There's a weird smell coming from one of the units in section G-18 on deck 24. Okay, thanks." They walked in silence after that.

Back aboard the *Osprey*, Jax was pacing while Naomi worked on a tablet at the small kitchen table. She looked up. "Cut it out!"

"What's taking so long?" Jax looked over her shoulder.

She looked up. "Skip and I are spoofing the tablet's hardware address, so it looks like it's in Joe's—that's the fence's name—quarters."

"This is quite fun," Skip said.

Jax looked at the ceiling, eyebrow raised.

Naomi slapped his arm. "Hey. Done. Invites sent." She set the tablet aside. "I set up a forward so the replies will come to Skip."

Jax nodded. "Perfect."

He looked at Rudy, sitting in his charging cradle. "Okay, pal, time to do your part."

"I thought my part was breaking your aunt out?" The navigation droid disconnected and rolled over to the table.

"Okay, part one of two." He gestured to Naomi. "We hide the data in Rudy."

Naomi looked from Jax to the rust-colored droid and nodded. "This won't hurt." She reached out to put a hand on Rudy's head.

"Damnit!" Agent Two hissed. He tossed the tablet to the ground.

"Something the matter, young man?" Governor Singh asked. She was sitting on her cot in the detention cell. She

THREE

had finally grown tired of angrily berating her captor after the man had stunned Jeffry as a warning.

Jeffry rolled over in his cot. "Is it so much to ask for some quiet? My head still hurts."

Agent Two stood and paced. "Your friends are playing a dangerous game."

"Oh?" The governor stood, small brown hands grabbing the bars. "Which friends would those be?"

"The terrorist ones," Agent Two replied. "The ones who stole Imperial data."

The governor clucked, "Don't know 'em." Jeffry groaned.

LOTS TO DO

The next morning, Naomi walked into the common area to find Jax on the sofa with a tablet. "Already seeing a bunch of RSVPs. Guess top secret Imperial data is worth scrambling for. Should be a full house, even with the short notice." Jax didn't look up. She snapped her fingers. "Hey. This thing on?"

He looked up. "Oh, sorry. RSVPs? That's good. I'm not sure how to feel about so many criminal organizations having a representative within a day's travel time to this station."

Naomi grabbed a cup of coffee. "Right? The joys of true sovereignty, I guess. I'm going to run to the tech shop and get some tablets."

Jax sat his tablet down. "Sounds good. I'm going to get the space rented and set up."

"You ever done something like this?" Naomi asked.

Jax shook his head. "Nope, this is a new one for me." He looked her in the eye. "Still good?"

She shrugged. "I don't know that it matters. We're in it now. No turning back." He nodded his agreement. "I

THREE

wanted to tweak the nose of the people who made me," she held her arm out, letting the bio-circuitry pulse, "*me*. Now we're dealing in state secrets, avoiding assassins and Imperial agents."

Jax grinned. "Only way to learn to swim is to dive into the deep end." He waved his hands. "And hope you don't drown."

Naomi looked at him. "Yeah, I don't think that's how learning to swim works. You should never have children."

Jax shrugged. "I think I'd make an outstanding dad." Naomi's face made clear her opinion on that. He stood. "Okay, I'm off. I'll take Rudy with me." Naomi nodded. Jax looked at Rudy, tilting his head toward the staircase. Rudy, who had been sitting in his charging cradle the entire time, said nothing but unclipped and rolled toward the stairs. Jax followed.

As Rudy and Jax walked from the *Osprey*, Rudy asked, "Are you sure this is a good idea?"

Jax looked down at his mechanical friend. "Sure? Not even a little. I just don't think we have any better options. The Crimson Orchid don't seem to be getting bored with trying to kill us, and this Imperial agent guy is a wildcard. Now he's got my aunt."

"And Jeffry," the droid added.

Jax shrugged. "Yeah, him, too. This agent thinks we're the ones responsible for the damage to the science academy."

"You are," Rudy pointed out.

"Well, yeah. Not directly, though. I mean, I kinda expected the Rebellion to take credit for it and all that," Jax defended, thinking back to placing the devices as instructed, near processing cores.

The two of them moved through the station without

further conversation: Jax lost in thought, Rudy likely thinking of a thousand things. The commercial section of Columbiana had an event space that occupied almost an entire deck. Meeting spaces of various sizes made up the convention area. Each was able to be combined and divided to create larger and smaller spaces as needed.

"Hello, sir," an older woman said from inside a small kiosk at the entrance to the convention area.

Jax smiled. "I need to rent a space. Nothing too huge, a dozen or two people."

The woman smiled. "Of course. Will you be needing any food and beverage services? Audio-visual help or furniture?" She produced a tablet that she began busily tapping on.

Jax shrugged, looking down at Rudy, who also shrugged in his own way. He looked at the woman. "No, no food or drink. We'll need a few tables, that's it." He snapped his fingers. "Throw in a few chairs, too."

She nodded as she tapped on her tablet, then offered it to Jax to review. He filled in the details: date and time, number of hours, and such. He placed his gPhone against the device to verify his identity, a fake one, and process the payment for the rental.

When the woman took the tablet, she smiled and swiped up, causing Jax's gPhone to buzz, alerting him he had just received a copy of the order. "See you tomorrow, Mr...." She consulted the tablet. "Palmer."

As they walked away, Rudy said, "You're going to have to start keeping track of the identities and accounts that you are using."

Jax shrugged. The more confusion he could create in the various electronic paper trails, the better.

REUNIONS

After Jax left the ship, Naomi finished her coffee. She was making her way down the stairs when Baxter called out, "Oh, good, you're here."

"Of course, I'm here. I'm sure Skip told you I was," she replied, stopping on the cargo deck.

"He did. I was trying to make this more organic," the battle bot said.

"I don't think it worked," Skip said from the ceiling.

Naomi shook her head. "What was it you wanted?"

Baxter pointed back inside engineering. "Help. That foam crap is everywhere." He wiggled his thick metal fingers. "Not made for intricate work."

Naomi sighed and headed for engineering. She worked with Baxter to dislodge the remaining foam and last few bits of the exploded droid, putting it all into a rolling cart with the Columbiana logo on its side.

Using the cargo arm, Skip lowered the cart to the deck of the docking facility. On her way out, Naomi wheeled the cart away to a recycler. Each domed landing pad of the space dock area had a recycler, allowing visitors to dispose of trash without dragging it through the station proper.

Naomi and Jax had planned to meet up for lunch after their respective errands. Helping Baxter had eaten up most of the buffer she had, so she hurried to the commercial district to get her shopping done before meeting her partner.

The lift doors parted on the lowest level of the commerce section. Unlike most of the station, the three levels of the commerce section were open in the center, forming a bowl with three concentric circles. The lowest level had the smallest open courtyard. Behind the shops that paid enough for visibility were the two rings of shops that were okay being less visible. The black- and the bit-less-black market. So long as you weren't skittish, you could find most anything you wanted on that level of the commerce sector.

The two levels above were home to the more upscale sellers, the name brands like Spacer Wares and Galaxy Goods. She looked around the first level but eventually made her way to the third floor and into Spacer Wares. The technology section alone was bigger than most of the storefronts on the two levels below. She picked five nondescript base model tablets and checked out. Since she wasn't going back to the ship before lunch, she had the purchase delivered, letting Skip and Baxter know to be on the lookout and to not shoot the delivery bot. With her primary goal addressed, she visited some of the other outlets on the third level.

Walking out of Basic Bitch with a bag under her arm, she spotted someone in the crowd that caused to her to stop walking and do a double-take. A tall man in an immaculately pressed suit was standing on the opposite side of the

THREE

ring terrace fronting the shops on that level. He made eye contact and raised a hand.

Naomi recognized him from the still image Skip had captured before his logs and memory files were erased. She started walking again, moving slowly along the terrace toward the mystery Imperial agent.

At five feet, Naomi stopped. "Hi."

The man, a head taller than her, nodded. "You don't recognize me." It wasn't a question.

She searched his face. It was familiar, but she knew that when she saw the captured image from Skip's cameras. She shook her head.

He held his arms out, immaculate cuff links glinting, the logo of the Empire. "I grew into my arms."

Recognition dawned on her. "Martin?" The man nodded. "Oh…I…" she stammered, hand coming to her mouth. "I thought…"

He nodded.

"I don't understand. You escaped. You were with us when we got out. We escaped." She looked him up and down. "You work for the Empire now? How? I don't understand."

Martin shrugged and gave her a lopsided smile, a smile she remembered. "I tried. I didn't make it off-planet but tried to get by." He shook his head. "I couldn't. I didn't know what to do, where to go. I lived on the streets until I couldn't take it anymore." He looked her in the eye. "They took me back. Five of us, actually."

"Five?" Naomi's mouth was still hanging open. Martin nodded.

"I have to take you in, all of you," he said.

Naomi stared at him, her mind racing as she ran through the possibilities and repercussions. Five of her friends had gone back to the people who had implanted state-of-the-art biological circuitry in them. The people who put organic data storage and processing modules throughout their bodies. The people who injected millions of nanites into their bloodstreams.

"You what?" she finally asked, shaking her head.

"You and your boyfriend, or whatever, you blew up the Academy of Sciences building."

"That wasn't us. Wait, blew up?" Martin nodded once. She shook her head. "The Rebellion's devices weren't bombs."

Martin's eyebrows shot up. "Rebellion?"

Naomi ignored him. "You broke into the ship, deleted data."

"You stole government secrets."

"You're...you're building super weapons," she countered.

CHAPTER FIFTEEN

JITTERS

By the time Naomi sat down with Jax for lunch, the shakes had mostly subsided.

"What's wrong with you?" Jax asked, looking up from the thin tablet he was looking at with the menu on it.

Mostly.

She shook her head. "I just ran into an old friend."

Jax raised an eyebrow. "Like...sex?"

Naomi looked at him from across the table. "No. What's wrong with you? Are you twelve?" She held up a hand. "Never mind."

Before Jax could respond, the server came by. "Get you two something to drink while you look at the menu?"

Jax again opened his mouth, but Naomi answered, "Two New Terra Lagers. Please." When the server turned to leave, she said, "The agent, the Imperial who..." she grimaced, "whammied the droids."

Jax stared at her, his mouth hanging open. After a heartbeat or two, "Wait, what?"

She nodded slowly. "Yeah. In the commerce section. He must have been watching the ship."

Jax shook his head. "So, what? You know him?" He leaned forward. "And he didn't arrest you?"

She dipped her head again. "The kid I told you about, Martin? The one who could reach the data cable that allowed us to know what was going on outside the bunk room? Him."

The waiter returned, depositing the drinks on the table. "Any decisions on food?" He smiled as he looked at Jax and Naomi.

Jax looked up. "What? Oh, uh, two burgers, please." The waiter nodded. Jax looked at Naomi. "I don't understand. What's that mean? Are we screwed?" He looked around. "Is he gonna arrest us? Call in the Imperial forces? Where is he?"

Naomi raised a hand. "I don't know. He said hello, told me who he was, we exchanged words. I left."

Jax looked around the restaurant again. "Words?"

Naomi said, "I don't know how, but he's a believer now. He's all in with the Empire."

"Oh. Goody," Jax quipped, then looked around again. "He say anything about my aunt?"

"Or Jeffry?" Naomi added. "Yeah. He said they were fine and if we turned over the data, and ourselves, he'd let them go."

"You believe him?" Jax leaned forward.

Naomi shrugged. "I don't know. He knows the data isn't aboard the *Osprey*. He assumes it's on one of us."

The server returned, depositing two plates to the table, burgers on each, top bun sitting to the side. A pile of fries filled half of each plate. "Get you two anything else?"

Jax looked up. "Oh, ranch dressing?" The man nodded and left. Naomi stared him. "What?"

They ate in silence for a bit, each thinking about the

THREE

absolute mess they had gotten themselves into. To herself, Naomi admitted that this was all because she'd wanted some revenge on the Empire for what they had done to her.

"He heard about the auction," she mumbled around a bit of french fries.

Jax sat his burger down. "What?"

She nodded, not adding anything further.

Martin hadn't moved from where he and Naomi exchanged words. He was watching the crowds below, his knuckles white on the railing.

When he and the others escaped the science academy building, they'd agreed that splitting up was their best bet to avoid capture. Martin had been nervous but agreed.

For a day or two, he had trailed one of the other kids, Lisa, without her knowing. He slept near where she slept, scrounged food from the same places. Martin had expected to approach Lisa after a few days, once it was clear neither was being pursued, but on the third day of his shadowing her, she made her way to one of the smaller spaceports and vanished. He assumed she had hacked herself passage on a shuttle, though he hadn't seen her interfacing with many computers.

Alone again, Martin did his best to get by, stealing from shops when no one was looking, bypassing locks to sleep indoors. He eventually found a group of street children mostly his age and fell in with them. Things got better after that until the woman that turned out to be the pimp of the little tribe of children found someone interested in Martin. He fled.

Back on the street, alone, it didn't take long for Martin

to get sloppy. Out of desperation, he started hacking into banking systems and food programs. He started offering his services to criminals, always careful, he thought, to keep his abilities hidden. When a pair of Shock Troopers showed up one afternoon, he knew his precautions had been insufficient.

Walking back into the bunk room, being captured, had been embarrassing. He had expected to see the kids who had stayed behind. Instead, he found only those who had escaped with him and been recaptured.

The other children huddled around Martin, welcoming him back. Rose-Marie told him about the body bags she had seen when the Shock Trooper brought her back. She was the first to be recaptured.

DISTRACTIONS

Naomi didn't wait for Martin to respond. She turned on her heel and stormed off. She figured it was fifty-fifty whether he would pursue her. He didn't. When she looked over her shoulder, the walkway was empty; he was gone.

Besides the three-level commerce section that Naomi had visited earlier, Columbiana had a massive public parkland near its center that helped with the station's atmospheric processing: tree-lined walkways, grass and shrubs everywhere. It was where tourists gathered to enjoy a bit of openness and nature away from the more cramped confines of the rest of the station. It was also where the sex workers looked for clients.

Jax strolled over to one such worker. "Hi."

Naomi sat on a bench watching her partner and keeping an eye out in case her onetime friend Martin showed up.

The woman looked Jax up and down. "Hi, yourself. What're you looking for?" She was just over two meters tall, ebony skin, her hair teased out into a chalk white afro.

"Nothing for me today." He smiled. "Unfortunately."

She turned to leave, and he reached out, pressing two fingers against her upper arm gently. "But, I do have a proposition for you."

She looked over her shoulder, hand on her outthrust hip. "I'm not into weird stuff." She tilted her head. "Well, not too weird. The rest just costs more."

He laughed. "Nothing weird. I promise." He looked around, "We'll need some of your friends, too, if they're amenable."

"Won't be cheap," she countered. Jax nodded. She squinted at him. "What're you up to?"

He laughed. "I swear, nothing weird or illegal." He motioned to a bench. "Let me explain?"

Jax spent a few minutes explaining what he and Naomi had in mind. The tall woman smiled and waved over a few of her colleagues.

After Jax came back over to Naomi, they walked along one of the pathways through a grove of pine trees. Naomi said, "How do you know they'll do it?"

Jax shrugged. "Sex workers are some of the most fun people you'll ever meet. I'll have to introduce you to Billy and his friends on Kelso. They're a hoot. Anyhow, I told her it was a gag for a friend's birthday." He rubbed his finger and thumb together. "That plus a not insignificant amount of money. They'll come through." He looked around. "Now we just need to designate our target."

Naomi looked around. "He should be here any time. I used one of the public terminals to send him a tip that we would be here trying to sell the stolen data."

They bought hot dogs from a vendor near the north entrance and sat down to wait. After chewing a bit of his probably-not-meat-from-an-animal hot dog, Jax asked, "You think he'll buy it and come running?"

THREE

Naomi took a bite of her hot dog and thought about her answer. She would never have pegged Martin as a joiner back when they were teens. He was one of the angrier kids in the group—an orphan, his parents miners on one of New Terra's moons. A recruiter had found him skulking around the transport hub, digging through a recycler.

She nodded. "Yeah, he doesn't have any other leads right now. He'll show."

They did not have to wait long. Martin walked through the hatch without even looking around. He strode down the pebble strewn path until he reached the first intersection. Walkways, branching out like spokes, bisected the park and its concentric rings.

Jax put his gPhone to his ear. "He's here. He doesn't suspect a thing." A pause. "Awesome! Thank you so much. I wish I could see his face. He's gonna be so embarrassed! He hates surprises." Jax lowered his gPhone and took a picture of Martin, sending it to his new friend. He put the device back into his pocket and hitched his head toward the nearby hatch. "Let's go."

As they walked through the hatch, a half-dozen men and women swarmed the Imperial agent, screaming and making as big a scene as they could.

Jax pulled his phone out again. "Rudy, we're on our way."

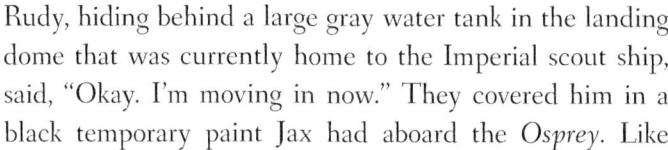

Rudy, hiding behind a large gray water tank in the landing dome that was currently home to the Imperial scout ship, said, "Okay. I'm moving in now." They covered him in a black temporary paint Jax had aboard the *Osprey*. Like

Baxter, it hid him from most common sensors. He rolled under the large Imperial ship.

Skip, I'm ready, he beamed over the shared channel.

Copy that. I'm ready here, the ship replied.

Rudy opened a small panel in the deck, turning several dials. He moved to another panel, disconnecting several hoses leading to the Imperial ship. From the compartment normally reserved for knives, the small droid removed two cylinders.

After placing each cylinder into the hoses, he reconnected them to the valves in the deck. After that, he rolled around, undoing what he had done earlier, turning valves back on. He quickly rolled to another panel closer to the large clamshell doors that allowed ships to enter and exit the massive dome. Opening that valve, a backflow to the valves connected to the Imperial ship's umbilicals, he waited.

It was not a long wait to see the fruits of his labors. The boarding ramp of the Imperial ship deployed, and before it hit the deck, Imperial naval officers were streaming out of the ship, coughing and retching. One stumbled to the deck, puking up their last meal.

Orange lights popped up from the deck around the perimeter of the dome and began to strobe. "Atmospheric contamination detected. Evacuate the area immediately." It was Skip's voice, coming from the docking bay's speakers.

Rudy rolled back further behind the gray water tank to make sure the fleeing Imperials did not see him.

The ship's captain stumbled down the ramp, coughing. He looked around. "Everyone out!" He pointed to the pink hued mist clinging to the floor, roiling down the ramp. "Head to the medical center!" He followed his crew to the hatch connecting to the gangway that led to the customs center and rest of the station.

THE FRAME UP

"What took you so long?" Rudy demanded as Jax and Naomi entered the docking bay. The pink hued mist had faded, sucked out through the emergency purge system after the captain and crew left.

"Sorry, it's not exactly a quick hop from the main arboretum to here," Jax said. He added, "They all gone?" He looked around the large domed space.

"Yes, they should all be in the med center. Skip already cleared the call the captain put into the station administration." He rolled toward the ship. "We should still hurry."

Naomi looked at the ship. "That's pretty. Think we can trade up?"

From the bottom of the ramp, Rudy said, "I won't tell Skip you said that." He rolled up into the ship out of sight.

Naomi followed the nav droid into the ship. "Wow," she said, looking around the cargo hold.

Jax followed her up. He whistled. "Okay, this is nice." His gaze moved toward the back of the hold. "Is that—"

"A cage? Yeah," Naomi said. She stared at it, then pointed to the stairs. Jax nodded.

The common deck of the Imperial ship was nowhere near as homey as the *Osprey*. There was no lounge area; instead, the deck was divided up into work areas and the engineering space in the rear. The deck above that was crew quarters and above that the bridge deck.

"A whole deck for the bridge?" Jax wondered aloud, looking at a wall mounted display that was showing the ship's layout. Naomi's hand was resting on the edge of the display, her bio-circuitry tattoos pulsing.

Jax tapped the display. "There. That's gotta be his quarters." His finger was resting on the quarters at the bow of the ship, labeled VIP. He turned and headed up the stairs. Naomi followed. Rudy rolled by with what looked like a brand-new steak knife in his hand. He rolled toward the forward section, a label over the hatch that read *machine shop*.

Up on the crew quarters deck, Naomi and Jax rushed from the staircase to the forward berth.

It took Naomi only a few seconds to override the locking mechanism.

"Not very VIP, if you ask me," Jax said, looking around the sparse quarters. He pointed. "There."

Naomi walked over to the terminal set under a large display screen. The default view of the screen appeared to be a camera on the hull, showing a view of the dome that enclosed the ship. "Rudy, get up here!" she shouted.

The droid answered from the hatch, "I'm here! This ship is an accessibility nightmare! Not everyone has grav assist technology. Or legs." The angry droid pointed back through the hatch. "I had to drag myself up the stairs. It was embarrassing."

"We can leave a note," Jax said, pointing to the terminal and Naomi.

THREE

Rudy rolled over to the desk set into the bulkhead. Naomi put a hand on Rudy's head and one on the processing core set into the desk under the display. Her biocircuits lit up, pulsing from the hand on Rudy to the hand on the desk terminal.

"Captain, you should hurry," Skip said over the shared channel. "The med bay here is better than I would have expected. They have discharged most of the crew already."

Jax tapped his ear. "Are they on their way?"

"Negative. They appear to be waiting for everyone. The captain is yelling at someone from the station about the incident." The SI chuckled. "Poor sap has no idea what the captain is talking about and keeps trying to show him that the docking bay is clear."

Jax looked over at Naomi. She was on the same channel. Her eyes were closed. He cleared his throat, and she said, "I heard. This takes time."

Jax decided to explore the ship a bit. "Skip, keep us posted." He left the VIP berth and walked down the corridor. Berths lined both sides, likely bunk rooms, with the captain's quarters at the exact opposite end of the deck. He came back and went up to the bridge.

"Hot damn," he said, running his hand over a console. The bridge was only about a third the length of the ship, but still more than double the size of the bridge of the *Osprey*. Windows lined the back section of the space, almost floor to ceiling, while duty stations and a single command chair occupied the forward section. He put a hand on the back of the command chair. "So nice," he whispered.

"Jax, I'm done," Naomi said over comms. "Meet us in the computer core."

He looked around. "Copy that." He left the bridge.

SLIPPING AWAY

From the relative safety of the gray water storage tank, Jax, Naomi, and Rudy watched the crew of the *Watchful* return to the docking bay. Several of them still looked a bit green, but otherwise, the gas that Rudy subjected them to seemed to have had no lasting effects.

The *Watchful*'s captain strode in, looked around, and pointed at the ship, issuing orders. His small crew scrambled back up into the ship. The captain got to the ramp and looked around the dome one more time, then walked up into the ship. The ramp rose as he walked up.

Jax looked at Naomi. "You're sure you wiped the security feeds? That's the first thing they're gonna look at."

The look that she gave him spoke volumes, but she added, "You were standing there when I did it."

He put both hands up, palms out. "Okay, don't be testy." Once the *Watchful*'s boarding ramp had sealed, Jax looked around. "How do we get out of here? Won't they see us?"

Rudy pointed to the deck. They were kneeling on a

THREE

section of decking that was a hatch. Naomi looked at the droid. "No."

"Afraid so," the droid replied. He reached down and opened the hatch on its hinge.

"I can't," Naomi protested, pinching her nose as she backed up.

Inside the opening was a tangle of conduits and pipes, many leaking things that Jax was certain he wanted nothing to do with. He looked from his partner to the small nav droid. "Seriously?"

The droid bobbed on his wheel. "You can walk out and hope they don't see you." Rudy rolled around the opening, then rolled off the edge into the narrow crawlspace. He tipped over and began dragging himself out of sight. When Jax and Naomi didn't immediately follow, he said, "Fine, stay there."

Jax looked at Naomi and shrugged. He slid into the opening, doing his best to avoid touching any of the various substances, mostly failing.

Naomi looked around, calculating her odds of running from the shelter of the gray water tank to the hatch of the docking bay. Not great odds. Swearing under her breath, she dropped into the crawlspace, pulling the hatch overhead closed behind her. The crawlspace was big enough that the human pair could shimmy on their elbows.

"This is so gross," Jax complained up ahead.

"Stop complaining," Rudy replied from further ahead.

The crawlspace was a service tunnel. Similar tunnels ran under each docking arm, pulling gray water, waste, and anything else from docked ships into the central waste and recycling center of the station.

Half an hour later, crawling out of an access panel in

the main space dock facility, to the curious looks of several passers-by, Naomi asked, "Okay, now what?"

Rudy's head spun a complete circle. "I've got to get to my next assignment." Jax and Naomi nodded.

It took Rudy twenty minutes to make his way from the space dock facilities to the security substation Skip had tracked the Imperial agent to.

Go around the next corner. What's down that way? Baxter asked from aboard the *Osprey*. Rudy was acting as a scout, since a combat droid stomping around the station would draw a fair bit of attention.

Rudy wheeled around the next corner. *Looks like storage mostly*, the navigation droid sent back. *Looks like it's all municipal. Oh, wait. No, I see a few that spaces seem to be rentable storage units.* He rolled around another corner to find another corridor of storage units, a mix of station-owned and private. Mixed in were a few small shops set up in the inexpensive spaces.

That could be useful, Skip said over the shared channel the droids were using to communicate. *I'll see what I can dig up*, the ship's SI added.

Baxter added, *Do me a favor and do a full circuit around the substation. I want to make sure we have to most up-to-date information.*

Rudy rolled up and down the corridors that bracketed the security substation. Most of the units were self-storage and empty at the moment. That section of the station wasn't one that folks loitered in. The few units that were shops were closed down for the day.

Interesting, Baxter said as Rudy turned back into the

main corridor. *That last corridor is marked as closed for renovations, according to the main computer.*

Rudy stopped and looked back down the corridor he had just come from. It didn't look any different from any of the others, at first, until his sensors picked up the newer wall panels on the right side of the corridor. The side nearest the substation. *They did some work on the wall. Looks like something to do with the substation, maybe.*

Rudy, I just saw our Imperial friend on a camera feed. Get out of there, Skip warned. Rudy sped toward the service elevator section of the deck.

CHAPTER SIXTEEN

DRESS THE PART

Despite Naomi's run-in with Martin, the Imperial agent had not shown himself again. It was possible the troupe of sex workers that Jax had sicced on him in the arboretum were still occupying him. She and Jax retired to the *Osprey* after their adventure aboard the Imperial ship.

"You ready for today?" Naomi asked as Jax walked across the common area toward the ship's head the next morning. He looked over his shoulder. "As ready as possible, I guess." He didn't slow down, closing the hatch behind him.

Rudy rolled over. "I've arranged for the pickup in ten minutes. Baxter is ready." Naomi nodded. "Okay, let's go get him situated."

Down in the cargo hold, the tall matte black combat droid was standing motionless in the middle of the space. When Naomi and Rudy arrived, he turned his head, red optical scatter light swishing left and right. "You better not forget me."

Naomi pointed to a large open crate sitting next to the

large cargo door. "Don't worry. We paid for return shipping, just in case." She motioned. "In you go."

They had fabricated the crate overnight. The interior was made to Baxter's exact measurements to help hold him in firmly place during transport. The droid stepped backwards into the crate, letting the interior conform to his arms, legs, and torso. "See you on the other side," he said as Naomi hefted the front of the crate in place. Rudy quickly fastened the lid to the rest of the crate with the provided self-sealing stem bolts.

"Skip?" Naomi said.

The large cargo door slid outward from the hull, then forward, exposing the domed docking bay beyond. With a loud whir, the thick cargo arm track slid out to its full extension, three meters. A powerful cargo grasper slid along the track until it was over the crate containing Baxter. It lowered, grabbed the crate, then retracted, raising the crate off the deck. The assembly slid along the extended arm until it reached the end and lowered the crate to the deck below, setting it down with barely a thud.

As the entire assembly retracted back up and into the ship, a team of cargo movers arrived. From the large opening, Naomi waved. "Hi there. That's the one." She pointed to the crate.

"Just this one?" the taller of the two cargo handlers asked, running a hand through his red hair. He pointed his other hand to the crate, directing a heavy cargo droid. The massive machine rolled over on thick treads, bending to lift Baxter's crate. The other human guided the droid back the way they had come.

Naomi nodded. "Just the one. Thanks!" She retreated into the cargo hold, the heavy door sliding into place and sinking back into the hull.

THREE

As Naomi cleared the staircase landing on the common deck, she spotted Jax walking back toward the crew bunks wrapped in a towel. She moved to the kitchenette to get a fresh cup of coffee.

Jax re-emerged from the crew berth section a few minutes later. He was wearing what might have been the only pair of trousers he owned that had no patches on them. His shirt was clean and bore no logos. Over that, he had a leather jacket she had seen him wear once or twice before.

"Look at you," she said, making a show of looking him up and down. "So dapper."

He smirked. "Figured I should look the part, right?"

"No argument." She offered him a travel mug of coffee. "Ready?"

In two bags, they carried the five tablets that Naomi had purchased the day before. Naomi had worked on the devices earlier, making sure they were ready.

Arriving at the convention space, Jax was a little surprised that not only were there no Imperial security forces waiting for him, but Naomi's friend Martin was nowhere in sight. "Think your pal will come?" he asked.

"He kind of has to, right? He knows we have the data. He can't let it fall into the wrong hands."

"I guess we're lucky that this is so secret he can't just have a garrison of Shock Troops swarm all over us."

"He doesn't have a garrison, so that helps," she replied. She looked around the small meeting room. At the far end was a table with lectern next to it. The rest of the room was empty. "Nice digs."

They had just reached the table and lectern at the front of the room when two men in dark blue suits walked in. "Mr. Van Buren?"

Jax thought for a moment, then nodded. He looked at

Naomi. "Security. Licensed to carry heavy stun pistols." He motioned the two men over. "So, I just need to you two to stand on either side of the table, make sure no one picks the tablet up. They can see the file listing, but that's it."

"Got it," the more heavily muscled of the two said.

SHOW TIME

Naomi had invited ten criminal organizations. Nine had replied in the affirmative. The tenth said nothing. The Crimson Orchid was among the nine that had replied, which was good.

In both of their ears, Skip said, "The agent just left the security substation."

"Any sign he figured out where we are?" Naomi asked.

"Well, he didn't look at the nearest camera and say, *I know where they are*, so I think you're good," the Sapient Intelligence that ran the *Osprey* replied. Jax and Naomi exchanged a look.

Everyone arrived promptly, and despite representing competing criminal enterprises, were cordial. A few of the representatives seemed to have legitimately friendly relationships with their rivals.

Jax received two complaints regarding the lack of snacks or drinks, which he found beyond confusing given the auction and its clients.

"This isn't a social club," he whispered to Naomi as a bald-headed man with a thick accent Jax couldn't place, walked away after voicing his annoyance at the lack of alcohol.

She shrugged. "They're all here."

He cleared his throat. "Excuse me, everyone. Hi. Welcome." He looked over to Naomi, who rolled her eyes. "Thanks for coming. Please form a line. We've locked this tablet down so all you can see are the file listings and a summary of the data. Everyone will have time to look it over before making your bid."

As the various criminal organizations from around the Empire lined up, Jax continued, "This data is not available piecemeal. It's all or nothing. You can look through the file list as long as needed. After that, you can place your offer via the contact details in the initial invite."

"Where is Joseph?" a woman near the back of the line asked. "I don't know about the rest of them, but I dislike dealing with people who aren't him."

Jax coughed. "Yes, well, you're going to have to get used to it. He's dead." The room burst into shouts of surprise and anger. Jax held up both hands. "We didn't kill him!"

"How do we know that?" another woman asked. This one was dressed in a leather catsuit with a gun belt draped over her hip, the empty holster obvious.

"How did you get our details if Joe is dead?" a dark-skinned man demanded.

Jax made a face, looking at the woman first. "Well, you don't, I guess." He turned to the man. "Does it matter? You're welcome to leave if you have an issue here." He pointed at the tablet that as yet no one had approached. "We're getting a little off track. If you don't want to bid on these files, by all means," he pointed to the door at the back of the room, "there's the door. I'm sure your competitors can find a use for higher throughput long range comms, or high compression wormhole tech."

The man at the head of the line jumped ahead to the table, leaning down to examine the files.

An hour after Jax and Naomi departed for the auction, Rudy left the ship. *Wish me luck*, he beamed to Skip as he exited the lift at the deck of the security substation.

You won't need luck. You'll be with me, Baxter replied before Skip could. *Just as soon as you come get me.*

Rudy rolled over to the storage unit he had rented the night before. He keyed in the passcode and rolled backward as the segmented door slid upward. Inside the two-meter-wide by three-meter-deep storage unit stood a single two-and-a-half-meter tall crate. Rudy scanned the area. No one around. He rolled into the storage unit. From a storage compartment in his cylindrical body, he withdrew a pry bar. The self-sealing stem bolts popped off with little effort.

Baxter moved both arms in a slow circle, looking down at his partner in crime. "You ready?" he asked in his deep baritone.

The much shorter droid said, "What could go wrong?"

The combat droid nodded. "Exactly." He stomped out of the storage unit, Rudy on his heels.

Can you get into the substation's systems? Baxter sent to Skip.

Negative. He has completely rewritten the software of the local processing cores, Skip replied. *I'm locked out. For that matter, so is the rest of the station.*

Old school it is. He's still out and about? Baxter asked.
He is.

The two-droid heist team moved to the corridor and the reinforced hatch to the security substation.

Rudy offered his pry bar only to have his taller companion wave it off. Baxter forced his fingertips into the seam of the hatch. Metal groaned as the hatch bent and separated.

SALES HUSTLE

One of the Crimson Orchid men that Naomi and Jax had run into earlier looked up from the tablet. "How do we know this is real? You don't exactly have a stellar reputation."

Jax glared at the man as he raised a hand, with one finger pointed up. "Hey, your boss is a liar. Ichiko tried to set us up, have us killed." Jax waved off the man's rebuttal. "Maybe this will help." He picked up the tablet, tapping on the screen. He offered the device to the man. On the screen was one of the least dangerous things he and Naomi had found in the files they stole: plans for a more efficient mid-level ship reactor. Almost twice the output as what was currently on the market, yet requiring less than twenty percent less reaction mass.

The man studied the tablet then looked up at Jax. "You make sure we get this, and I can make sure Mr. Ichiko calls us off." He leaned forward. "All of us." He smiled a not-at-all-even-close-to-a-friendly smile as he handed the tablet back to Jax.

The Crimson Orchid goon moved away from the table to talk excitedly with his companions.

The other groups looked at the tablet in turn. Each asked questions that Jax and Naomi answered as truthfully as possible. Most groups drifted toward the door, leaving after viewing the tablet. As each group departed, Jax reminded them where to send their bids.

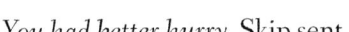

You had better hurry, Skip sent.

The two pieces of the hatch slid apart with a final groan. Baxter's powerful grip had pressed into the metal, deforming both pieces.

At the far end of the space, Jeffry and Governor Singh were standing at the bars watching.

Rudy rolled past Baxter. "Hello, Governor, Jeffry."

"Well, it's about time," the governor groused. "I thought Jackson had left us here to rot."

"You've only been in custody a day and a half," Baxter replied, walking into the substation. His sensors immediately cataloged everything in the space: weapons locker, secure processing cores, workstations.

"You hush, robot," the aged Indian woman said and wagged a finger at the menacing combat droid. She then added, "But hurry up, rip these bars open."

Baxter made a noise that Rudy knew to be his version of a sigh. The bars should have presented less of a problem than the hatch, except that as Baxter approached, a low hum appeared in the air. Red lights in the corners of the substation came to life, strobing.

The substation was nothing more than a long rectangular space, desks in the front for those assigned to

THREE

the station, a small closet off to one side that served as the armory, and the detention cells against the back wall, three of them. Only the center cell had occupants.

"Step back!" Baxter snapped a moment before arcs of static electricity moved along the length of the bars. Governor Singh and Jeffry let go of the bars, stepping back with barely a second to spare.

Rudy's head made two full rotations, taking in the scene. "That's a lot of current." Baxter said nothing, nodding.

"Well?" the angry old woman demanded, tapping a foot on the floor.

Rudy moved to the wall that would back up to the recently renovated corridor outside. One of his circular sensor arrays shifted colors quickly as he scanned the wall. He rolled backwards, then pointed. "There."

"There what?" Governor Singh and Baxter asked in unison.

"Blast, there." The nav droid turned to the two humans. "Get down."

Jeffry and the governor got down on the ground, the younger man sort of covering his employer.

The metal of Baxter's back shifted and whirred, freeing the twin railguns. They clicked into place, a low whine building from within the combat droid's torso as the weapons' super capacitors charged.

Without warning, each powerful weapon barked once. The sound of fast discharge capacitors dumping their energy faded quickly.

The wall that Rudy had pointed at was now a smoking ruin. Sparks erupted from ruined conduits. Water trickled out of a waste water supply line, filling the substation with a stench that sent Jeffry to the small privacy field surrounding the toilet. The red emergency lighting had died.

As his railguns folded back into his back, Baxter reached the cell and grasped the bars. With a single pull, he yanked the cell door from its frame.

"Let's go," he said, dropping the door with a clang.

CHAPTER SEVENTEEN

MUGGING

Jax and Naomi thanked the security team they had rented and left the convention section of the station. They had only walked a few hundred meters before running into the Crimson Orchid goons.

"Hand it over," demanded the man they had determined must be the head of the group on Columbiana. His colleagues were arrayed behind him, blocking the corridor.

"Did you place a bid?" Jax asked, stalling. Out of the corner of his eye, he saw Naomi lean down to rummage in the bag with the tablets. She kept herself between the bag and the Crimson Orchid man.

The goons all produced pistols. The leader said, "I think this bid wins."

Jax raised both hands. "Woah, be cool." Naomi stood and handed over a tablet. The lead man took it, handing it to one of his men. Jax added, "This still squares us, right? I mean, now you're getting it for free."

The lead goon smirked. "We'll see." They turned and left.

Jax looked at Naomi, and they continued on.

"This way," Rudy said, rolling ahead of the group. He made a turn down the corridor that housed the rented storage unit Baxter had been delivered to earlier in the day.

He entered the code and ushered the two humans inside. "Quickly."

Baxter pressed the control, lowering the door.

Rudy rolled over to the empty crate, pulling a panel off of the side. He manipulated the material for a minute, turning it into a low bench. "Here you go."

"I beg your pardon?" Governor Singh said, looking from the smart plastic origami bench to the small nav droid.

Baxter moved to the crate and began disassembling it. He constructed several large poles. He moved to each corner of the small space, setting a pole up in each. Once in place, the top of each pole turned blue, a light pulsing slowly.

Rudy made a gesture to the nearest pole. "Those are providing a damping field to shield this unit from scans. Until we can make sure the agent is no longer after you, we need to keep you off the radar. Those will mask your bio-signs," the small droid explained, pushing Jeffry towards the bench.

"Jackson will pay for this," the elderly woman growled as she eased down next to her young assistant on the bench, the smart plastic creaking.

Rudy rolled over to the door, his head spinning to look back at the others. "I'll be right back." The door slid up and he rolled out.

From several intersections over, the small navigation droid leaned into the corridor in time to see Agent Two, Martin, come around the corner. He stopped at the ruined

THREE

hatch and swore loudly. After looking up and down the corridor, he rushed into the substation. Rudy could hear more swearing from inside the station. The Imperial stormed out and headed off the way he had come.

"He's on the move, probably coming for you," Rudy reported over the shared channel. He rolled back to the storage unit.

Once the door dropped closed behind him, he looked around. "Now we wait."

The next group to intercept Jax and Naomi was the woman who had initially not wanted to deal with them without the fence, Joe, involved. Four freakishly muscled—in Jax's opinion—men were flanking her. Each man held a pulse pistol.

Jax looked at Naomi. "I guess everyone ignores the no guns rule." She shrugged.

"You will give me the tablet," the woman demanded, stepping forward.

Jax watched Naomi turn and stoop to reach into the bag of tablets. She kept her body in the way so that no one else could see that there were four tablets left in the bag. She withdrew one, handing it to Jax with an exaggerated sigh.

Jax looked at the device. "You know this will make you a target, right?"

The woman smirked. "I think I'm okay with the risk based on what I saw on that thing. Hand it over." She held her hand out, fingers wiggling. Her eyes were bright with the profit she was expecting to see.

Jax deposited the tablet in her outstretched hand, backing up and raising his hands in a single motion.

She looked Jax and Naomi up and down. "Don't fret, you'll get better at this. Everyone gets screwed their first time out." She winked at Jax and turned to leave, motioning her muscle to fall in with her as she moved.

In Jax's ear, Skip said, "That Imperial ship, it just opened up. Six spacers just departed. Armed."

Jax and Naomi exchanged a glance, then waited until the woman and her men had rounded a corner a hundred meters ahead. Jax said, "Not Shock Troops?"

"Negative. Naval regulars."

IT'S COMPLICATED

Jax and Naomi continued walking the corridors, guided by Skip. The SI had tapped into the station's security feeds in order to make sure the roving criminal organizations looking to mug the pair and steal a tablet, succeeded.

Twice they had to scramble to avoid a group of criminals looking for them once the bag of tablets was empty. Naomi pointed out that not being able to hand over a tablet might be dangerous, so after the fifth and final tablet was taken from them, it became a game of cat and mouse.

By the time Martin turned the corner ahead of Jax and Naomi, the shopping bag she had kept the tablets in was empty.

The Imperial agent rounded the corner with six Imperial Navy security officers behind him.

Naomi and Jax stopped in their tracks. The former said, "Hi, Martin," dropping the empty shopping bag.

"What the fuck are you two up to? You broke into the security station! Where is Governor Singh and her assistant?" His eyes narrowed. "Where's the data you stole? It wasn't on your ship. I know Naomi can't carry that much." He looked at Naomi's empty bag, lying at her feet. "What was in there?"

Jax looked around. "Don't know what you mean." He leaned to look at the six Imperials standing behind the agent, looking a little confused. "What data?"

Martin huffed, understanding dawning on his face. "You sold it. That was you, the *private event,* earlier today. I didn't put it together. That's why this place is crawling with lowlifes." He tilted his head. "Well, more lowlifes than normal. What? You had an auction or something?"

Naomi shrugged. "We're not sure what you mean?"

Jax held up a hand. "You know what, though? I did see a bunch of unsavory-type folks all walking away from the convention section, with identical tablets. Seemed weird. I just assumed Spacer Wares had had a sale or something."

"Do you know what you've done?" Martin demanded, stepping closer to Naomi and Jax. The six security officers shifted their weapons. "Selling state secrets? To organized crime syndicates?" He turned to his men. "Take them into custody."

Jax held up his hands. "Woah, woah, for what?"

Martin gave him a crooked grin. "Didn't you hear me? Selling state secrets." He motioned to his men. "Take them to the ship." The naval officers rushed to surround Jax and Naomi, weapons drawn.

Naomi leaned over. "Is this an improvement?" Jax shrugged.

Martin was pacing back and forth, running his hand through his close-cropped blond hair. He slammed a palm on the wall. "Let's go back to the ship." He stormed past his men and their charges. The troopers shoved their charges forward, falling into formation around them as they moved.

THREE

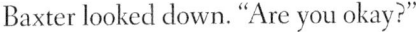

Baxter looked down. "Are you okay?"

Governor Singh looked up at the imposing droid. "Of course not!" she snapped. "I'm tired. I've been kidnapped by a government agent who thinks my nephew and his girlfriend are terrorists." She smacked a withered hand down on the smart plastic bench. "I'm thirsty, too." She pointed at Rudy. "Go."

"Go where?" the droid replied.

The governor grunted, "Find me a drink." She motioned. "Shoo." Rudy made a noise and rolled over to the largely disassembled crate that Baxter had hidden inside of earlier.

Jeffry had been pacing for almost an hour. When he got close to the bench, he sat down next to her and looked at Baxter. "Are we safe?" He patted the bench and gestured to the corridor. "I mean, here?"

Baxter nodded. "I am not detecting anyone in the immediate vicinity." He made a slow spin, arms raised. "A veritable fortress, this storage unit."

Rudy returned with two bottles of water. He offered one to each of the humans.

Governor Singh made a face. "Have those been in there this whole time?"

"Yes." Rudy bobbed on his smart material wheel.

The aged Indian woman glared at the droid. "Why didn't you offer them earlier?"

Rudy made a noise. "I didn't know you were thirsty."

The old woman made to lunge at the droid. Her assistant barely caught her in time. Rudy rolled backward as Baxter made a metallic barking noise, his laugh.

The combat droid said, "They should be heading back to the ship."

"Should?" Jeffry asked after making sure his employer was not about to leap off the bench.

"I have not heard from them since the auction began," the small droid said.

"Auction?" Governor Singh repeated.

"We should get going," Baxter said, turning to the roll-up door.

BEAR POKING NEVER GOES WELL

"Nice ship," Jax said as he and Naomi walked up the boarding ramp of the *Watchful*. Like the *Osprey*'s, this ship's boarding ramp led right into the small cargo area. Despite its size, running cargo was not that ship's purpose. The cargo hold was mostly full of foodstuffs and other perishables that the ship would need to scout long distances. Of course, at the rear of the space was the cage that Naomi and Jax saw earlier.

One of the naval officers pushed him forward. "Move." Right toward the cage.

Martin followed the procession into the ship, pressing the control to raise the boarding ramp behind him. "Put 'em in the cage." He walked toward a staircase built into the bulkhead.

As the cell door slid closed, Jax looked around. "This looks like they built it for you."

Naomi nodded. "Indeed." She made a slow circle, taking in the space; it was four meters square, spacious, with no bulkhead within arm's reach through the bars.

From a speaker in the ceiling, Martin said, "I had the

crew build the cell just for you, Naomi. You won't find a data line anywhere within reach, including under the deck, if you could get the paneling up."

Naomi looked up and flipped off the camera. She turned to Jax. "And now?"

He shrugged. "Well, I hope the boys got their part done."

"And us?" she pressed.

Jax dropped to the cot opposite where Naomi was standing. "By now the tablets are in play. We just need Martin to do his part." He looked up at the camera.

"Where are they?" Governor Singh asked as she arrived on the common deck of the *Osprey*. She looked around as Rudy zipped up the center of the spiral staircase from below. "I thought we were leaving."

Rudy wirelessly beamed to Skip, *Do you know where they are?*

Afraid so. They're aboard the Imperial ship, four levels up, arm Charlie-7, the ship's SI replied.

Rudy rolled over to the kitchenette, removing two bottles of water from the refrigerator. "Jax and Naomi are still working on the final parts of getting us out of this," he informed the small Indian woman who was tapping her foot on the deck in the middle of the space. He held the water bottles up in offering.

Governor Singh glared at the nav droid as she took the offered water. She turned to Jeffry. "I'm taking a nap." She stomped off down the short corridor that led to the crew and guest berths.

Rudy wirelessly asked Skip, *Are the tablets online?*

THREE

Three of five are online. They're still trying to figure out how to circumvent the copy protection Naomi and I set up. That won't last forever, however. I am ready to begin whenever the captain sends word.

Rudy rolled to the staircase, zipping up to the small bridge. "Come on, Jackson," he vocalized as he plugged into his navigation console.

Back aboard the *Watchful*, Martin came back down the stairs. "I've called in reinforcements."

"Is it Stacy? Did they catch her, too? She was always such a flake; I don't know how much I'd rely on her." Naomi smiled.

Martin reached the cell door, resting his hands on the horizontal bar of the door. "You always were the class clown."

Jax looked at Naomi sitting on the cot opposite him. "Her?" He pointed. Martin nodded once. "I guess it must depend on the audience." Naomi made a rude gesture.

Martin continued, "Not another agent. I called in the Imperial regulars. There was a cruiser only a few hours away. They'll lock this shithole down and we'll find that data."

Jax leaned forward on his cot. "Maybe once someone with some authority arrives, you'll see that we're not who or what you think we are."

Martin shrugged. "She's an Interface. The emperor will be interested in that no matter what else happens."

Naomi stiffened. "You wouldn't." She stood and moved to the opposite side of the cell, putting herself as far from Martin as possible.

Martin cocked his head. "It's not so bad, you know."

"After everything they did to us, how can you say that? How can you serve that monster?" She spun to look him in the eye. She didn't move to cross the space. She knew he'd step back from the bars. She crossed her arms. "What happened to you?"

He frowned. "I told you, not all of us were as fortunate as you. We didn't get far."

That time Naomi took a step towards Martin. "Fortunate? Fortunate? You have no idea the things I had to do to get off the planet and continued to have to do for years to get my feet under me." She took a deep breath. "You think I —what? Lucked out? That it was easy and my life has been all flowers and candy?"

Martin turned and stomped off back up the stairs to the rest of the ship above.

Jax looked at her. "Now I want candy."

CHAPTER EIGHTEEN

SPRINGING THE TRAP

All five tablets have connected to the station network, Skip informed Rudy and Baxter.

I guess the next part starts now, then, Rudy replied. He disconnected and moved to the staircase.

Governor Singh and Jeffry were working at the small dining table. Each had a tablet in hand and several others scattered between them. The elderly Indian woman looked up. "Hello, Rudy." The droid recoiled a bit at her tone.

"Governor." The droid bounced twice, changing the density of his smart material roller ball. "I believe we're almost done."

Jeffry looked up from his tablet. "That's good." He turned to his employer. "Right?" She growled.

Throughout Columbiana station, including three modified freighters docked in domes like the one the *Osprey* was sitting in, the corrupted data tablets were doing their job. Skip and Naomi had spent several hours crafting a virus that made the ship's SI nervous. The data they stole had helped. It turned out that the Empire was also working on terrifyingly advanced computer virus. The virus they had built had one job. Once the tablet connected to a network, the station's or a private shipboard's network, it would infect everything it could, opening as many back doors as possible, and connect back to Skip.

Rudy moved to his charging port, plugging in. *Skip, you can patch me in to help*, he sent.

I'm ready to help, too, Baxter added from his dock in engineering.

Here we go, then, the managing intelligence of the *Osprey* said. The two droid's intellects joined Skip over the ship's network. They went to work immediately, copying and moving data from place to place. The virus-opened back doors were giving them access to criminal enterprises across the Empire.

Those organizations who came to Columbiana via ship —ships connected to the organization's network back home, wherever home was—opened doors for the attacking droids. Even those, like the Crimson Orchid, who had people on the station already, were not safe. Rudy electronically hopped from the tablet sitting on a table to a processing core that housed the local operation's files. From there, he was able to use their secure connection to Themura to get into their main computer.

Aboard the *Watchful*, an ensign looked up from her console on the bridge. "Uh, Captain, sir. There's something weird going on with the station's network."

The captain walked over to look at the ensign's console. The display was a mess of lines that were growing and shrinking, appearing and vanishing. "Weird how, Ensign?"

She pointed at something on the display. To the captain,

THREE

it resembled nothing more than a mass transit map from New Terra. When she looked up to the captain's blank expression, she said, "This is network traffic on and off station. Since we arrived, I've been monitoring the network." When the captain continued to stare, she added, "Someone is transferring a lot of data on and off station. To a lot of different places."

The captain stood. "Why?"

The ensign shrugged. "No idea, sir." She looked around the bridge. "Maybe it has something to do with our guest?" She tipped her head down toward the lower decks.

The captain frowned. "Could be."

The captain turned toward the stairwell but stopped when another officer, a lieutenant, said, "Sir, we're being hailed."

BAD NEWS

A tablet smashed against the wall, shattering into many tiny parts. A well-dressed man spun to face one of his lieutenants. "What the hell is going on?" he shouted.

The younger, equally well-dressed man shied away from his boss. "I don't know! The processing core is going nuts." He pointed to the pair of processing cores sitting on a shelf in the corner of the rented office space. "We're getting data packets from who knows where, and sending data out to who knows where." The fronts of the processing cores were awash with lights flickering.

The young gangster pointed to a screen. "This, this looks like accounting records from one of Black Sun's shell companies." One thread of data thickened. "That, that I think is an inventory for one of our warehouses on New Terra."

The Crimson Orchid man looked at his lieutenant, then at the processing cores and their blinking lights. He removed a pistol from a shoulder-mounted holster, firing a single burst of energy into each core. The devices sparked and went dark.

THREE

The local boss looked around. "Get on the horn with Themura. Mr. Ichiko needs to know about this." He looked at another man who had until then kept silent in the office's corner. "Go find me that Caruso kid." He frowned as he watched the screen: data packets moving all over the place. One minute he saw the ledgers for their retail outlet on the commercial level, and the next it was gone, replaced by the payroll records for a business that sure looked like it was a front for the Lorax Syndicate.

HACK THE HACKER

Jax and Naomi were sitting on their respective cots staring at each other when Martin returned. "What are you doing?"

Jax did not turn his head or blink. "Staring contest."

Martin stopped dead in his tracks. "What?"

Naomi did not turn her head or blink. "Which word was confusing?" Her right eye twitched, and she blinked. "Damn!" She turned to Martin, sighing, "What do you want?"

The Imperial agent stammered, "What? I don't..." He took a deep breath, running his hands down the front of his well-pressed dress shirt. "I don't know what you two are up to, but you're never going to see the light of day after this."

Jax looked around. "Will we be seeing the light of day soon, then? So that it can be the last time?"

"You're terrorists. You blew up the Imperial Academy of Sciences building."

Jax shook his head. "No, we didn't."

"We have you on video," Martin countered.

THREE

"We took a tour," Jax pointed out. "It's an interesting building." He looked at Naomi. "She wanted to see it again."

"I wanted to show him where I grew up," Naomi added, straight faced. "You know, where you grew up, too."

Martin shook his head. "Times change. You two can talk around the issue all you like. We have you on video entering the academy building and not leaving it. We also know what files you stole. Now I have you not only on the theft of those files, but the selling of them."

Before Martin could say anything more, an Imperial officer came down the stairs. He was in a hover chair gliding down the staircase with ease, lieutenant bars on his shoulders. "Sir?"

Martin's shoulders hunched as he took a breath. "What?"

"Sir, the *Polaski* has arrived and is preparing to dock."

Martin spun to face the officer. "Very well." He moved to join the junior officer as they returned to the bridge.

Naomi looked at Jax, who shrugged and leaned back on the cot against the bars of the cell.

I think that is about all we can do, Skip said.

Agreed, Baxter said.

The two droids disconnected from the *Osprey*'s main computer while the managing intelligence erased as much presence as possible of their trespass on the network.

Think it worked? Rudy asked.

Assuming the captain and Naomi survive their run-in with the Imperials, we'll find out.

Rudy disconnected from his charging base and rolled back over to where the governor and Jeffry were working. "I think it's time, ma'am."

The elderly governor nodded. "Okay, let's do this."

PROPER PAPERWORK

Naomi and Jax watched a dozen Shock Troopers march up the boarding ramp, taking up positions along the port and starboard sides of the hold.

Once the troopers declared the cargo hold secure, several men and women in crisp maroon uniforms walked up the ramp into the large space. The officers fanned out, moving to speak with the crew of the *Watchful*. Martin waited next to the cell until a balding black man approached.

Martin inclined his head. "Captain Abumwa. Thank you for coming."

The dark-skinned man looked Martin up and down. "So you're one of the emperor's *agents*." It wasn't a question, and he couldn't hide the derision he felt for the idea.

Martin did not seem to notice the other man's expression, or care. He said, "These two are responsible for the explosions at the Academy of Sciences complex and the theft of state secrets. I need you to deploy troopers to secure this station. I believe they sold the stolen data to criminal elements."

The captain held up a hand. "What proof do you have of all this?" He looked past Martin to the captives.

"Captain, need I remind you of my place in the chain of command?" Martin asked, finding some iron to put in his voice.

Captain Abumwa growled under his breath. He turned to an officer who had followed him over to the impromptu brig, staying a respectful distance away from his superior officer. "Commander Cutler, see to it." The man nodded once and turned, issuing orders to those gathered around the cargo hold.

The captain of the *Watchful* came over. After exchanging pleasantries with Abumwa, he turned to Martin. "Anything you need my people to do?"

Martin shook his head. "No, Captain Abumwa's Shock Troopers can do the rest."

Captain Lancaster nodded, then said, "Actually, I have something you might be interested in."

Martin raised an eyebrow. "Oh?"

Lancaster continued, "One of my officers noticed a significant increase in station network traffic. Petabytes of data moving around the station, terabytes moving on- and off-station. It choked several of the public network routers to the point of crashing."

"What?" Martin stepped closer to the scout ship captain. "When? You're just now telling me this?" He spun to look at his captives. "What are you doing? What are you up to now?" He held up a hand. "Captain Lancaster, please have one of your officers log all the *weird* data transfers." He turned again to glare at his captives. "I suspect it will be evidence."

Jax and Naomi exchanged a look, then turned to Martin and the captains, shrugging.

THREE

Captain Lancaster whispered orders into his commset, then turned his attention back to the prisoners.

Jax then said, "Sirs, we don't know what he's talking about. He and a bunch of officers stopped us in a corridor and dragged us back here. We haven't done anything wrong. We run a transport business."

Martin's cheeks flushed a deep red. He spun to face the two captains. "We have them on video taking a tour of the Academy of Sciences. They clearly enter the building but aren't seen leaving it." He continued, "We detected a massive data theft had occurred moments before the explosions."

From the cell, Naomi said, "We took the tour. The science academy is such an interesting place." She looked at Jax, then back to the captains and Martin. "I don't know why the cameras didn't see us leave, but we did, with our tour group."

Captain Abumwa's eyes narrowed. "What were you doing on New Terra?"

"My aunt is the governor of Kelso station. She was attending some summit the emperor hosted for independent colony and station governors," Jax answered. "Since we had just finished a delivery job, we brought her to the summit." He grinned. "We thought it would be a fun little vacation. Our work keeps us out near the outer colonies. Coming to New Terra was a bit of a treat."

Captain Abumwa stared at the two prisoners for several tense heartbeats before turning to Martin and Captain Lancaster. "Does all of that check out?"

Martin stammered, "I...yes. I had the governor in custody at a security substation, but someone broke her out."

The dark-skinned captain's eyebrows shot up. "You

detained the governor of an independent station?" He held up a hand. "And didn't bring her here, to Imperial property? You involved locals?"

Martin shook his head. "No, I ensured that the local security forces were not using the station and wouldn't be for the duration."

"You took it over?" When Martin stammered, the senior captain continued, "A security substation on a sovereign space station. You have literally no authority here. Did you clear any of this with station management?"

Martin opened his mouth but closed it when Captain Abumwa continued, "I'm not surprised someone busted her out. This station is crawling with criminals and anti-Imperial malcontents." He crossed his arms. "Do you even know where the governor is now?"

CHAPTER NINETEEN

CLOSING THE TRAP

Two elderly women strolled through the corridors of Columbiana station. One turned to the other. "Who do you suppose will pay the repair bill on that security substation?"

Governor Singh turned to her colleague and friend. "Oh, I don't know, Ivanka. I'm sure you'll find someone to bill or tax for the repairs. I believe the Empire currently has a ship in one of your docking bays?"

The other woman smiled. "And another connected to a docking arm. So many Imperials." She looked at her friend. "I have you to thank, I assume."

Governor Singh clucked, "After a fashion." They reached the central elevator column. Behind them, a matte black combat droid was keeping a respectable distance.

They boarded the lift, and Governor Singh continued, "You've done well keeping this place together."

Her friend nodded. "Being the largest producer of Helium-3, and a few other rare elements in the sector, helps keep Imperial mitts out of my hair." She grinned a coffee-stained, toothy grin.

"The massive guns hidden all over the place probably

help, too," Governor Singh said. Her friend inclined her head in agreement.

As the lift descended toward the space dock facility, Governor Ivanka Rostova looked up. "You know, I could really clean this place up with a few of him." She hitched a thumb towards Baxter.

Governor Singh clucked again. "Is that a thing you want? To clean this station up? It was my understanding that Columbiana was exactly as you liked it, mostly lawless."

Her friend grinned. "True. Maybe 'cleanup' was not the right phrase." Her grin turned wicked.

From behind them, Baxter said, "I am sure Jax could come up with a suitable hourly rate for my services." Both women laughed.

The doors parted, and they continued on their way.

"Well, no. I was attempting to locate her when I found those two." Martin hitched a thumb over his shoulder. "The governor was never a suspect, of course. I was holding her to draw these criminals out."

This time it was Captain Lancaster that looked at Naomi and Jax. "So, those two are criminal masterminds? No offense." He looked at Martin. "You've searched their ship, I presume?"

Martin nodded. "I did. They must have moved the data off the ship, probably to keep it close and safe."

"Sirs, if I can offer a suggestion?" Naomi stood and walked over to the cell door.

Martin glared at her but said nothing. Captain

THREE

Abumwa, being the senior of the two captains, answered, "Of course."

"I assume he," she inclined her head toward Martin, "has the file signatures for the stolen data?" Martin nodded, unsure where she was going. "It sounds like you've tapped into the station's network. Couldn't you scour it and all connected ships, devices, etcetera, for those signatures?"

Abumwa looked to Lancaster first, then Martin. Martin finally nodded. "Yes, we could." He added quickly, "But if, as I suspect, they have hidden the data on a device not attached to the network, such a search would be fruitless."

"Uh, Captains, sirs," an ensign said from the top of the boarding ramp. Both captains turned. "I have two old ladies and a combat droid outside. They're demanding to speak to someone in charge."

"Are they specific old ladies, or..." Captain Lancaster snapped.

"Sorry, sir. They say that they are the governor of this station, and another. I didn't catch the name. I can go ask." The nervous ensign made to turn back toward the ramp.

Captain Abumwa glowered at Martin. "No, send them up." He added, "The droid stays out there. Place a guard on it." The junior officer nodded and hurried back down the ramp.

Jax and Naomi watched two older women ascend the boarding ramp. "Hi, Auntie," Jax waved.

"Hello, dear," she shouted back as the two women walked toward the group at the rear of the ship.

The taller of the two women spoke first. "Who's in charge here? Someone destroyed one of my security stations." She glared at the two captains. "I need to know who to send the bill to."

Governor Singh added, "That man," pointing at Martin,

"abducted myself and my assistant the other day." She turned her attention back to the captains, switching from angry auntie to diplomatic governor. "I am beyond late returning to my duties on Kelso station." She pointed at Jax and Naomi. "You've detained my ride."

Before either captain could answer, the lieutenant in a hover chair descended the stairs. "Excuse me, sirs, we've been inspecting the network traffic as ordered and have found some weird stuff."

"Stuff?" Abumwa and Lancaster asked in unison.

TURNING OF SCREWS

The lieutenant continued as his chair hovered to a stop, "I believe, sirs, that several criminal syndicates here on Columbiana and elsewhere within the sector are being hacked, like right now. The data we're seeing is a mishmash of accounting, secure file storage, personnel records, payroll, and more. It seems to move from one organization to another at random. Files clearly belonging to the Black Sun syndicate appear to be showing up in Galiardo family servers."

The uncomfortable looking officer then added, "Several of the files' streams also have Imperial coding."

"See!" Martin shouted, making both elderly women flinch. "I told you. They sold the stolen data to organized crime!" Martin punched the air. "I knew it!"

The lieutenant added, "Several streams also seem to have our ident encoded in them."

Captain Lancaster dropped both hands to his sides. "What do you mean, our ident?" He turned to Martin. "I think it's time to search the network, and ship, for those archive signatures." He turned to Governor Rostova. "I understand we have not consulted you of late. With your permission, I would like to deep dive the station's network for any indications of the allegedly stolen data."

The two older women exchanged a look, Rostova asking, "Do I have a choice?"

Captain Lancaster smiled. "Not really, no. Of course, you're welcome to lodge a formal complaint later."

The governor of Columbiana station nodded. "Then by all means."

Captain Lancaster looked at the lieutenant. "Get the agent a tablet."

With all eyes on him, Martin grudgingly uploaded the archive signatures to the tablet. When his own bio-circuitry pulsed blue, several officers nearby gasped, as did one of the two governors. He handed the tablet back to the waiting lieutenant, who guided his hover chair back to the staircase and up to the bridge.

Seeing an opportunity, Jax pointed out, "You know, it sounds like organized crime in this sector is going to be shaken up for quite a while. Probably a great opportunity for the Empire to swoop in and do some cleanup, right, guys? Bring that light of civilization and all that." He looked at Governor Rostova, who smiled.

The two captains looked at each other, then Jax. They said nothing, turning their backs on the cell to face the two elderly station governors standing before them, looking bored.

Governor Rostova said, "You know, Captains, while this current situation sounds like it spans the sector, it seems to be focused here on Columbiana. My security forces are more aligned with local code enforcement, not mopping up organized crime. I could be convinced to invite your forces onto the station, briefly. I assume," she looked over her

THREE

shoulder to the nearest Shock Trooper standing at parade rest along the bulkhead, "those shiny troops of yours would make quick work of these criminals."

Governor Singh chimed in, "If what your lieutenant said is true, I'd assume your forensic investigators will be quite busy, as well, dismantling the syndicates. A mighty win, to be sure." She grinned. "The emperor will surely be pleased."

The lieutenant from before descended the stairs, this time with two security officers trailing behind his chair. "Sirs."

The two officers with the lieutenant fanned out. The Shock Troopers took notice and moved, as well. Jax and Naomi remained where they were in the cell, watching.

The young officer said, "We found the stolen data. A definitive match of the archive signatures." His gaze flicked to Martin, then back to his superiors. "A terminal in the forward VIP cabin."

Martin gasped as the two security officers and four nearest Shock Troopers moved to surround him. "This is preposterous! I am an agent of the emperor!" he protested. He spun and lunged for Jax and Naomi through the bars of their cell. "You did this!" Both of them stepped back, hands up in front of them.

Captain Abumwa took in the situation, then turned to the lieutenant. "With the data you've collected, do you think we have enough to move on the criminal organizations you mentioned?"

The lieutenant tapped the side of his chair as he thought. "Almost certainly, sir." He turned to his captain. "It's hard to know exactly how many organizations are involved, but we traced several pathways to spaces here on the station, in the commerce section."

Lancaster turned to Abumwa. "My ship doesn't carry any Shock Troopers." The older captain turned to another officer. "Dispatch squads where," he pointed to the hover chair bound lieutenant, "this man says." Both officers nodded and departed.

Captain Abumwa turned to his colleague. "What say we see what secrets might be in your forward VIP cabin?"

FAKE NEWS

"I would like to see, as well," Governor Rostova said before the two captains took a single step.

"Me, too," Governor Singh added.

Captain Lancaster sighed. "Very well." He motioned to one of the troopers nearest Martin. "Bring him."

When the group was out of earshot, Jax leaned over to Naomi. "Moment of truth."

She threw him a look. "You doubt me?" He held both hands up.

The VIP cabin, while spacious, had not been designed to accommodate six people at one time, especially when one was a Shock Trooper in two hundred kilograms of bulky Shock Trooper armor. The trooper shoved Martin in ahead of him, then stood in the hatch opening his carbine, held at the ready.

Captain Lancaster sat down at the terminal, using his credentials to override the personal lockout used by Martin. He pulled up the report from his lieutenant on his gPhone while browsing the files on the local processing core. After several tense minutes, he turned to face the others, then looked directly at the Shock Trooper in the doorway. "Put him in the brig."

Martin's screams and shouts of protest died out as the trooper dragged him bodily down the corridor to the staircase. The small scout ship's regular brig was on the common deck, a single small room with two even smaller cells in it, near the aft med bay. By comparison, the cell that Jax and Naomi were sitting in was downright spacious.

Governor Singh was the first to speak. "So." She looked around sweetly. "My nephew and his business partner, free to go?"

The two captains escorted the governors back down the two levels to the cargo hold. Captain Lancaster opened the cell door. "You're free to go."

Captain Abumwa added, "But we'll be looking into the other allegations the agent leveled against them." He turned to the two prisoners, nodding.

Jax and Naomi walked out, the former hugging his adopted aunt.

Governor Rostova said, "I would most appreciate any updates on your actions against the criminal elements on Columbiana."

Abumwa nodded. "I'll have my second in command put together a report when the squads check in." He consulted his gPhone. "I can't imagine it taking more than a day, given that we've tracked the data pathways." He pulled Jax aside. "Captain Caruso, your name isn't unknown to me. I'm aware of your recent run in on Jebidiah." His eyes narrowed. "You'd be smart to keep a low profile." He looked at Jax. "A lower profile."

He smiled. "Especially after this." When Jax opened his mouth, he made a motion, silencing the reply. "I don't pretend to know what all is going on here. I had my people

THREE

check into Martin's story about the attack on the science academy building. It is weird that you're not seen leaving, but that doesn't justify all of this." He waved a hand toward the cage sitting a few meters away. "You already made an enemy of the Crimson Orchid, and it sounds like you've added quite a few names to the list today. In fact, you seem to be exceptionally good at collecting enemies."

Captain Lancaster joined in. "I feel compelled to warn you that," he nodded his head toward the general direction of the brig of his ship, "he will not forget this. I can't even begin to guess what all is going on, but I am sure he's not actually guilty."

Jax flashed his biggest smile but said nothing.

Once Jax, Naomi, and the two governors were in the corridor outside the landing bay, Jax let loose a deep sigh. "I wasn't sure that would work."

Faster than anyone her age should have been able to move, his aunt spun, lashing out with several open-palmed slaps to his chest and arms. "When we get back to Kelso, you're grounded," she hissed. Baxter, trailing behind the group, took a step back.

Governor Rostova and Naomi exchanged a look and picked up their pace, putting some distance between themselves and the irate Indian woman and her adopted nephew.

"Auntie," Jax whined as the two women moved further ahead.

The older of the two looked up at Naomi. "So, dear. What was all that about?"

Naomi took a deep breath, then smiled. "Long story."

The other woman nodded once. "Fair enough, and honestly, I don't care." She looked over her shoulder at Governor Singh and Jax. "I am pretty happy that somehow the two of you managed to get the Empire to clean up not just my station but a portion of this sector."

CHAPTER TWENTY

TTFN

"Welcome back, Captain," Skip said. Jax, Naomi, and Governor Singh were filing up through the embarkation room. Baxter took up a position at the bottom of the ramp.

"Let's get ready to go," Jax said, moving through the common deck to the quarters he was currently sharing with Jeffry. He mumbled something about changing his clothes as he disappeared from view.

Jeffry had been sitting in the large chair in the lounge space when the others arrived. He was up and out of the chair the moment the ship's SI notified him of their arrival in the landing bay. He was hovering next to Governor Singh until she swatted at him, driving him to the dining table.

Rudy rolled over to Naomi. "Glad that all went according to plan."

The governor looked over. "There was a plan?" She gestured to Jeffry as she dropped into the sofa. "Jeffry, I need a drink, whatever the stiffest thing Jackson has."

Jeffry stood, but stopped when Naomi said, "He keeps the strong stuff here." She walked over to a bookshelf set against the bulkhead opposite the large entertainment display. Three of the books were fake, revealing two bottles, both whiskey.

The governor grinned. "I'm glad not everything I taught him was for naught."

"Oh, come on, Auntie," Jax said, emerging from the short corridor that led to the crew and guest quarters. "I learned a ton from you, not least of which is an appreciation for alcohol." He grinned. He had changed into his customary shipboard uniform of loose-fitting denim pants and T-shirt with a logo no else recognized. Their time locked up had been made even more uncomfortable by his being dressed for the auction in tight-fitting trousers and a nice shirt.

He moved to the kitchenette, opening one of the high cabinets, removing four tumblers. Setting all four on the coffee table in front of the sofa, he took the bottle from Naomi. "Skip, go ahead and get the pre-flights started, please."

"Copy that, Captain," the ship's SI replied. Rudy bobbed his metal fist, nodding. He rolled to the staircase and shot up the center to the bridge above.

Once Jax had poured the drinks, he distributed the glasses. Holding his own up, he said, "To things never going according to plan."

Everyone took a sip. After coughing, Jeffry said, "That doesn't seem like a thing you would toast to."

Jax grinned. "You just haven't been around us long enough." He made a gesture to himself and Naomi.

Jeffry took another sip, shuddering. "No offense, Jackson, but I hope to never, ever, EVER travel with you again."

"That's fair," Jax said.

THREE

"Captain, we've got clearance to depart," Skip announced.

Jax stood. "On my way."

From below, the sound of Baxter coming up the ramp echoed. "We're sealed up," Skip announced.

THEY NEVER LEARN

The *Osprey* slid out of the domed landing bay into space. Local space was no less busy than when they had arrived. Dozens of massive freighters jockeyed for position to dock and load or unload. The biggest difference that time was the Lightfoot class corvette docked at one of the longer docking arms. Jax watched the busy local space, expertly moving the *Osprey* out of the way of vessels larger and smaller.

"Someone just scanned us," Skip announced.

Jax tensed. "Who?"

"Working on it."

Jax looked over his shoulder. "Get a course plotted for home."

Rudy bobbed his fist. "On it."

"Light freighter sliding in behind us," Skip announced. "No ident being broadcast."

"One guess," Jax groused. He slapped the communication console, opening a channel. "I'll say this once: don't do anything stupid." He muted the channel. "Skip, just in case, see if you can reach our Imperial friends." He adjusted their course,

THREE

trying his best to make it look like he was simply trying to avoid a large bulk freighter instead of trying to keep the *Osprey* and their new friend in weapons range of the Imperial corvette.

The communications console blinked. He pressed a button. One of the overhead monitors came to life. It was one of the Crimson Orchid goons he had seen at Leonard's. "You really have a death wish, don't you?" the man said. He continued, "You could have been free and clear of us. We'd be off your back and you could go back to hauling grain or whatever you do."

Jax grinned. "No, not really. I'm hoping to live a long life and to die when medical science has done everything humanly possible to extend my life. I've even thought about having my head preserved in a jar, but then, I don't know if I could live without sex." He grunted. "I mean, what kind of life would that be? No physical pleasure?"

"Shut up!" the man on the screen shouted.

An icon appeared on the screen, a microphone with a red slash through it. Skip had muted their side, then said, "He's targeting us."

Jax nodded as the mute icon vanished. "You know, it'd be highly insane to attack me here. I mean, sure, Columbiana normally wouldn't care, as long as you didn't hit the station. But you know, right about now, all your guys and all your competitors' guys are being rounded up by Shock Troopers. I'm kind of in the good graces of the station governor." Jax beamed. "Plus, you know, that Imperial corvette."

"You're just space trash. Nothing more," the man retorted.

"That's just mean," Jax replied.

The mute icon appeared again. "The *Polaski* said, and I

quote, you are on your own," Skip said. The mute icon vanished.

Jax did his best to mask his annoyance as he adjusted their course again, this time angling away from the station and as much traffic as he could.

The man said, "You could have just handed it over. Cleared your debt to us. But no, you had to be cute."

As the *Osprey* cleared the nearest inbound bulk freighter, Jax consulted the navigation display: more or less open space for a few hundred thousand kilometers, not counting the handful of well-armed asteroids in the vicinity. He moved as inconspicuously as possible, arming the ship's weapons systems.

On the screen, the criminal leaned forward, filling the screen with his wicked smile. "Goodbye, Mr. Caruso. Mr. Ichiko sends his regards."

"He is firing," Skip announced, not bothering to mute the channel.

Jax laughed, pulling the ship into a tight corkscrew as a missile flew past. "Here's the thing." He brought the *Osprey* into a turn in the opposite direction, using the maneuvering thrusters to slide the ship laterally as it turned wide, bringing the nose of the much smaller ship to bear on the modified freighter. "You're in a freighter. A well-armed one, pretty thick armor too, I'm sure."

On his primary flight display, he watched as the targeting computer went to work lining up the powerful plasma cannon mounted amidships on the ventral section of the ship, just aft of the boarding ramp. It had a limited firing arc, requiring the Valerian Coop Infiltrator to be above its target.

"But," Jax said, "I've got this." He squeezed the trigger on his flight control as the rectangle on his main display

THREE

turned green. A purple line appeared between the two ships, causing Jax to squint until the transparent portion of the bridge turned dark.

The freighter immediately listed to the side, atmosphere venting from a five-meter-long cut in the ship's side. The damage was still glowing white as the escaping atmosphere pulled a body through the hole.

On the small communications screen, the Crimson Orchid man was shouting orders at someone, red lights around him strobing. He looked back at the camera, scowling.

Jax slapped the communication console to close the channel, then lined up another shot as the *Osprey* sailed past the stricken freighter. A turret on the dorsal of the ship tracked the smaller craft, firing blaster bolts that splashed against the shields, rocking the much smaller ship. Jax's own turret came around, lining up on the freighter. The moment before the targeting rectangle was going to turn green, a nearby asteroid opened fire with a single railgun shot that vaporized the freighter.

"Governor Rostova says, you're welcome," Skip announced.

Jax adjusted their course to clear the remaining asteroids. He looked over his shoulder. "We good?"

"Course plotted; wormhole generator is online," Rudy replied.

Jax smiled as he reached for the blinking button that would open the rift in space-time directly ahead. The green and purple vortex opened, and the *Osprey* leapt into it.

WELCOME HOME

The rest of the trip was uneventful. The new alluvial damper for the wormhole generator worked without issue. Jeffry and Naomi bonded over a trilogy of movies that Jax had forgotten were even in his archive. Something about sharks in a hurricane or something. He only made it through half of the first one before finding something to read in the cabin he and Jeffry were sharing. It was beyond Jax how someone thought making more than one was a good idea. He spent the trip going through the files they had stolen, deleting most of them. Most of the data they had stolen was far too dangerous in anyone's hands, especially anyone Jax would likely sell it to.

There were a few gems that he was hopeful could fetch a good price or even benefit him directly as upgrades to the *Osprey*.

As they neared Kelso station, Governor Singh joined him on the bridge while Naomi, Baxter, and Jeffry wrestled with the mountain of luggage she had brought along.

"I'm sure you're excited to get your quarters back," she said, putting a withered brown hand on his shoulder.

THREE

He grunted. "Yeah, your boy Jeffry has some seriously weird dreams." He tapped the console. "Nightmares might be more accurate. So much screaming." He looked over his shoulder. "I bet you'll be glad to be home."

She nodded. "You have no idea. Apparently, there was a bit of a labor issue in engineering, and my lieutenant promised everyone additional holidays and hazard pay." She shook her head. "Idiot. I might have to promote Jeffry. He's far more competent than that boob, Robert."

The large outer door of the Caruso family mechanical bay slid open, orange lights strobing. Jax let out a sigh of relief. It wasn't much, but everything in that bay was his, and it was home.

The *Osprey* touched down with a clang. Jax flipped switches, powering down the reactor and engaging the standby routines. He looked at his aunt. "That was quite the adventure."

She smiled. "Yeah, it was. I never want to do that again."

Jax laughed, standing up. "Can't argue. I've had more than enough of New Terra and the Empire for a bit."

"Good, because I was serious when I grounded you," the small Indian woman said, walking to the staircase.

Jax froze, watching her vanish down to the common deck below. He turned to Rudy, who spun his squat cylindrical head so that his optic sensors were facing away from Jax. He rushed to the staircase. "Auntie, wait."

Governor Singh joined Jeffry and Naomi as Jax came down. "You can't be serious! I'm a grown ass man. You can't ground me." He looked at the others for support.

Naomi made a deliberate show of looking at her fingernails. Jeffry held both hands up and pointed to the small woman next him. "She signs my paycheck. Sorry, man."

Jax's face fell. "Auntie?"

She smiled. "Sorry, Jackson. Maybe some time not off gallivanting around the sector will give you time to think about your actions and how you can be more responsible."

Naomi tapped Jeffry, and they both grabbed suitcases and moved to the staircase. Baxter, who until then had been standing quietly near the hatch to the ship's head, said nothing but grabbed several suitcases and followed the other two humans down to the cargo deck.

Below, Jax could hear Naomi, Jeffry, and Baxter working their way further down to the embarkation room and the already deployed boarding ramp.

Governor Singh pointed to some more bags. "Grab those, dear." She made for the stairs.

Jax grabbed the bags. "Auntie, you make it sound like I'm out racing, or...I don't know, something dumb like that." He stumbled on the last step and nearly fell on the small woman in front of him.

Catching himself and his breath, he continued, "Naomi and I, we're out trying to make a living. Things cost money. You know that."

As Governor Singh stepped off the boarding ramp onto the deck of Kelso station, she inhaled deeply. She watched Jax come down the ramp. "That may be, but this little adventure has shown me you take far too many risks. Not just with your life, but others' lives, mine in particular." She poked him in the stomach. "You could have just lounged around the pool while Jeffry and I were busy. Instead, you robbed the emperor, destroyed public property, started a cross sector chase, and nearly got Columbiana station sanctioned, or worse." She headed off toward the hatch out of the mechanical bay.

THREE

Jax groaned. "Allegedly." When he saw her face, he added, "That wasn't even my idea!"

She clucked, "Oh? If someone said you should walk out an airlock without an EVA suit, would you?"

"Of course not."

"Well, then. I guess a month staying here on Kelso will give you ample time to reflect. Maybe take up yoga."

Jeffry and Naomi had moved out of the way as the two argued. The governor's assistant leaned over. "You may need to find a new partner, at least for a while."

Naomi groaned. "I haven't even finished breaking this one in." She rubbed her chin. "Maybe those Delphino brothers need a hand for a bit."

"I heard that!" Jax shouted in from ahead of them.

The hatch opened before Governor Singh arrived. Lewis from customs walked in. He beamed. "Well, hi there, Governor Singh! Welcome home." He dipped his head.

She smiled warmly. "Thank you, Lewis." She slowed down. "When you're done with your inspection, please issue a one month lockdown on the *Osprey*. She doesn't leave the station without my express authorization."

Lewis' eyes bugged out. "Oh, uh...okay, ma'am." He turned to Jax and shrugged helplessly. He mouthed, *What did you do?* Jax scowled and turned away.

The governor walked into the corridor, motioning Jeffry to join her. She looked at Jax. "It's only thirty days, dear. I'm sure it won't kill you." She turned away, then turned back. "Don't forget to have Baxter deliver my bags to my quarters." She did not wait for any reply. She turned and vanished into the corridor.

Lewis rocked on his heels, looking at Jax, then Naomi, then the ceiling. Finally, he turned to the two of them.

"So…" He tapped the tablet in his hand with the index finger of his other hand. "How was New Terra?"

Jax sighed. "Fine." He looked at Naomi. "At least we got coffee."

His business partner looked at him and shrugged. "Did you get some? I was busy not dying."

Jax looked at the ceiling of the large hangar space. "Kill me now." He looked at Naomi. "No coffee." She shrugged, patted his shoulder and headed towards the hatch his aunt had just exited through. "Wonder if Tony is busy?" He mumbled.

"So…nothing to declare, then?" Lewis pressed.

The End.

CONTINUE THE ADVENTURE

If you enjoyed this story, I'd love it if you left a review.
Seriously, reviews are a big deal.

Reviews help readers find authors. Reviews help books get discovered.
Even just "I liked it" means a lot!

STAY CONNECTED

Want to stay up to date on the happenings in the Grand Human Empire?

Sign up for my newsletter at
johnwilker.com/newsletter
Visit me online at
johnwilker.com
You can also join my Patreon page for all sorts of awesome goodies!

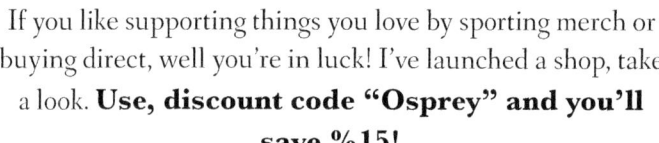

If you like supporting things you love by sporting merch or buying direct, well you're in luck! I've launched a shop, take a look. **Use, discount code "Osprey" and you'll save %15!**

OFFER

As they say, there's no harm in asking, so here we go.

If you can help connect me with someone who can get The Grand human Empire on a screen (Big or Little) I'll cut you in for 10% (Up to $10,000) of whatever advance is paid.

Send me an email and we can discuss.
rights@johnwilker.com

OTHER BOOKS BY JOHN WILKER

The Space Rogues Series. Wil Calder and a bunch of alien misfits somehow keep finding themselves in the thick of it. No one ever checks qualifications when it comes to saving the galaxy!

The Grand Human Empire Series. Jax, Naomi and the droids are just trying to get by. New droid parts ain't cheap after all.